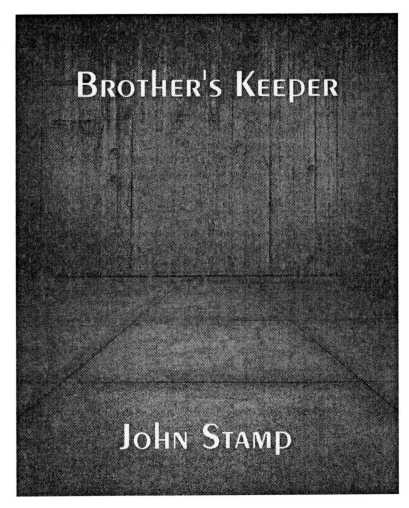

BROTHER'S KEEPER

JOHN STAMP

Cover Art:
Michelle Crocker

http://mlcdesigns4you.weebly.com/

Publisher's Note:

This is a work of fiction. All names, characters, places, and events are the work of the author's imagination.

Any resemblance to real persons, places, or events is coincidental.

Solstice Publishing - www.solsticepublishing.com

Brother's Keeper
John Stamp

Dedication

This book has to be dedicated first and foremost to my mom, who has read through every line of everything I've ever written, to include the sixty-five page "novel" I hand wrote instead of paying attention in sixth grade math class. She didn't have the heart to tell me it sucked then and I still can't get any objective criticism from her now. Thanks Mom.

Chapter One
Charlie
2013

Charlie Bowman made the left-hand turn off North Meeting Street, deep in the Neck of the Charleston Peninsula. There were no streetlights in the Neck and very few road signs. There were even fewer intact windows on the many abandoned and crumbling buildings. The last vestiges of civilized society had escaped the Neck long ago, fleeing the city as it fell apart.

The headlights on the 1997 Jeep Wrangler fought against the darkness in a sad attempt to light his way. Charlie glanced at his watch and pulled to a stop beside an old, tin-roofed machine shop, long abandoned to the degradation that had eaten up neighborhoods throughout the no-man's land between the adjoining cities of Charleston and North Charleston. Charlie snuggled the Jeep between an old, rusting dumpster, and the cinderblock wall of the timeworn shop, hoping that would camouflage the vehicle against any scavengers who might be patrolling the dark and silent street.

Charlie slid out of his old Jeep and gently eased the driver's side door closed so as not to make too much noise. He paused at the corner of the dumpster that still carried the stench of decades of rancid garbage. He peered into the darkness, listening while his eyes and ears adjusted to the night. It was after one o'clock in the morning and the Charleston sky was heavy with clouds with not a lick of moonlight to help him on his way. Rain could fall at monsoon strength at any moment.

Charlie retrieved his Kimber 1911 chambered for nine millimeter from his waistband and press-checked the weapon. He gingerly retracted the slide of the weapon backward against the frame, and then slowly let the slide return to battery when the faint glint of a brass shell casing caught his eye. He breathed slowly in, then out, took one last glance around the area between himself and the old warehouse across the street, and moved out.

Charlie ignored the front door closest to his path from the machine shop, and slipped down an alley where he found a side door. The rusting, battered steel door had been tagged at one point by some wannabe gang, but the spray painted symbols, once proud, had peeled away with time.

The door creaked on old iron hinges. Charlie cringed. The squealing signal sounded like a blow horn in the desolate neighborhood. He opened the door just enough to squeeze through. He moved laterally along the wall, careful to avoid banging into ancient appliances and rat-infested furniture. Pausing about twenty feet from the doorway, he crouched, and listened, again adjusting to the new environment.

Nothing.

Just as he was about to resume, he caught movement. A dark form crossed the dim light filtering through a shattered window. Charlie froze. He watched the figure as it moved quietly through the open spaces from one abandoned piece of old machinery to another. The figure, bulkier than most street scavengers lacked the slow, uncoordinated herky jerks of addicts or other bums, slid through the darkness. Charlie kept an eye on the form as he moved to concealment behind an old steel tool shelf. He watched the figure draw near.

When the man was within ten feet of him, Charlie whispered, "I've been watching you since you came in. Very stealthy, Milligan."

Keith Milligan yelped as he stumbled and knocked over a rust-encrusted metal chair.
"Jesus Christ, Charlie! What the fuck is wrong with you? I could've shot your wise ass!"

"Not with moves like that, you couldn't," Charlie

said.

The two closed on each other and shook hands.

"How you doin'? You okay?" Milligan asked.

Charlie sighed. "I'm all right." He was silent for a long moment. Charlie could feel Milligan watching him, for any signs that he was cracking. Charlie didn't hold it against Milligan; it was part of his job. Finally, he continued, "But I think we're going to have to wrap this up soon. That last one was rough. It could have brought the whole thing down on my head."

"I know, I know, another pregnant girl comes out of one of those shipping containers, and I don't know what you can do to save her. The Marshals say the girl is doing pretty good, though; the baby is still okay as far as anyone can tell."

Charlie nodded slowly. "But …?" There was always a but.

"She wants more, Charlie. She thinks we need a better link from Westchase to the operation itself."

Charlie Bowman's heart felt like it was going to shoot out of the top of his head. He looked Keith Milligan in the eye. "That's an easy call to make from behind a desk."

"I know it is, Charlie. But at the end of the day we both know that you run this game. You're the one on the pointy end. If it gets too hot, you bug out, fuck 'em."

Easy for you to say, Charlie thought, and was about to say when the hairs on the back of his neck stood up. The pressure in the old garage changed. He held his breath while his eyes searched the darkness.

Milligan had picked up on his cue. The older man shuffled around in his light jacket for his gun. "Wha—?" His voice was drowned out by the staccato thunderclaps of submachine-gun fire.

Milligan dropped as Charlie dove behind a five-foot-high steel toolbox, landing in a crouch with the

Kimber in his hand. The fire poured in on him. Zipping and popping hornets of lead and copper singed the air.

The old cinder-block building reverberated the sound of the gunshots keeping him from identifying where they were coming from. He turned to face the toolbox as he backed off the cover a pace or two and chanced a look around the side.

Keith Milliganwas on his ass, leaning against the wheel of an old, beat-up Gremlin. Bullets snapped and splatted against the engine block and hood of the old car. Milligan had his Glock in one hand and pressed the other to a gaping wound in his thigh.

Charlie slid back around the toolbox and peeked out. Muzzle flashes burst from three separate gunmen on the other side of the shop. The men were spraying the general area where he and Milligan crouched.

"Go! Go! Go, Charlie!" Milligan yelled.

Charlie could barely hear him over the din of gunfire. The man sounded tired; he must be losing a lot of blood. Charlie cringed but knew the older man was right. It was time to move. He took a deep breath, let it out slowly.

The firing continued, though the pace had somewhat slackened. The three assailants hadn't moved from their general position. The one closest to him was maybe twenty feet away. The assailant wasn't shooting directly at him, rather spraying around the old, beat-up car Milligan was hiding behind. The man turned a fraction of a degree and Charlie burst from his crouch, opening fire .

He flanked the three gunmen, firing continuously at the one closest to him. His first two shots missed but got the man's attention. Charlie could see the man had not been ready for a gunfight. When he jumped in response to the nine millimeter round smacking the wall next to his head. He spun toward Charlie in shock but wasn't reaching for his gun then Charlie's third round hit him in the chest. The man stuttered back into the cinderblock wall and collapsed.

Charlie saw him fall out of the corner of his eye while he fired three more rounds at the next closest assailant. He hit the man somewhere in the side. The gunman leapt straight into the air and seemed to curl in around the impact of the round. His momentum slammed him into the third gunman.

The third man had zeroed in on Charlie, who was advancing, exposed over open ground. He fired just as his stricken partner, who had absorbed two more jacketed hollow points from the Kimber, barreled into him, knocking his aim off by a fraction. That fraction meant life, not only for himself but for Charlie Bowman. The round meant for Bowman's aorta tore into Charlie's hip on his gun side. The bullet Charlie fired a thousandth of a second before and had been aligned with the bridge of the man's nose, impacted harmlessly against the cinderblock with a *whap*.

Charlie spun around and landed on his ass in the middle of the dust-covered floor before he realized he'd been hit. It took him another second to realize his right arm would not respond, and another to know his gun was gone, lost in the darkness. Then, he felt the searing hot coals burning in his shoulder.

He started scrambling, but then froze upon hearing the click of a fresh magazine being loaded into a gun. Before he could turn to face the threat he was struck across the temple and knocked unconscious.

Chapter Two
Alex and Charlie
2002

Alex Stillwater was exhausted. He'd spent the majority of the last three days standing in lines. Lines at graduation from Basic Training, lines to be dismissed from basic training, lines at the gate leaving Paris Island—a place he hoped never to see again.

After a brief visit with his mother and father in Charleston, South Carolina Stillwater had made his way to Geiger Camp Geiger, North Carolina, where he was ordered to attend the next level of training as a United States Marine at the School of Infantry. Alex was a zombie by the time he in-processed, was assigned his gear, and allowed to head for a bunk. It didn't matter what bunk. At this point, he'd sleep on the floor if he thought it wouldn't lead to pushups or some other form of non-judicial torture at the hands of his instructors.

The leave spent between Paris Island and Ft. Geiger had been for the most part peaceful--ten lazy days spent on the beach and fishing on his dad's boat. It wasn't until his last day at home that his high school friends, Terry and Matt, decided to give him a proper farewell, and Alex was hung over. He had seventy pounds of gear in a sea bag on his back and just wanted to drop his shit and squeeze out a couple of seconds' rest.

At this stage of the game, the very beginning of training, the swarm of young Marines surrounding him who were likewise trying to find a sliver of rest all knew the same truth. They were being watched. Like Ospreys eyeing a river full of trout, instructors were everywhere, waiting for the same thing—someone to make an example of to create a cautionary tale for the rest of the class. One of the young Marines milling about the wide bay stacked with bunks was going to set the tone for this leg of training, Alex

Stillwater was determined not to be that Marine.

Alex spotted a bunk toward the rear and headed for it. Not far enough out of the way to be thought of as trying to hide, but far enough out of the way to give him an extra second or two to get his shit together when they suffered late-night surprise inspections. Alex reached the bunk he intended to make home for the next two months. With his eye on the rough, green wool blanket so thin it couldn't keep a man warm in Death Valley, he just wanted to sleep. Lurching to build momentum, he slung his heavy canvas sea bag toward the paper-thin mattress of the bottom bunk. Then, he watched as, from out of nowhere, an identical sea bag slammed into his own, knocking it to the floor.

Alex felt the rush of heat rising in his neck and face as he followed the trajectory of the interfering bag to a set of brown-and-tan fatigues identical to his own. The Marine wearing the earth-toned stared at Alex. In turn, Alex stared at the name tag that read, "Bowman." Barely contained hostility fueled by lack of sleep and the jailhouse mentality that ruled the inhabitants of the close living arrangements won out. The two young warriors attacked each other in a blind, uncoordinated fury. The battle was short but notable—at least that's how the lead instructor liked to recall it.

Alex couldn't remember if there were any words traded or insults offered. The fight didn't last long, but he was pretty sure he'd landed a couple of good shots. All that didn't seem to matter much anymore, however, as he stood at attention next to his adversary. They were surrounded by the shaven-headed, pimpled faces of their classmates, who looked on with hushed relief that it was him and not them.

Before him stood Staff Sergeant McGregor, head instructor for Class '02-'09. The brim of the sergeant's Smoky-the-Bear hat was razor-sharp. The man's steely eyes bored into his and those of his nemesis, and conveyed a very simple message: They were screwed. McGregor barked for nearly seven minutes straight in that clipped, bullhorn volume that rattled Alex's brain. McGregor made the two Marines into that cautionary tale Alex had warned himself not to be. McGregor expounded on the merits of teamwork, controlling aggression, and other traits of a good Marine of which Alex and his sparring partner had lost sight. Obviously content with the example he'd made, McGregor leaned back and studied the two wayward Marines.

He then shared a look with the unseen cadre of instructors to his rear and growled, "Follow me."

Four hours later, Alex Stillwater and Charlie Bowman were filling their two hundredth sand bag. It was the ultimate exercise in teamwork, and a lesson McGregor wanted to ensure the two Marines understood. Bowman held the burlap sack open while Alex worked the entrenching tool over and over into the North Carolina sugar sand, moving scoop after exhaustive scoop into the bag.

Charlie seethed. Shit like this, dumbshit rich boys, were how he ended up in situations like this. He wasn't doing anything wrong, keeping his head down, going about his business, just like the judge and his father told him to do. Sure, he saw the kid angling for the bunk he wanted, but what the fuck? Out of sight out of mind was the plan of the day, every day, for the next four years 'til Charlie could get himself out of this shit and back to the real world.

Charlie watched as the kid dug into the dirt, then mechanically dropped the sand and mud into the sack. His hands were caked with dirt from the stupid ass missing the bag so many times. They had last switched off maybe ten sacks ago. Charlie counted the bags he'd tied off since taking over and figured it was time to switch.

Alex dropped the last scoop of dirt into the bag, and Charlie said, "Switch."

The two locked eyes for the briefest of moments

and each could see in the other that manual labor had not cooled either one of them.

Good, Alex thought. Asshole. He grabbed his plastic water bottle from the grass and while he was at it he grabbed Bowman's. It wasn't that Alex was showing weakness or conceding to the prick, he just did it without thinking. Bowman turned as Alex tossed the bottle to him.

He caught it, then looked at Alex incredulously. "This doesn't mean shit."

"Fuck you," Alex retorted, stepping forward.

Bowman closed the gap until the two were less than a foot apart.

Alex was watching the kid's shoulders, knowing that he was going low. Once he got Bowman on the ground, he'd pummel him. Alex Stillwater, Low Country High School Wrestling Champion four years running, had yet to find anyone in the Marine Corps or anyplace else for that matter, who could hang with him on the ground.

The two didn't flinch, didn't breathe, each just waited for the other to act, to ring the bell.

"Hey, Mo-Tard's! Who told you to stop fuckin diggin?"

The instructor's million-candle-power spotlight blistered the two young Marines' eyes and they both shriveled back to the sand pit.

Alex grabbed the nearest sack and Charlie grabbed the entrenching tool. Neither spoke while each watched the instructor out of the corner of his eye. After the man seemed content that his two examples were back to work, he turned his back and moved on to the nearby smoke pit.

Alex looked to Charlie for a minute and saw the disgust on the other's face.

"Hey," he finally whispered.

No response.

"Hey!"

"What?" Bowman hissed.

"This isn't over."

"No shit."

"But they're gonna be hounding us the whole time."

"Lucky for you."

Alex ignored that. "I got a deal for you."

Bowman ignored him but Alex kept talking anyway.

"Night we graduate, we settle this, until then you go your way, I go mine. That way no one can get in the way, and we don't fill any more goddamned sandbags."

Bowman froze before spilling his next load of dirt into the waiting burlap bag. "Deal."

There was no handshake.

Chapter Three
Alex and Charlie
Two Months Later

For the Marines graduating from the Combat School at Camp Geiger, Jacksonville, North Carolina might as well have been Manhattan. Class '02-'09 was unleashed on the unsuspecting city like a tempest with pockets full of cash.

During training, Charlie Bowman had hooked up with a group of guys he'd known in basic. He, Mack, Duggins, Harris, and Paulson would shoot out from the base with two cases of Pabst Blue Ribbon and a carton of Marlboro Red "Cowboy Killers." Charlie was not a big smoker, but after enough beer they'd start finding their way into his hand. Like many of the guys he knew from Basic, Marines were given regular smoke breaks. Smoking was a way to get a precious few seconds to one's self while being run like a mule through that twelve weeks of hell. Charlie had tried it during basic but for some reason the taste of cigarette smoke when he was sober disgusted him. When he started drinking, he found that after four or five beers, he started to crave cigarettes.

After grabbing a bite to eat at Applebee's, one of the classier restaurants in Jacksonville, Charlie and the others made their way to Lou Ann's. Lou Ann's was packed to the gills with the breadth of Jacksonville's population. Charlie sipped casually on a beer while his classmates scoured the dance floor for females, in whatever form they came. Charlie hung out for the most part by himself, people watching, and keeping an eye out. Jacksonville, North Carolina would never be on anyone's "must see" lists. The patronage of the expansive nightclub was a mix of redneck, Marine, underage high school kids, and even some retirees trying to relive the good old days. The various groups melded into an undulating mass of bodies on the giant

15

dance floor as a DJ spun everything from Hank Williams to Ludacris.

Charlie appreciated the good times his friends were having, and intended to fully enjoy all that the rural night club had to offer. But first there was business to take care of. He watched the door for over an hour before Stillwater showed up. He was mixed in with another throng of their classmates. Charlie took one last swig of his Pabst Blue Ribbon beer that had gone warm while he nursed it. He remained still, leaning on the bar as he surveilled his quarry.

Stillwater hung at the back of his crew. Charlie could tell by the way he moved that he was not nearly as drunk as the rest of the crowd. He stood a little bit taller than the others. His movements were more defined, eyes more alert. Stillwater was twenty feet past the bouncer at the door when their eyes met.

As his anticipation grew, Charlie had hoped to see shock, fear, any kind of flight response he could revel in. He and the rest of his classmates had been training to kill people in the name of God and country for the last twelve weeks. Preparing to go to war stirs up the predatory nature in any human, that's what it's designed for. Charlie Bowman had been itching for a fight for almost three months while confined under the restraints of decorum in the training environment. When he looked at Alex Stillwater he saw the same aggression in the way his brow furrowed, his shoulders bunched and he'd started leaning forward.

This was going to be fun.

Alex made a beeline for Charlie, who fought his growing tension and forced himself to remain leaning casually against the bar.

"Figured you'd be here," Stillwater said when he reached him.

"Where the hell else would I be?" Charlie asked

rhetorically and rose from the bar to face him.

"You still in?"

Charlie motioned with his arm toward the exit sign near the bathrooms. Stillwater marched toward the red warning light.

The back of Lou Ann's was exactly as one would expect. A fence-lined alley full of garbage. The dingy battleground reeked of decades of stale booze and cigarette butts. Alex shed an orange polo shirt and tossed it on to the fence as Charlie unbuttoned a plaid short-sleeved shirt and did the same. Neither spoke as they squared off and began slowly circling one another.

Fists raised, each measured the other. Charlie had three inches and fifteen pounds on the slimmer Stillwater who was thin, but tightly muscled. They circled again, and one more time, then just as Charlie got set to unleash a haymaker, and Alex was going to shoot through Charlie's legs, a clipped scream shattered their focus.

The scream was so loud, so shocked, that both of them straightened and took a couple of tentative steps toward the parking lot. It was a feminine cry that repeated and was suddenly hushed. A lower tone, garbled in the distance could just be heard. Moving shoulder to shoulder now, Charlie and Alex exited the alley to find four rednecks clad in grubby flannel, t-shirts, jeans, and truckers' hats had a girl surrounded while a fifth clamped his hand over her mouth and held her in a chokehold.

They were toward the back of the parking lot where a field of scrub opened up for overflow parking.

"Come on, boys," the one holding her mouth shut said. "Train's leavin' the station."

Alex and Charlie didn't say a word as they covered the distance between the alley and where the group was sliding away from the lights of the bar. To her credit, the girl was a fighter. Charlie saw her trying to stomp the guy's foot who was holding her. She twisted and bit at him but he was still able to control her. He and the others laughed at her. As they closed in, Charlie saw her look toward him, she was scared, but she was pissed. He didn't know if she had really seen them coming or not, but at that moment she must have gotten a piece of the meaty paw clamping her mouth shut. The guy, grimy, wearing a dirty flannel. He looked like a trucker had too many miles alone on the open road, yowled. He let go of her mouth, spun her around and back-handed her with his non-bleeding hand. The girl dropped, eliciting a growl from Charlie Bowman.

The fat bastard had just enough time to look toward the sound, and realize what was coming as Charlie blew through the four surrounding men and took the prick off his feet with a clothesline to the throat.

Like all fights, things became a blur after the first impact. Alex recalled seeing the bottom of the guy's boots two feet off the ground after Charlie hit him. That was impressive. Alex attacked the closest of the assholes by kicking out the guy's legs from behind and following with a boot to the jaw when the guy hit the ground. He was tackled by two of them after that. They got him to the ground, but eight years' of competitive wrestling and twenty weeks' of Marine Corps training trumps redneck any day. Alex spun and rolled, attacking joints and leveraging one body in front of the other until he was in a crouch over both of them. He saw one bleeding profusely from the nose and the other moaning drunkenly as he twitched in the dirt.

The ringleader was out cold, sprawled on his back like a baby lying in a crib. The fifth guy, who must have gone after Charlie, lay curled in the fetal position crying like a six year old at the grocery store. Charlie stood over him brushing dirt off himself. His white t-shirt was ripped and wrecked, much like Alex's own. The big Marine mumbled something about women and gave the asshole one more shot in the ribs before moving on. He looked at

Alex with a grin, which faded quickly as the darkness was filled with flashing blue lights.

***

When Staff Sergeant McGregor walked into the Onslow County lockup he thought it was funny the amount of laughter he was hearing in a place specifically designed to stomp out any and all mirth from a given situation. When his corporal on duty called him he had to see for himself. While most see drill instructors as ass-chewing automatons the vast majority took great pride in seeing young Marines excel. The instructor corps, though loud and brash more often than not, watched the dynamics of their classes diligently. They watched personalities merge and diverge. Saw conflicts grow and boil over or simmer and cool.

On that first night, after the posted instructor overseeing Stillwater and Bowman's extracurricular training told him about the deal the two struck, he was both impressed and intrigued. In his ten years' training Marines for combat, he'd not once seen the kind of big-picture-thinking in two twenty-year-old Marines. The majority of his instructors didn't buy it. They didn't believe that two twenty-year-old hardasses, one of whose ticket to the Corps had been punched by a judge in lieu of jail time, could keep it under control for the extended period of training.

McGregor wasn't supposed to know about it, but there was a pool with a defined set of parameters to keep any given instructor from interfering with the natural dynamic. Last he heard, the pot was almost two grand, with betting about equal on which of the two would break and not make it through training without taking the other's head off. However, as time went on and training progressed, interest had waned. He and the instructors had figured by the end of the eighth week that the two had cooled and the feud forgotten. McGregor couldn't figure out if he was impressed or disappointed in the two as he came to rest in front of the cell containing two of his Marines.

One was lounging on a paper-thin cot and the other was leaning against a cinderblock wall, blathering about some garbage like they'd known each other for years. It took them a moment but when they realized they had company the two snapped to attention, but did not salute.

"My God, as I live and breathe," McGregor said. "Now as I have come to understand it, you two clowns overcame a force of double the strength of your own and secured your objective with no loss or casualties tonight. Is that correct?"

They were hesitant to answer. McGregor raised an eyebrow at their silence.

"Yes, Staff Sergeant!" they answered in unison.

McGregor nodded and slowly started pacing back and forth in front of the tiny cell. "On top of that fine performance, is it true what I heard, that you two just happened to be in the midst of settling a score from the first night of your training when you just happened upon the situation and took action?"

"Yes, Staff Sergeant!"

McGregor continued, "So you two held a collective grudge for twelve weeks, only to have your collective revenge soured by five rednecks and some gap-toothed waitress?"

"Yes, Staff Sergeant!"

"And now"—McGregor gestured toward the Onslow County Sheriff Shift Supervisor—"according to our brother-in-arms, you two have not shut up since you got here. According to our brother in blue, it's like a goddamned little girls' sleepover in here. Have you tried to braid each other's hair yet?"

"No, Staff Sergeant," was the subdued reply.

"Huh, mortal enemies to girlfriends in less than two minutes flat. That's pretty good."

"Thanks, Staff Sergeant," Bowman replied which gained him a look from both McGregor and Stillwater.

"Don't mention it, young'un," McGregor said. He put his fists on his hips and leaned into the bars to study his heroes. "So we're all friends now? You didn't just reschedule your mutual ass-whoopin' for maybe Valentine's Day next year?"

"No, Staff Sergeant."

"Well, good." McGregor turned back to the Shift Supervisor. "Lieutenant, would you be so kind as to let my boys out of there?"

The lieutenant unlocked the cell with a set of ancient, skeleton keys. "You boys aren't bein' charged with nothin', just policy to keep you under wraps if there's any violence. You did a good job on those five tonight. But don't tell anyone I said so."

Charlie and Alex filed out of the cell and looked to McGregor for their next move.

"Now that we're all besties, I want you girls to hold hands real tight, cause you got a plane to catch." McGregor smiled broadly and his eyes lit up, "I pulled some strings. I have a special place I'm sendin' you."

Chapter Four
November, 2004

When Lieutenant Danforth, Charlie and Alex's CO, shook the hand of each man in his platoon before mounting up in the APC, the two friends shared a look. They'd known something was up for the last couple of days. All the officers were on edge, and troops of Marines were joining them at FOB Ar Ramadi.

Staff Sergeant. McGregor wasn't kidding when he'd told them he had someplace special he was sending them. East Coast Marines normally joined units at Camp Lejeune after training. McGregor had been a West Coast Marine before becoming a drill instructor. Those strings he'd pulled had bucked the system and sent the two East Coast Marines to California's Camp Pendleton to join the First Marines

At the moment, Alex was wondering if McGregor had thought he was doing them a favor when he'd pulled off the transfer. When they'd mustered that morning, dressed out in full battle rattle, they'd been told they were going to Fallujah.

Charlie being Charlie, had quipped, "Sounds like a shithole."

Thanks to McGregor, Alex and Charlie were about to be part of the biggest Marine action since the invasion of Panama in 1989.

***

On any other day, Danforth would have shot back a sarcastic answer of his own. On that morning, though, the man had silenced Charlie with a look

That brought Alex back to the present.

No one spoke inside the cramped, stuffy confines of the Armored Personnel Carrier. Fallujah was a reported hold-out for Al Qaeda in Iraq. The Marines were going to flush out the terrorist group.

It was quiet, as quiet as the inside an APC can be, anyway.. Some of the guys checked and re-checked their weapons. Some guys listened to their iPod like they were riding the bus to a Friday night high school football game. Others just stared blankly at the boots of the guy across from them.

Charlie feigned disinterest. Alex could tell. He had noticed Charlie as had watched the buildup, growing more and more alert as each new unit flowing into their small FOB.

Alex scanned the rest of his unit. He was just a PFC, which equated to a private with a little extra color on his lapel, but he had grown an instinct for watching after his squad mates not only in the shit, but on their downtime, too.

His team was tense, to say the least.

Though this would not be their first journey into harm's way, this was not going to be a patrol along a road of talcum-powder sand hiding improvised explosive devices where you prayed with every bump in the road your truck wouldn't being blown inside out.

This was going to be a fight—United States Marines versus Muslim extremists from a hundred countries around the world.

Alex wondered for a brief second what Julie Majistrano was doing at that moment. He'd had a huge thing for the girl back in Charleston. That girl could sure fill out a sundress .... He imagined the flowing fabric teasing him as it revealed her tight, golden, sun-drenched legs every time the breeze picked up. She was at the College of Charleston last he heard. He could see her lounging against a backpack in the park at King Street and Calhoun, reading a cheesy romance novel in lieu of some god-awful text book. Alex was going to look her up as soon as he got out of this mess.

Then reality shoved away the vision of her

greenish-hazel eyes and curly, sun-glazed dirty-blond hair, and threw him back to the present. He scanned the faces of his squad mates and realized, although he yearned to be elsewhere, there was an equal, if not stronger side of him that wouldn't want to be anywhere else.

After his first tour, and the first four months of his current tour, it seemed like they were walking on eggshells in this Godforsaken place. Enemy fighters from all over the Middle East had flooded Iraq. These mercenaries—or crusaders, depending on who you talked to—mingled with the local population, and made fighting them without collateral damage impossible. Charlie and his fellow Marines had been like boxers forced to fight the first six rounds with their hands tied behind their backs. But not today.

Today they were going to cut loose. Alex and the rest of his Marines were not just ducking punches and playing defense today. Today they were unbound and bringing all their rage with them. His gloved hand slid down the frame of his M-4 rifle, which hung on a sling barrel toward the floor in front of him. He began an inventory and didn't want it to look like he was nervously fidgeting, so he slowly moved his hand down the weapon as he scanned it with his eyes. While he did this he recalled the feeling of the grenades he had stashed in his vest and the nine millimeter Beretta on his right thigh.

***

Two days later, the Marines of 3rd Battalion, First Marines, were weary to the bone. Door-to-door fighting had been the order for almost forty-eight-hours straight. Nerve-wracking, moment-by-moment as the men formed stacks and busted through doors of mud-brick homes with no idea what was on the other side. Sometimes there was nothing at all; sometimes a huddled mass of wailing women and children, and sometimes a withering barrage of 7.62mm bullets.

So far, they'd lost three of their brothers. Private Zedneck had been first in line, in front of Charlie. A monster of a Marine—a nineteen-year-old farm boy from Pennsylvania—and their door man for six hours, Zedneck caught a round in the hip on entry. He had crumpled as the bullet shattered his pelvis right in the doorway of a mud-brick shack full of amped-up fighters. Charlie dragged the wounded man out of the line of fire while Alex, right behind him, tossed two grenades into the middle of the throng.

After the ear-splitting explosions he'd gone in, M-4 blazing, to find that he'd killed all but two of them with the explosives. The two survivors moaned in shock, rolling on the fine talcum powder dust that covered everything. Alex shot each one in the head as he cleared the little room while the others tended to Zedneck, who was screaming outside.

It didn't occur to him at the time, being in the zone, doing his job, but that was the first time in almost two tours at war Alex could actually see the person he was killing up close. He'd fired his weapon during nighttime ambushes and what not. But that was always at a distance, firing where he thought the rounds coming in, were coming from. Not like that, up close, killing six men in a matter of seconds

***

This was their third day of almost constant action, of kicking in, or blasting through door after door with shotguns. The Marines, as much as they could, rotated the stack so the same guy didn't have to be on point every time. Everyone took their turn. There wasn't much talking among the men. No dark humor, no short, witty quips. They were playing Russian Roulette, but with buildings instead of a six-shooter.

When Alex and Charlie rotated back to the front, Alex was in the lead because Charlie, who was carrying his M-4 rifle with an underslung grenade launcher, was not really equipped to be on point. The lead guy on a stack was the man to put his boot through the door or shoot out the latches with buckshot. As practiced, the first man through made contact and announced their presence to the enemy, then was supposed to back out of the way and let the stack pass into the house with momentum and coordination.

Adrenaline and males in their early twenties kept the practice from being perfect, but with Charlie carrying the grenade launcher and being the biggest son of a bitch on the squad no one wanted him out of the action for a minute. Despite his cursing, arguing, and threatening, Charlie was ordered over watch with the big gun more often than breaking doors down.

For Charlie, having to watch other people break things while not getting to do so himself was absolute torture.

Alex positioned himself to one side of the door while the squad, with Charlie at the rear, formed up on the opposite side. Squad Leader Corporal Riggins gave hand signals when it was time to go. Alex had studied the door he was about to destroy. The building, a two-story mud-brick thing was nicer than most of the single story dumps they'd broken into in the last three days. It must belong to the mayor or something, Alex thought. When Riggins gave him the signal he went on automatic. Alex hefted the sledgehammer they'd been given as a field expedient breaching tool and planted it just under the brass lock.

The door flew open with a splintering crash and six United States Marines charged through the gap, roaring like Vikings storming a village. They were met by silence. Charlie was the last through the door and Alex followed him in. Weapons up, each man had his own field of fire, careful not to "laser" any other man on the squad with their weapon's muzzle. Using standard tactics, the first two men went left, the next two, right, clearing the corners and danger areas to the entry point. They were followed by the next two who cut a little deeper into the building, and so on as the Marines shuffled slowly deeper into the two-story house.

The squad moved forward in a line of six muzzles, each covering a field littered with potential enemy hiding places. Their heavy soled boots squeaked on the dust-covered marble floor. They were in what would equate to a foyer back in the States. A hall opened to a wide great room with doorways splitting off to the left and right. Straight ahead of them, across the large marble room was a courtyard that appeared to be surrounded by a five-foot fence. Each man tried to keep his eyes on as much ground as he could, and though no one would admit it, the men were exhausted and had almost lost their edge.

Alex and Charlie had taken positions on the far left wing of the line. They were creeping forward, abreast with the rest of the squad when Alex heard a barely perceptible click. Maybe he felt something … saw something in a window …he could never tell. He reacted.

In their exhausted state, the men failed to note the loft situated over the front entrance.

Alex shoved Charlie to his right, almost butt-stroking his friend with his rifle as he spun toward the landing. He never got a good look at what happened next. The impacts—1-2-3-4slammed into the chest plate in his vest and drove him backward. Alex used the momentum to carry him further away, toward any cover from the barrage of the automatic weapons fire

The staccato burst in his ears and the adrenaline reaction to the impact of bullets hitting his body threatened panic. Alex reverted to pure muscle memory. He bounded through the left-side door, chased by an angry swarm of rounds, which pockmarked and shattered the walls of the house. Curling around the wall, he saw movement, having lost his rifle when he was hit, he reached for his Beretta 9mm hand gun and slid it out of its holster. He wasn't sure what he was firing at, he just knew he wasn't alone in the room, and he wasn't dying without taking some of these sons of bitches with him.

Alex burst through the door and opened fire at the three surprised *Hajis* who were fumbling with their own AK-47s.Alex expended a full magazine into the three men, none of which managed to get a shot off, then spun and slid to the ground with his back against the wall. In a blur of motion he ejected the empty magazine from his hand gun, replacing the carrier with a fresh one with fifteen rounds. He then holstered the sidearm and recovered his rifle, which still held a full thirty-round magazine.

It was when he tried to stop and listen, get under control, and back in the fight, he realized he wasn't breathing. Then he was hyper-ventilating. He squeaked and hissed, eyes watering against the burning, pounding pain in his chest and shoulder. Fighting with his own body and trying to keep an eye on the doorway he'd just come through, he painfully slowed his breathing, trying to force air into his battered lungs by counting the length of his breaths.

One, two, three, exhale, one, two three, exhale…

For aa millisecond he scanned the room for a way out. There was none. He was trapped. It was eerily quiet. He could only hear his own creaky wheezing while he stared at the three dead men sprawled across the floor. He wondered what happened to his guys. Nobody was shooting. Then a form flashed across the doorway, and the unmistakable kah-kah-kah-kah of the enemy's weapon sliced a swath of mortar out of the dusty wall above Alex's head.

As the form dodged from the doorway, he responded by filling it with as much fire as he could put down.

***

Alex scanned the room to be sure it was empty

save for the three corpses in the center of it. He knew that, sooner or later, the fighters in the great room were going to simply charge and overwhelm him. They'd either kill him straight out or try to take him prisoner.

After seeing some of the YouTube videos uploaded by Al Qaeda during the last year, Alex had long ago promised himself he would never be one of those poor souls decapitated by those animals and splattered all over the Internet. Alex freed a grenade from his vest and waited.

**

Charlie hadn't heard or seen or felt any threat coming at him until Alex, smaller than himself by at least thirty pounds, slammed him out of the field of fire. Charlie had turned in shock to see four puffs of dirt fly from the front of his best friend's body armor. He reached for Alex, but he was slow, like in a dream; he was moving through molasses while Alex might as well have had a jet pack on. Then a storm of bullets filled the gulf between them and Charlie felt himself being dragged away.

Charlie hit the ground outside the building and after he regained his senses, tried to charge back inside.

Riggins stiff armed him. "Fuck, no, Bowman! There's no way to get in through there!"

"Alex!" he screamed. Then he heard the sharper crack of an M-4 contrasting with the stuttered sound of the enemies AK-47. "Fuck!" he yelled.

The rest of the squad melded into a loose perimeter around the house, half turned away from the house to cover from other threats while the others trained on windows with one eye and Riggins with the other. Charlie did neither. He eyed the outside of the building, did some quick math in his head, made a guess, and took off around the corner of the building while Riggins barked orders at him.

Coming around the side of the house, Charlie met a wooden gate between the six-foot sides of mud wall. He started firing through the wood, shattering the dried gate.

Moving forward, he moved his finger to the trigger of the M-302 grenade launcher under the barrel of his M-4 and squeezed.

***

Alex heard them talking, babbling in their guttural language, and figured the enemy was trying to decide what to do with him. For a moment, Alex thought about charging them. Throwing a grenade into the room and following it, burning through as much of his ammo as he could before they got him. But that room was huge and he had no idea how many of them were out there. He'd begun shaking, and the arm supporting his weapon was burning. He was losing control of himself and it made him mad. He felt his grip on the grenade loosen. He could still breathe. He counted that as a positive, though it was through clenched teeth. He figured that if a round had penetrated his chest cavity he would already be losing consciousness as his lungs compressed. His logic told him he just had the wind knocked out of him, that the plates had stopped the bullets. He heard agitated shuffling outside; it was getting closer to the doorway. They were coming for him.

Fuck it, he thought.

"Come on!" he yelled, then pulled the pin on the grenade and chucked it out the door.

Alex grit his teeth and waited. Suddenly a shock wave flattened him. A mountain of shrapnel, mud and dust covered him. In a panic, he found the trigger on his rifle and started firing just as bullets bit at the air around him. He could see them in the dust pouring from the doorway. His grenade must have fired but there were too many of them. He felt a tug at his hip and ignored it. He could see the muzzle flashes outside the door lashing at him. He kept firing. There was another tug at his boot. Then the entire doorway disappeared in a searing white fireball. Alex flinched and tried to cover as burning debris swallowed him for a second time.

"MOVE YOUR ASS!"

The English surprised him. Alex turned in a scramble and saw Charlie Bowman moving at him through a crater in the side of the house big enough to drive a semi-truck through. Alex rolled toward his friend, who was firing on full automatic through the doorway he'd just tossed a second grenade through. When he rolled, he screamed. He looked down at his side to see his desert digitals were stained a dark crimson. His left side would not respond.

"I said MOVE!"

Charlie grabbed him by the collar ring on his body armor and both of them fired as Charlie pulled him through the hole in the wall.

Sunlight blinded Alex as he was pulled from the building. Charlie got them both out of the funnel and Alex managed to leverage himself up on his right leg. The two retreated through the gate Charlie had smashed, and collapsed in the midst of their squad.

Things went fuzzy after that. Alex only remembered that he was suddenly growing very cold. Charlie lying next to him, heaving, and there was blood draining down the side of his body armor. Right before Alex lost consciousness he heard his friend mumbling,

"I got you. I got you …"

Chapter Five
Alex and Charlie
2006

"Two-Thirteen Control! Foot pursuit! Suspect black male, early twenties, white tank top, dark pants. Drake and South, heading north!"

"Copy 213, all units hold channel. Foot pursuit in the area of Drake and South Streets."

Alex heard the confirmation come from the dispatcher as he sprinted ten feet behind Antwan Jenson. The two men had met for the first time approximately two minutes prior to his radio traffic to Dispatch.

Antwan Jenson had emigrated to the East Side of Charleston, South Carolina by way of Baltimore. He was twenty-four years old, a high school dropout at the age of fourteen, and a semi-successful heroin dealer.

Antwan had heard about Charleston, how the turf was up for grabs. The Charleston heroin game was anyone's bet, that was the story Antwan got from the old-timers in the Baltimore projects. Those forty-year-old, broken-down ex-cons had some great stories. Antwan never thought to ask himself what they were doing in Baltimore if the streets of Charleston ran with gold. Antwan was never much of a thinker.

Three months ago Antwan had scored an egg, which is almost a half an ounce of uncut heroin from Kwame Rolston. Kwame ran the heroin game in west Baltimore. Antwan got the dope on consignment after he managed to sell Kwame on the idea that Charleston, SC was unclaimed territory, that it was open for expansion. Antwan was going to make him and Kwame rich, "Scarface rich," was how Antwan sold it.

A week later Antwan and his boy Jones got off the bus in North Charleston, the egg stuck in his ass in case they got stopped or hassled along the way. The two men had been small-time crack and weed dealers from the time they were children. As they made their way to the broken-down hotel where they set up shop off North Meeting Street, Antwan could smell the money already starting his way.

Antwan and Jones stepped on the heroin, diluting the purer form with various ingredients such as inositol and corn starch until they'd stretched their initial stash from a little less than a half ounce to about an ounce and a half. In street value, they had tripled their profit margin. Antwan and Jones circulated around town for the next week, learning the clubs and the locals.

They seeded a bag here and a bag there, laying the groundwork. Both men managed to hit up a pair of strippers at the Southern Belle Gentleman's Club after dropping a bindle of powder on them while getting lap dances. Anna and Mirabelle—Antwan doubted they were their real names—were their first regulars.

Soon word and business spread and the two men from Baltimore were serving strippers all over the Charleston metro area. Their stash went so fast they had to re-up from Kwame twice in that first month they were there. Money started rolling in, and Antwan was neck-deep in pussy. That was until Mirabelle, also known as Karen Tennent, was pulled over in West Ashley while she pushed a mailbox down the street with her Volkswagen Beetle. From what he picked up from some of the other girls after the fact, "Karen," didn't even realize she was locked up until Anna got her home and in a shower the next day.

Unfortunately for Antwan, he didn't hear that from Anna until after Jones was taken off in an undercover sting. Antwan was out collecting some cut when Anna showed at the hotel where Jones was holding down shop. She bought three bindles and left like she was in a hurry or something, at least that's what Jones told him when he called from County. Five minutes after the sale, the door to the room was smashed in and Jones, their dope, and fifteen grand cash was taken by the police.

That was two weeks prior to Antwan's current flight from the two blue uniforms chasing him through the East Side projects. First Jones gets taken off and Antwan is left broke. The next day Kwame calls and is looking for his piece. Antwan went back to the club to see if he could squeeze Mirabelle for some cash since it was her fault. He didn't even get a look at her before two bouncers, some redneck with a red ponytail, and a brother the size of a dump truck beat his ass in the parking lot. Antwan figured maybe Mirabelle was fucking them, too.

Like any good survivor Antwan knew two things: 1. He could not go back to Baltimore any time soon; and 2. How to break into cars.

His first three days Antwan had pretty good luck. Hondas were common and they were easy. He patrolled the areas around the college downtown; the students were stupid, always leavin' shit like cell phones, computers, and other shit in their cars he could pawn. Antwan cleared sixty bucks from the pawn shops those first two days before hitting the jackpot.

He took a gamble on a Ford F-150 after spotting a GPS unit on the dash. He was able to crack the door in under a minute. He scooped the GPS up off the dash and froze when he opened the glove box. His breath caught in his throat when he saw the piece. A Smith and Wesson, semi-auto, polished chrome on black. It was a nine millimeter. Antwan was shaking as he made his way back to the tiny room he managed to pay for day to day.

He buried the gun under the tattered mattress he slept on, then hit the pawn shop to sell the GPS unit. He was able to get forty for it, signing his name as Peter Hampton, 'cause he knew from the old days that cops can track what you sell at the pawn shop. That night he sat with the gun, feeling it in his hands, racking the slide back and forth. He must have emptied and reloaded the fifteen bullets in the magazine a dozen times. This was it, he told himself, this was the money-maker.

The next morning at nine-thirty, Antwan walked into the Bank of America at the corner of Meeting and Calhoun Streets. He played it so cool. He didn't wave the gun around, didn't go all Pulp Fiction on them. He simply walked up to the fine-ass white girl behind the counter and pulled his shirt up. Her eyes popped wide when she saw the gun. All he said was, "Gimme," and the bitch emptied out the register right there, six hundred and fifty bucks! For five minutes of work! Antwan had hit the big time.

That night he scored some of that real dank, hydro weed from a college kid off St. Phillip Street, grabbed a 750ml of Courvoisier and went to his room. It was a one-man show. The next morning he was layin' in a pool of his own vomit, surrounded by an empty liquor bottle and a bunch of twenties. He had a little weed left so he got baked to clear his hangover, then went back at it.

This time `Antwan stayed a little farther north and hit a credit union up in the Neck. Same game, he didn't even have to touch the gun, he just said, "Give it." An hour later he was countin' out eleven hundred in his room. Shit was too easy.

After that hit, Antwan had about thirteen hundred total to his name. He thought about going back to Baltimore to see if he could give a little back to Kwame and make peace. After a second thought, though, he realized Kwame would just kill him and take his scratch, so screw that. Besides, Antwan suddenly had a good thing going here in Chuck Town.

Jensen hit three more banks in the next two weeks, putting his total at five bank robberies on the Charleston Peninsula and a little over four thousand dollars gained in the commission of his string of felonies. It was on the seventh, at a little bank across from the Medical University, where things went sideways.

At a little before ten in the morning, like was his style, Antwan calmly strolled, if not strutted, into the Charter Bank. There were only a couple of people in the bank, most of them wearing scrubs, Antwan figured they were all doctors of some kind and immediately hated them for it. He strolled up to the counter where he came face-to-face with a little sista'. The girl had purple contact lenses and some kind of color in her weave. Her three-quarter-inch fingernails matched her eyes and she chomped on gum like a cow chewing cud. She looked at him like he owed her money as he walked up to the counter.

Antwan grinned as he pulled his shirt up to show her the gun. "Gimme," he said.

The girl, her name plate read Kammie, arched an eyebrow and cocked her head to the side while sucking her teeth. "Wha-chu wan?" she spit at him.

Antwan was lost for a minute. Thrown off his game by this girl in front of him. "Gimme the drawer!" he growled, shaking his shirt to emphasize the gun in his belt.

Kammie sucked her teeth a second time as her lavender eyes drifted, unimpressed, to the hand gun. Then said, "No."

At this Antwan heard gasps from around the small business, and he noticed two of the other tellers on the phone. His mind, still a little faded from smoking a ton of weed the night before, screamed they were callin' the cops. He took one last look at Kammie, she moved her head laterally around her shoulders, sporting an "Eat shit and die" look on her face. Antwan thought for a second about actually pulling the weapon and shooting the bitch but part of him thought the girl might actually attack him and beat him to death with his own gun if he tried.

Antwan dashed out of the bank as Kammie yelled something behind him he couldn't quite catch. He hit Calhoun Street like he was still in high school trying out for the football team. His forty time out the door was awesome, and was bolstered all the more by the sirens and squealing tires he heard racing behind him. On instinct Antwan bailed from the busy street and took to running between houses looking for a place to hide. Then he heard the boots pounding the pavement behind him.

Antwan heard the cop calling out on his radio, chasing him through the maze of narrow old Charleston row houses. He leapt over fences and dodged between houses, changing direction in an attempt to lose the cop. He couldn't get done like this; Antwan needed a place to lay low. He knew from past experience that where there was one cop, more will follow.

***

Alex saw the skinny black man wearing a black hoodie and blue jeans leap over a fence and duck in between two houses.

"Control, suspect is between houses in the area of Wilson and Minor Streets," he huffed into the radio.

Coming up to the fence, he vaulted over the four-foot chain link and tore off after Antwan. He spotted him once more about twenty yards ahead of him, running down a narrow corridor between two row houses. Alex tried to close on the man but he was carrying an extra thirty pounds in gun belt, body armor, and boots. The suspect was pulling away and Alex could see the suspect would have open ground to escape after he cleared the houses. The suspect would be out in the open again, and gone.

Alex cursed, and shouted, "Stop! Police! Get down on the ground!" When the guy looked at him over his shoulder, Alex was sure the guy grinned a little as he left Alex in the dust. The suspect turned to the left just as he cleared the house and broke out onto the street. Alex feared he was gone when he lost sight of him for a split second. As he raced around the corner, he stopped short when he saw the skinny man's gangly limbs akimbo as he crashed into the trunk lid of a Honda Civic parked on the street.

Alex forced a final burst of speed when he saw Bowman step into the gap, closing on the suspect he'd just taken out. Alex's eyes flashed to the suspect as he slid off the car and a hand went up his shirt. The suspect was just out of Bowman's reach and he was too close in to draw. Alex had the momentum with him as he threw himself out of the alley and smashed into the suspect just as he pulled a dark, heart-stopping object from under his hoodie.

Alex hit him with everything he had and scrambled to break the gun out of the suspect's grip as the two collided. He hit under the weapon and broke the man's grip over his thumb. The man yelped and Alex heard a crack as he rolled away from the man, gun tucked to his chest like a fumbled football. For a moment, he sucked wind, laying in the middle of the street. Then mustered the strength to haul himself to his feet.

He heard sirens in the distance and engines roaring in their direction. He saw Bowman holding the man between two cars. He straddled him, pounding the man's face into dog meat.

"You gonna shoot me, Bro!" he bellowed between blows as the suspect tried to curl into the fetal position beneath him. "Fuck you!"

Alex recovered the suspect's handgun and ejected the magazine from the semi-automatic pistol. He racked the slide back to clear the chamber. Once it was clear, he shoved the weapon in the small of his back and looked around. They were close to the college and he could see several pedestrians watching tentatively from corners and from behind trees.

"Eyes, bro," he hissed. "Get the cuffs on him."

"Fuck him!" Bowman yelled, hitting him again.

"I said *eyes*, asshole," Alex hissed again, shouldering Charlie to the side and rolling the broken man onto his stomach. Alex cuffed him and patted him down, then left him face down in the mud. When he stood up, Bowman was looking at the handful of people who had seen him "effecting" his arrest. When he looked at Alex, Alex shook his head and tapped a finger to his temple.

***

After they booked Antwan Jensen into jail, Stillwater and Bowman received the call Alex had feared was coming. Their shift supervisor, Sergeant James, wanted them at the team office to meet with the lieutenant.

Ten minutes later, Bowman and Stillwater were lounging as calm as they could, outside the shift commanders office waiting for Lieutenant Wopat to finish a phone call. They each tried to listen in as much as they could, but the small snippets of conversation weren't enough to give them an edge.

Alex watched the team commander, looking for signs that would tell him the seriousness of the problem they were facing. But Wopat always seemed pissed about something, always carrying around a stat sheet griping about the production of his team, or the amount of vehicle break-ins they had had the night before. Stillwater felt Bowman watching him and turned his way.

Charlie Bowman slouched in an old, broken-down office chair, grinning. He swiveled a little back and forth. His vest had ridden up toward his chin and framed his face. The man who had become Stillwater's constant companion since that fateful day in North Carolina five years before looked like an orphan who'd stolen an extra bowl of porridge.

"Quit being a pussy," Bowman mouthed.

Stillwater ignored him and turned back to studying the Lt. Mere seconds went by before he was kicked in the foot. He looked at Bowman, who again mouthed the word, "Pussy."

Stillwater pointed at himself and arched his eyebrows.

Bowman, still grinning, nodded.

Alex kicked his boot away. "At least I'm not a fuckin retard," he hissed, trying to keep it down.

Bowman scoffed, "I'm not the one who threw a beating on a guy in front of a bunch of college kids, dumb shit." Bowman leaned back in the chair once more, shit-eating grin now replaced by one of satisfaction: Mission accomplished. He spread his hands out to his sides. "Tough love, baby." The grin returned.

Alex had been taken by his friend; he'd let him push a button and he knew it. Alex had received a complaint a couple of months back after he had to wrestle a drunk Junior at the College of Charleston to the ground during a brawl at one of the fraternity houses. Alex had been cleared but he'd been put through the ringer by internal affairs. Bowman knew he could piss him off whenever he mentioned it. Alex was lunging from the chair toward an equally advancing Bowman when they were both stayed.

"Get your asses in here!" Wopat yelled.

Wopat was staring at his computer screen as the two cops filed in and took their seats in front of his desk. Alex and Charlie shared one final look before Wopat looked up from the screen, consternation layering his features. The three men stared at each other for a long moment. While Stillwater and Bowman stared back with dead-eyed sterile countenance. .

When Wopat finally looked away, he grabbed a sheet of paper from his desk and held it in front of them. "Do either of you know a Ms. Emily Coughlin?"

"No, sir," they said in unison.

Wopat smiled. "Well, Ms. Coughlin is a resident of Smith Street. She is an English major in her first year at the college, an unnecessary point she offered to tell us. She has concerns that our police force abused a man she saw arrested on her street earlier today."

There was no response from the two patrolmen.

"Now, you two miscreants have been my best performers since you invaded my fair city two years ago. That's why I put you together in the same squad. That's why I give you lenience when you don't write tickets or do your required number of community liaison communications. That's why I don't keep you two confined to your beats like the rest of the flatfoots patrolling my peninsula. What you boys make up for in felony arrests have made this team's stats the strongest in the Department. With performance comes opportunity .... Are we understanding each other?"

"Yes, sir," was the tandem response.

"This ..."He held up the email that he received from Internal Affairs after Coughlin made her complaint—"...is the kind of thing that makes all those perks disappear, gentleman. An email detailing a complaint sent to me from IA. This is the kind of thing that gets a good team broken up. This ..." he pointed to the email with his free hand for emphasis. "... Is where all the stats in the world don't mean jack shit if every arrest comes with an excessive force investigation. So, before the circus starts, what happened?"

Bowman and Stillwater stirred just a smidge in their seats and looked at each other.

"This is not the time for teamwork, boys. Tell me what happened. Now."

"Sir, the suspect was armed and refused verbal orders to comply with a lawful arrest. He led us on an extended foot pursuit, at the end of which he attempted to pull a firearm on Officer Bowman as he tried to effect an arrest," Stillwater reported.

Wopat looked to Bowman.

"Sir, the suspect and I were in close proximity and I was out of position to see the weapon as it was being drawn. Officer Stillwater disarmed the suspect and in the process took the both of them to the ground. While Officer

Stillwater rendered the weapon safe, I attempted to subdue the suspect, who continued to try to flee."

"Did you hit him?"

"I struck him in response to his attempts to strike me as I continued to try to effect the arrest."

Wopat looked at Bowman.

"Sir, Officer Bowman issued verbal commands during the altercation which the suspect continued to ignore. Once I was able to secure the suspect's weapon I assisted Officer Bowman and the two of us were able to subdue the suspect and make an arrest."

"The suspect ended up with twenty stitches and a broken jaw."

Neither of the two responded to that.

They watched as Wopat again searched them for some form of deceit he could lock onto. After a moment he seemed satisfied and slid back in his chair with a chuckle. "You two are like my own demolition crew. You get the job done and you keep me looking like a hero at the damn comp stat meetings. I've read your reports, and what you just told me coincides with those reports. I'm going to report back to Sergeant Hilmire that this complaint seems unfounded."

The two officers breathed for the first time since they sat down.

"But," Wopat continued, "don't think for a second that the brass upstairs can't put an end to you two in a hot second. Complaints like these, founded or unfounded, will put an end to good cops quicker than a bullet, you two understand me? You're good cops and you make me look good, that is our arrangement. The second that changes, we have a problem. Get back to work and keep your shit clean. Dismissed."

Chapter Six
Six Months Later

Charlie and Alex were sitting on a known crackhouse one of Charlie's buddies in Narcotics had dropped on them as a possible quick score. It had been a quiet couple of weeks while on day shift and the two cops were getting antsy for a good arrest.

The house, in only the loosest sense of the word, sat back on the dead end of Romney Street. Charlie had parked their cruiser three blocks down on the opposite side of the street to watch for cars or conspicuous foot traffic making the turn off King Street. There were only three houses on the dead end. One of the three was abandoned and literally caving in on itself while the other was still inhabited by an eighty-nine-year-old lady who still trimmed the flower beds on the stoop every morning.

"Poor old lady," Charlie had said while they were reconnoitering the location. "Probably been there in her dream house for sixty years, and had to watch all this shit fall down around her."

The two were on their third day in on a four-day nonstop shift. They had managed to dodge calls and sit on the place for the last two. It was Friday, their last shift day, and the fifteenth, which meant every slinger in Charleston was picking up or stealing a welfare check. The two had high hopes, as long as they could keep from having to run and cover the garbage calls that had been dogging them. Three calls in the last hour for vagrants and one for shoplifting at the Winn Dixie planted dead center in the hood.

"I don't know why they even bother calling in shoplifters from that place, Jesus!" Alex commented as he slammed the radio down after another unit thankfully picked it up.

It was going on four, two hours into their stakeout,

when a gray minivan slid around the corner from King Street heading for the target location. The guys perked up as the vehicle pulled to a stop in front of the house and a black female stepped out of the van and went inside.

"Did you get the tag?" Alex asked.

"No, too far away," Charlie said.

The girl was in the house for almost ten minutes before exiting. When she left the house both men noticed a backpack slung over her shoulder. As the girl got in the van they saw her hand the bag off to a second person in the passenger seat who they hadn't seen. From the distance, the two passenger was only a shadow. After a minute, the van pulled away from the house and made a U- turn at the end of the street.

The gray van was heading for King Street when Charlie asked, "What do you think?"

Alex sighed. "Kind of thin, but it would make really good cover to move some shit around."

The girl piloting the van was watching traffic when she stopped at the corner of Romney and King Street. She had her blinker on and didn't even look their way. The party next to her, however, was locked onto the black and white. From what they could see he was maybe white or Hispanic, wearing a wife beater. His head might've been shaved but they were too far away to know for sure. The passenger watched them like a rabbit watches an owl while the girl driving made the turn. Every traffic law was observed to the letter. The van turned and Alex and Charlie watched for any violation before pulling out into traffic.

It was Alex who laughed first when he came eye-to-eye with the third passenger in the van.

Charlie laughed as well when he saw the three-year-old boy sprawled across the side window of the van like a Garfield cat with suction cups on its paws.

'That made it easy," Alex scoffed.

"Pff, there isn't a kid in a car seat within ten

blocks," Charlie said as he pulled out into traffic.

"That doesn't make it any less illegal." Alex called dispatch and notified that they were pulling a traffic stop at King Street and Stewart. He gave the dispatcher the description of the Honda Odyssey and the South Carolina license plate.

Charlie flashed the blue lights and turned on the siren while Alex cracked his door.

To their surprise the guy in the passenger seat didn't run. Alex checked traffic before walking up to the driver's window while Charlie covered the passenger. As they walked up, the three year old bouncing around the center row of seats slammed into the window, making Alex jump just a little. When he saw the little kid with a gapped-tooth smile waving at him he gave the kid a quick nod before continuing.

The black female lowered her window as Alex approached. The sweet, tart stench of marijuana rolled out of the window. Alex didn't respond to the smell.

"Ma'am, I'm Officer Stillwater, Charleston Police Department. Do you know why I pulled you over today?"

The girl sucked her teeth. "I dunno. 'Cause I'm black?"

"Exactly," Alex responded. "You're black in a predominantly black neighborhood; we've been waiting for someone like you all day."

Just then the kid leaped into the space between driver and passenger, and yelled, "Po-wice man!"

"Can you think of anything else I might have stopped you for?"

While Alex was engaging the driver, Charlie knocked on the passenger window and gestured for the white/Hispanic/Italian/whatever-male to roll his window down. The man grimaced before lowering the window. The glass wasn't lowered by an inch before Charlie got a lungful of weed smoke.

Lacking the discipline of his partner, Charlie burst out laughing. "Damn!" he yelled. "Get outta the car."

The passenger's eyes flared and he looked to his lap. Charlie dropped a step back and in less than a half second was aiming his department issue Glock model 21, .45 handgun at the man's forehead. "Hands! Now! Show me your goddamn hands, now!"

When Alex heard his partner break leather and start belting out commands, he instinctively dropped back and likewise drew his weapon. "Outta the car right now, ma'am!" he said.

The girl rolled her eyes as he opened the door with his free hand. As she slid from the vehicle like a limp rag doll, Alex one-handed her wrist and put her face down on the street.

The three year old started bawling.

The passenger hesitated just a second too long and Charlie took the offensive. Freeing his left hand from his weapon, Charlie back-fisted the guy on the bridge of his nose. Two empty hands shot up to his face but failed to protect him when Charlie grabbed a handful of the guy's greasy black hair and dragged him through the window and bounced him off the curb.

"Partner?" Alex yelled.

"Oh-four! You!"

Alex didn't respond, instead the two met eyes across the open cabin of the van, a three year old screaming hysterically in the middle. Alex made sure the cuffs were secure on the female and did a quick pat down to ensure she had no weapons. He then looked into the eyes of the screaming little boy and tried to reach for him. "It's okay, little guy. Everybody's okay."

The kid looked right through him and continued to scream.

"What's your kid's name?" Charlie asked as he opened the passenger door.

The male, handcuffed and bleeding from the nose, spit a gob of blood and phlegm on his boots, and yelled, "You don't talk to my kid, motherfucker."

Alex heard the exchange over the blaring sound of a frightened three year old, and warned, "Partner—"

Charlie wasn't listening. "Your kid?" He loomed over the asshole. "What kinda dad smokes a shit ton of weed with his kid in the car?" He punched the handcuffed man in the face twice. The man's curses turned to dribbling babble. When the man started bawling like his son he rolled him onto his back. "Your kid," he growled again. "If I get my way you'll never see that kid again, asshole. Cry about that."

***

Three hours later, young Brian Thompson was spending the night with the Charleston County Department of Social Services, Brian senior and Veronica Union, Brian's baby mama, were tucked away in the Charleston County Jail. Charlie and Alex were again sitting in front of Lieutenant Wopat.

"Veronica Thompson states that you struck her handcuffed baby-daddy in the face in front of their child. That true?"

Bowman was sitting rigid. "No, sir. I only used force necessary to effect the arrest."

"Right." Wopat looked at Stillwater. "You?"

"Sir, I was detaining Ms. Union. I could not see Officer Bowman or Mr. Thompson."

Wopat stared down the partners long enough to make each of them squirm just a fraction in the uncomfortable chairs they'd become accustomed to. Finally the older man sighed. "Boys, these phone calls from IA are becoming a regularity. Now, I don't know and don't care how valid these complaints you are accumulating are. Most assholes you two run into deserve to have the fear of God beat into them, good on you. And this asshole in particular had thirty pounds of weed in the car with his kid, so fuck him."

The two officers breathed for the first time in over a minute.

"But," Wopat continued, "someday one of these is going to take root. Some asshole in this dear department of ours, or one of our local do-gooders is going to make some shit like this stick and it will be the end of our ride together. You will either end up running traffic, walking a beat, or selling lures at Bass Pro Shop, and it will be for some asshole you wanted to teach a lesson to."

Bowman started to argue but when he saw Wopat was giving him a chance to step on his own dick, immediately thought better of it.

Wopat broke his glare at Bowman. "I don't want that any more than the two of you. Now, it's the last day of the tour. Go home, drink it off, spank the old lady, I don't give a shit. You guys have been slipping. Work it out over the break and come back with your shit together. Or change will be coming. Read me?"

"Yes, sir," was the tandem reply.

"Dismissed."

***

By the time Alex got to Sammy's, Charlie and Sammy O'Laughlin were halfway through their respective repertoires of war stories. Sammy had been a Charleston PD cop during the 'seventies and 'eighties. In nineteen eighty-eight he was working an off duty detail at a Piggly Wiggly on James Island when two thugs pushing shotguns stormed the place right before closing. Sammy was fast on the draw, but, that night he wasn't fast enough. He took a full bore of buckshot to the chest before he could get his first shot off.

But Lamar Charles and Pinky Eldridge were not aware of the fight they started, nor were they students of wound dynamics like their victim Sammy O'Laughlin.

O'Laughlin, who went down with the first shot behind a checkout counter. When Charles and Eldridge strolled around the edge of the counter to celebrate the cop they'd just killed, Sammy was waiting.

The two wannabe bad-asses had never gone up against a Vietnam veteran before that night. Charles' last sight was the muzzle of Sammy's .38 five-shot pistol spouting fire as he shot the would-be cop-killer through the bridge of his nose. Pinky lasted a moment longer and was able to pop off a wild round, which shredded Sammy's left knee right before Sammy butterflied the last four shots from his revolver, stitching the skinny little shit from his navel to his throat.

The way Sammy told the tale (over and over again) and the way other old-timer regulars at the bar recalled it, when units arrived they found Sammy whispering into Pinky's ear as the man died. Blood flowing from the cop's chest, mouth, and shattered leg, they swear they heard Sammy telling the stricken man in the midst of death throes that he was going to meet him in hell, and that he was going to shove a spit up his ass and roast him over the fires for the next millennia.

Sammy laughs when he tells the story, and there are two pump shotguns crossed over the door into the bar Sammy opened after he was medically retired. Eldridge had managed to cause enough damage to require the Sammy's left leg to be amputated below the knee. Sammy also had buckshot buried in both lungs that night, but that never stopped him from biting the filters off his Marlboro Reds before lighting up.

"Things were different back then," Sammy said with a chuckle.

"Justice was still a real thing back then." Charlie sighed as he recalled the bureaucratic nonsense cops have to deal with on the streets today.

When Alex bellied up to the bar next to Charlie, he

saw the old, cracked leather blackjack Sammy held gingerly in his right hand. He was catching him in the middle of his blackjack rant.

Sammy gave him a nod as he rotated the flat leather paddle with embedded ball of lead in the center on its side and did a tomahawk gesture. "See, if you turned this little beauty just so when smacking some asshole you could lay him open like you were cleaning a dear. Actually took a guy's ear off with that move one night. Ha ha, asshole," Sammy said, then downed a finger of Jameson. "Whiskey?" he asked Alex.

"And rocks."

"Done."

"What's up?" Alex asked his partner.

"Don't start," Bowman said, shooting back his own tumbler of amber liquid.

"What?" Alex asked.

"Don't what me. That asshole had it coming today. Fuck him."

Alex threw his hands up. "I didn't say shit, dude. Fuck you."

"You were thinking it, though."

"What?"

Bowman turned toward him. "You're gonna lecture me on how we're gonna get laid up for throwing these assholes the beatings they deserve."

"No, I wasn't."

"Right." Charlie turned back to the bar.

"We do need to watch that kind of shit, though."

Charlie's head dropped to the oak bar with a thud. "My God! I knew it."

Alex sighed. "Fuck it, let's just drink then."

Sammy arrived at that moment and slid a tumbler filled to the brim with Jameson to Alex. "What the hell are you girls bitching about?"

"He thinks we're gonna get done for excessive

force or some bullshit," Charlie blurted.

"Erickson, Henry, Geddrick …. Do I need to go on?" Alex was looking at Sammy, pleading his case. "And those were all bullshit. Righteous ass-whippings every one, and every cop is now out of the game. But, no one is coming to save us from bullshit allegations, and IA makes their bones on people like us. We need to be smart, is all I'm saying. What good will a wayward haymaker do for us if it costs us our badges?"

Sammy was swaying a little bit, either from the booze or the prosthetic leg, He just looked at the two of them for a moment, then said, "Ah, shit. You young guys are fucked either way you cut it these days." He jabbed a finger at Alex. "You do your job and deliver swift justice when required."

Then he jabbed a finger at Bowman. "And you, don't let that temper cost you good years on the street. This is the only job in the world where you can save the day every day you put that uniform on. Don't fuck it up."

Alex and Charlie glowered at each other until they were splashed with tequila as Sammy smacked two shots down on the wood in front of them; he had one for himself. "Now we drink to the only adventure left in the world, and you two get your shit together."

Chapter Seven
2012

"I'll handle it, Sarge," Alex called from the booking room behind the front desk at 180 Lockwood Avenue.

Charlie was signed up for an off-duty job outside of O'Henry's Bar on the Market so he could make a little extra cash. Since the department required an ounce of blood from its officers before approving any type of overtime outside of time spent in court, most cops worked almost as much time at off-duty jobs as they did on the department clock. In the past couple of months, Charlie had gotten it in his head that he needed a new pickup and he'd been working an extra twenty hours a week trying to come up with a down payment.

That left Alex in the booking room with Benjarvis Green, who, earlier that night, had decided to silence his nagging wife by wrapping her in duct tape and beating her with a broken axe handle.

The call had caught the two men off guard. It had been a clear night, quiet on the radio, so quiet that Alex and Charlie had opted for a rare sit down burrito at Juanita Greenberg's on Wentworth Street, downtown. Greenberg's was a dive, serving college kids on the Peninsula massive burritos, cheap beer, and other Tex-Mex food to speed them on their way to the dreaded freshman fifteen. Alex had just peeled the first layer of aluminum foil from the gut bomb of steak, refried beans, lettuce, rice, and cheese when both men's radios squawked an alert tone.

Alex had heard somewhere that a study had been done on patrol cops and firemen, and how they reacted to the random alert tones. Firemen dead asleep in the middle of the night waking up to a blaring siren, and cops just about to bite into a hot slimy mess of greasy food suffered the equivalent of a massive heart attack every time an alert sounded. He never heard how legitimate the study was, or if it ever really happened. But he believed it, no matter what was going on, when an alert tone sounded all activity ceased. The world came to a screeching halt and everyone just waited in silence.

After the tone died the dispatcher reported the domestic violence call eighteen, South of Broad, which meant someone was beating the shit out of that someone's loved one, and it was in the richest part of Charleston. Alex's burrito and Charlie's quesadilla were left steaming on tin plates on the table of a grimy booth at Juanita's while they ran for their car.

Response time was less than five minutes, and all the while the two cops were relayed reports from the dispatcher. Apparently the nine-year-old daughter of Ben and Markey Green was calling from her upstairs bedroom: She heard her mother crying, and her daddy yelling. When they pulled up they were met by Unit 224, a single-man cruiser piloted by another cop named Hanahan, who'd just beaten them to the scene. Alex and Charlie chased Hanahan up the front steps of an ornate, pastel-blue two-story house. They could hear what sounded like a male yelling from inside the residence. Hanahan didn't miss a beat between freeing his gun from his holster and kicking in the front door.

"POLICE!" they yelled simultaneously.

"Fuck you!" was the hoarse reply coming from deep in the house.

Alex broke left to clear a sitting room populated with ornate, antique furniture while Charlie broke right to clear an entertainment room, which was blaring the movie the *Dirty Dozen*.

Hanahan continued straight down a hallway toward what looked like a kitchen area. "Police! Show me your hands and get down on the ground."

"Fuck you!" he heard again.

Alex had paralleled Hanahan through a dining room, which swung around to the dining area. He cleared the corner a second before Hanahan reached the opening from the hallway, "Hold, 224!" Alex screamed at Hanahan.

Benjarvis Green was standing just to the right of the doorway, ax handle poised like a baseball bat. The man's eyes went wide when he saw Alex's Glock aimed at his forehead.

"Drop the weapon!" Alex commanded.

Green looked at Alex's gun again, then into his eyes. The wood club in his hand quivered just a bit.

"Drop it," Alex told him. "Do it now, sir."

Green's massive shoulders sagged. The man was built like a house, thickly muscled; his neck was as wide as Alex's thigh. Green hesitated another moment then dropped the ax handle to the floor. Alex circled to the center of the room, keeping a bead on Green.

"Come on, Hanahan," he called when he had a clear field of fire and Green had backed off his ambush point a couple of steps.

Hanahan slowly moved out from the doorway, triangulating the huge man with Alex. He came across the handle and kicked it down the hallway with his boot.

"Get on your knees," Alex ordered.

Green was slowly lowering to the ground when Charlie's voice boomed from the other room. "Two-eighteen Control! Get me EMS. Female down, unresponsive."

Alex watched in horror as all the rage that had drained from Ben Green's features roared back, the white man's stubble-covered face boiled red. "Get away from that cheating bitch!" The man spun and charged Charlie, who was on one knee, attending to an unconscious Markey Green.

"No!" Alex and Hanahan yelled together.

Charlie looked up in time to see Green's mass

block out the light coming from the kitchen like an eclipse. But Charlie was fast, he sidestepped the hulk, and drilled his fist into the man's floating rib, then followed with what should have been a lights-out punch to the temple. Unfortunately for Charlie, the guy was enraged, and as it turned, out lit up like a Christmas tree on cocaine and whiskey. The man backhanded Charlie, sending him flying into a coffee table. Green was about to stomp on his wife when Alex and Hanahan hit him, one high, one low, and the fight was on.

There was a point during the fight seemed to stretch on to eternity when Alex was pretty sure he caught an elbow in the temple from Hanahan. He was also pretty sure he straight-punched Hanahan in the face.

All the while Green was trying to beat on both men; all three screamed and cursed like a trio of demons fighting to break out of hell. Alex worked on the big man's face like a speed bag while the guy's flailing arms tried to choke him out. Neither the cops nor the coked up wife-beater gained ground. Just as quickly as the battle started it came to an end with a mighty crack. Alex felt the wind of Charlie's Motorola radio as it missed his cheek by a hair's breadth to smack Green directly across his forehead. Ben Green's body convulsed as his nervous system backfired and shorted out. The big man hit the floor, then curled into the fetal position, both hands nestled around his nose as a torrent of frothy blood spilled through his fingers.

Charleston County EMS responded and transported both Mr. and Mrs. Green. Alex rode in the ambulance carrying Ben Green to keep the man tame during his treatment. Three hours later, his wife slipped into a coma after surgery for closed head trauma. Green had suffered a couple of scalp lacerations and a shattered wrist, gaining seven stitches and a cast, then was cleared by the medical staff to go to jail.

By the time Alex and Charlie got to the booking

area their shift had been over for two hours and Charlie had to get to his off-duty gig. That left Alex, the Desk Sergeant, and Ben Green in the office. Green was still a little wobbly after the Motorola strike to the forehead. This made him less than cooperative and forthcoming with his identifying information. The cast on his wrist also made fingerprinting a bit of an adventure, though the man only howled twice while Alex tried to maneuver his arms around the live scan system. In fact, Alex's only point of amusement that night was Green's booking photo which clearly detailed the reverse imprint of M-O-T-O-R-O-L-A stamped squarely over his brow. Alex saved a photo for himself and Charlie, knowing that his partner would get a kick out of it.

An hour and a half after arriving, Benjarvis Green, a once well-respected and prosperous contractor, was dressed in prison orange and left in a cell surrounded by derelicts and drug dealers to keep him warm that night. When the adrenaline had decreased, Alex picked up on the chronic booking area stench of bleach, body odor, and feet. He moved the charging affidavit, investigative reports, and use-of-force statements to the roll call room.

Alex was finishing up, ready to head for home and a big shot of Jameson when the television blurted a breaking news alert. Alex was technically off duty and popped his head up to see what was happening. The older male anchor was framed in one shot. The freeze frame on the screen to the right depicted a police cruiser with a beaming blue light. Under the image were the words "Police Brutality in the Low Country."

"Ah, shit," Alex breathed and stepped closer to the TV screen.

The anchor grimaced into the camera. "Good evening, Charleston. We have interrupted our regularly scheduled coverage to bring this shocking piece of video received just minutes ago from a local viewer." The scene behind the anchor grew and overtook the screen, then faded to a background Alex knew all too well. It was the Market downtown. "I warn you these images may be disturbing to some viewers," the anchor's disembodied voice narrated.

Alex watched, his stomach reeling, as the dark and shaky video began to play. On it he saw the last person in the world he wanted to see: Charlie Bowman. There was no mistaking his best friend and partner, a hulking figure looming over a skinny black male, who lay underneath him. The black man kicked, trying to curl up and protect himself from a hail storm of punches thrown by Bowman. Alex slouched against one of the desks, mouth hanging open as he watched the video loop over and over showing Charlie beating a man on a crowded Charleston city street.

When the video finally ended Alex didn't even hear the anchor return to his commentary. He sat there alone in the empty roll call room, the room the two men had joked, pranked, and received their marching orders in night after night since coming back from the desert. It didn't occur to him then that they would never have a moment together again in the room or in a cruiser, running Charleston's darkened streets.

Chapter Eight
Alex
One Year Later
2013

Alex Stillwater was trying to get a sip of boiling hot coffee while his scrambled eggs finished cooking on the stove when his phone rang. The ringtone was a clip taken from Kansas' Wayward Son which meant his personal phone was ringing at six-thirty in the morning as opposed to the robotic beeps of his department issue cell phone that usually ruined his morning routine. Frowning at the number, he saw that it was Sammy, whom he hadn't seen in more than a year.

He paused for a couple of seconds, then answered, "Stills." He was greeted by dead air, "Hello? Sammy?" There was no response, then the line went dead.

Stillwater hoped that the old bartender had only butt dialed him or something, but the nagging worry that the old coot had had a heart attack or some other ailment gnawed at him. Stillwater figured he was just being paranoid. Then his phone chirped: It was Sammy's number again, this time with a text message: 911.

Alex grabbed the pan of still-cooking eggs from the stove top and tossed it into the sink, grabbed his coat and ran for the door.

Alex burned through red lights on the way to the bar. Beating on his horn and hitting his siren when needed, he blew down US 17 from West Ashley to downtown. He felt a little wave of guilt at the realization he hadn't been to the bar and hung out with the old man, since he'd transferred to the Central Detective Bureau nearly a year ago. He tried to tell himself that it was the hours he worked that kept him from going out. That maybe the fact he was a married man had kept him away, but in the back of his mind Alex knew he was just making excuses for himself. After the debacle that ended his career in patrol, Alex really hadn't felt like he should hang out at the bar at all. It just didn't seem right.

When he pulled up to Sammy's, the squat box-like two-story building was dark. Being a cop bar, the windows in the front were blacked out and there were very few advertisements that would draw a crowd. Alex hopped out of the car and tried Sammy's number again with no luck. He approached the front door and cupped his hands against the glass to look inside, then saw the aluminum and glass door was ajar by a couple of inches. Alex upholstered his Glock and, flipping on the small light from his belt, slid inside.

"Sammy?" he called tentatively.

The first shot pinged into the metal door frame to the left of Alex's ear. Instinctively, Alex juked to the right, and jumped behind the old oak bar as cover. The second and third shots silhouetted a figure at the rear of the dark room, near the restrooms and exit. Alex kept moving and fired three shots in return, using the assailant's muzzle flashes as his reference point.

"Police!" he shouted.. "Put the—" A swarm of rounds coming from now two distinct assailants zipped and popped in the air around him.

As he crouched under the bar, Alex caught sight of the heavy-set limp form sitting on the floor against the wood shelving at the other end of the bar. As his eyes adjusted, he could see an old pump-action shotgun cradled in his lap.

"Sammy?" he hissed.

H heard mumbling from the other end of the room. He popped up for a split second and saw light filling the space as they dashed out the back door. He could hear sirens in the distance; the cavalry was coming.

His gun trained on the rear doorway, he scanned

the room with his light and made his way to Sammy. Blood had soaked through a white t-shirt, his V-neck sweater, and a pair of old khaki trousers. Alex knelt next to the man and felt for a pulse.

As soon as he touched him Sammy bolted upright, grabbing the shotgun at port arms. "Muthafuckers!" He coughed a pink cloud of blood and immediately fell back.

"Sammy, it's me, Stills. Just lay back."

Sammy's eyes floated, confused and glassy until he was able to focus on Stillwater. He coughed again as he tried to say something.

"Not now," Alex tried to calm him. "Not now." Alex pressed a hand against the hole in Sammy's chest where he seemed to be losing the most blood.

The old man shoved his hand away while he gagged and reached for his leg.

Alex didn't know where the tenacious old copper got his energy from; he couldn't believe the man was still conscious given the amount of blood pooling around him. Sammy strained, hacking up a continuous gob of phlegm and blood as he ripped his prosthetic leg from under his knee and sat back in a huff. The old man wheezed as he tried to get the breath to speak. Alex went back to trying to put pressure on his wound. He felt the pressure build and fall on his palm beneath his hand as the air escaped and then tried to suck back in though the wound as Sammy wheezed.

"Hold on, old man. What happened?"

"Charlie!" Sammy finally spat and Alex froze.

"What?"

"Charlie," he wheezed through cyanotic lips and bulging eyes. "He's in trouble, Alex."

"What did he get you into?" Alex responded accusingly as he ripped an old, stained rag from the bar and tried to shove it into the chest wound.

"Fuck off, Alex. You don't know shit." Sammy

reached into his pants' leg and retrieved a tiny plastic square. He smeared it into Alex's palm with blood and grime. Then Alex watched as suddenly the lights seemed to dim; Sammy was fading away.

"Come on, Sammy," he tried, "stay awake, stay awake!" Alex slapped him lightly on his jowls, "Come on, Sammy."

The old man perked up for just a moment. "UC," he whispered, then went limp.

"UC? Come on, Sammy. No."

Screeching tires and blaring sirens sounded outside.

"Stay with me, Sammy. Can't you hear 'em? The cavalry's here!" he pleaded.

"He needs you," Sammy whispered His eyes closed and his body went limp.

Alex felt his pulse as the old man slid toward the floor. There was nothing. He noticed the blood boiling from his chest had stopped and there was no pressure on the palm of his hand anymore.

Chapter Nine
Charlie
2013

Charlie wasn't sure if it was the smell of diesel or antiseptic that drew him out of his stupor. When he opened his eyes to the dim lights, he saw a blurred, dismal figure hovering over him. He felt the pressure of a stinging burn in his shoulder that reminded him he'd been shot. The memory of the ambush roared back into his mind and he shot upright. He grabbed for the shadow in front of him, then felt a sudden jolt punctuated by a loud CLANG! Breathing in ragged, staccato gasps, Charlie found his wrists handcuffed to the cot he lay on. The figure above finally came into focus and in the gloom of the dim amber lights he saw the slight and sharp features of an Asian woman. As his senses began to return, he heard the low, droning sound he knew as a ship's engine.

"Whe—?" he started to ask the silent woman.

"Good, you're awake."

Charlie heard the voice and felt the warming rush of an adrenaline dump flood his system. Turning his head, he saw the organization's main enforcer, Billy Hopkins, about twenty yards away, standing under a halogen light in the middle of a cavernous dark area Charlie figured must be an empty cargo hold. Charlie saw Keith Milligan bound to a metal chair next to Hopkins. The man's right leg was soaked in blood, his head was bowed, and his body heaved with each breath.

"I was worried I might have rung your bell a little too loudly back at the shop. Luckily, we've got Mai there to bring you back to us." Hopkins smiled as he nodded toward the woman.

Charlie looked himself over and realized he had an intravenous connection running from his forearm to a saline bag hung above him. Gauze and tape covered his left hip.

"Shit," he breathed.

"You have no idea the depth of the shit you are in, my friend," Hopkins told him. He looked down at Milligan. "Now, old Keith here was a little more alert than you when we got here so he and I have kind of a head start on you. So far, from what Keith's told me, you are a fed, trying to catch us bad guys the old sneaky way. That so?"

Charlie didn't answer. He watched Hopkins' every move.

"Keith hasn't as of yet told us much more than that." Hopkins reached into his waistband and retrieved a six-inch revolver and let it hang in his hand. He crouched down to Milligan, who didn't lift his head to meet him. "Does that about sum it up there, Keith?" he asked.

Milligan didn't respond.

Charlie saw him squirm weakly against his bindings.

"Looks like it," Hopkins answered his own question and took a step away as he raised the pistol.

In his last moment Milligan's head lifted just so he could look at Charlie Bowman. The two men who'd worked in this dangerous and deadly world together, watching each other's backs for the past year, said, "Sorry, Charlie." The .44 in Hopkin's hand spouted fire. The shot reverberated through the metal walls of the cargo hold.. The heavy round threw half of Milligan's head six feet across the grimy deck plating.

"No!" Charlie yelled. "Motherfucker!"

Hopkins studied his work for a minute, then turned the weapon in Charlie's direction. He closed the distance between himself and Charlie, then leaned in close, "Save your strength, rat," he hissed. "You're gonna need it."

Sudden movement from above drew Charlie's attention from Hopkins and he saw the Asian woman injecting something into his IV drip. Less than five seconds later the world started to float away.

Chapter Ten
2011

Alex was moving on. Charlie had seen it coming for a while; his partner had started talking about becoming a detective after they were assigned special duty chasing an arsonist the year before. Charlie had seen how Alex watched the plainclothes officers, how he paid attention to the questions they asked, the notes they took, and the observations they made.

Charlie swirled the whiskey around the melting ice rocks in the tumbler he held and watched from the old wooden bar as Alex got congratulated and slapped on the back by the commanders, members of their patrol team, and other cops that had come to Alex's promotion party. Charlie felt the two were miles apart. He looked around the old, hazy bar and watched the party carry on around him for a moment, then he emptied his glass in a silent toast and slid away.

***

Luckily, the rear patio was vacant. Charlie didn't feel like chatting when all the small talk would surround the "breaking up the band" as everybody called it. The lieutenant had already told Charlie he'd be taking on a rookie once Alex made the transition to the Central Detectives Bureau in a few months. Though Alex was now technically a detective, he wouldn't leave the street until a slot vacated by a retiring detective came open in another six months or so. It seemed a little funny to be celebrating already when Alex wouldn't really move on for a while but cops never needed much of a reason to get drunk.

Charlie wasn't jealous of his partner, far from it. He knew Alex Stillwater would make a great detective, whereas Charlie was always in the moment, dealing with life as it unfolded. Alex could see through even the wildest of situations, rise above the chaos, and see how things would play out. Charlie always harassed him for overthinking things, but he had to admit Alex always seemed to be right. Somehow the man had a knack for strategy Charlie couldn't fathom and that was fine. Charlie was happy running from call to call, dealing with life in small hectic packets. Handle the crazy and move on, that's how Charlie liked it.

Charlie was alone on the darkened patio for about ten minutes before Alex popped through the back door and plopped down in a metal patio chair next to him.

"What's up, man? You pissed?" he asked.

Charlie raised an eyebrow and scoffed, "Nah. I always knew you couldn't handle it on the street. I was actually going to suggest the move myself at some point. Getting tired of looking out for your ass."

"Dick," Alex said, taking a pull off his drink.

The two sat in silence for a long moment. They'd been together almost daily for the better part of a decade, through hell and back. The fact that they would no longer be side-by-side seemed to hit both of them right there.

It was Alex who finally broke the silence. "When are you going to make the jump? You know they would take you."

"I know. I don't know, though. I'd have to wear a tie. And I'm not sure I could give up jumping hot calls, not sure I'd fit into a nine-to-five shift. Shuffling paper back and forth."

"I hear ya," Alex said scanning the bottom of his glass. "Anyway, it won't be 'til Redman retires in a few months. We still have plenty of time to save the world between now and then."

"Right."

The two chuckled.

Just then the back door popped open and Erica, an EMT Alex had hooked up with during a call to a traffic accident a couple of months before, poked her head out.

She was dressed in a form-fitting skirt and heels; her dirty blond hair danced about her shoulders. She had a smile that melted men's hearts every time she flashed it. She slid out the door and sat on Alex's lap.

"They're asking for you inside," she announced, "and I think Sam is trying to get me hammered."

"No, he tries to get everybody hammered," Charlie told her as the three stood to return to the party.

Charlie lingered for a moment as the couple went ahead. He watched them together and knew things had definitely changed between the partners. He figured it had changed for the better ...as long as you looked at the big picture.

***

Two months later Charlie was hovering over a drink at The Blind Tiger on Broad Street. Alex had a dinner date with Erica and Charlie didn't feel like hanging out at Sammy's, listening to old war stories he'd heard over and over again. He'd decided he needed a change of pace and he liked The Blind Tiger; it was kind of out of the way and had a big outdoor bar where he could disappear if he wanted to.

When he arrived, he'd found Cindy Webber tending bar. Charlie and Cindy had had an on-again off-again thing going for a couple of years, ever since he and Alex responded to a break-in at her and her roommate's loft on Coming Street. Charlie hadn't talked to her in a while and was surprised to find her at the bar when he walked in. The last time they'd hooked up, she was a hostess at one of the fine dining restaurants off East Bay. The two had a shot of tequila together, then chatted about absolutely nothing for almost an hour till the bar began to fill up.

Charlie found himself alone in a crowd, watching Cindy debating whether or not to try to re-ignite things. He re-upped for another Maker's Mark and rocks, returned a wink from Miss Webber, and was just about to retreat to the patio when his drink was nearly knocked from his hand as an older guy wearing khakis and a polo shirt took the stool next to him.

Charlie set the drink on the bar and sat back down for a second to wipe the liquor from his hands. When he finished with the wadded-up napkins he looked up and the guy who had bumped him was facing him and watching him dry his hands.

Charlie asked, "Can I help you with something, pal?"

The guy in the polo shirt was older than Charlie by a good bit, he guessed maybe pushing fifty or so. His hair was gray and formed a sharp widow's peak atop his forehead. He carried a beer gut but had once carried some muscle around his upper body. The look in his eyes told Charlie this was not a chance meeting.

"Did you just motherfuck me, son?"

The old man's question caught Charlie off guard and he almost laughed. "Pal" was a term saved for those times when cops were not in a position to call a citizen a motherfucker or any number of insults. It was old-timer code Sammy had educated him and Alex on when they'd first started drinking with him. The fact that the old-timer knew the term and had called Charlie out told him two things: 1: He was a cop. 2: He was here for Charlie, which meant he was Internal Affairs or some other bullshit.

"What do you want?" Charlie asked.

"Your name came up as a potential candidate for an operation I'm putting together. I wanted to talk to you in person, away from prying eyes. This seemed as good a place as any. Keith Milligan, Immigration Customs Enforcement. You got a minute?"

***

After he was relieved of duty, Charlie made sure to run into Alex while returning his equipment to the department.

The two half-circled each other for a second before Alex greeted him tepidly, "You okay?"

Charlie paused for a minute before answering, "Put me on the suspension until trial. Who knows when that's gonna be."

"Yeah."

"You're gonna take the stand for me, right? As a character witness?"

Alex's eyebrows creased when he heard the question. He sputtered, "Well, … er …."

"What the fuck, dude?"

Alex threw his hands up. "Fuck you! What the hell am I supposed to say under oath? That you're a fuckin saint? We ain't saints! I can't cover for you anymore, man, not this time."

Charlie circled his friend. "Nice. When the goin' gets tough, huh? Fuck, you're not even a detective yet, and you've already turned into a pussy. What? … Erica got your balls in her med bag or something?"

"Don't put this on me, you fuckin prick," Alex said, jabbing a finger at him. "How many times have I had your back, covered for your dumb ass in front of the brass? You never fuckin listened when I said to cool down. No, instead you just went fuckin cowboy whenever shit got a little hot."

"So you're a fuckin martyr now?" Charlie raised his voice. He noticed they were starting to draw a crowd. "Well, shit, my bad, then. I didn't listen to your sorry ass and got the job done. You know that fuck deserved the beating he took. He saw Alex fuming, and made his move. Fuck you, dude," he said as he turned his back on his oldest friend.

It took less than a second to get the desired result. "Where you goin, asshole!" Alex hissed, grabbing Charlie by the shoulders.

"Get off me," Charlie shouted, spinning and stiff-arming Alex.

Alex rushed him and Charlie met his charge. He ducked a punch to the jaw from Alex but missed the knee to the ribs. He rolled with the strike and caught his friend with a roundhouse punch to the face that every uniform present could clearly see. The two friends and former partners rolled around in the muck behind 180 Lockwood Boulevard in full view of ten uniformed cops. To Charlie's surprise the other cops let them go at it for longer than he thought they would. After the two managed to score a strike or two, a couple of uniforms jumped in and pulled them apart. Charlie winced at his bruised ribs but saw Alex, blood running down the side of his face, was fuming. He fought the cops for a couple of seconds then stormed off without a word.

A sergeant from the West Side who had stepped in, leaned in close to Charlie, and whispered, "You should go before the brass gets wind of this. Not a very graceful way to go out, Bowman." Charlie was then let go and left alone to limp away, feeling sorry for instigating the fight

As was expected, less than a week later the prosecutor added the charge of assaulting a police officer to his already impressive list of charges. As was expected, Charlie pled guilty out of court and in the "deal," received a sentence to include six months in the Charleston County Jail.

Chapter Eleven
2012

He remembered those last moments before Milligan dropped him off at the county jail.

"This is it, kid," he'd told him, "last chance to get out."

Charlie had been close to taking the out. Even when he was a cop he'd hated jails. The smell of too many humans lacking a sense of hygiene all crushed in together. The stench of a mix of dirty socks, unwashed ass, and bleach lingered even after you left the place, stuck in your clothes and nostrils.

But Charlie had made the deal, given Milligan his word. "I'm good," he'd said.

Charlie was housed in the same pod as Steve Tyrell, one of the targets of Milligan's investigation. Tyrell was a low-level guy who'd gotten popped on a battery charge after he'd tuned up his girlfriend, Mindy, after she'd used grape jelly and not strawberry in the peanut butter and jelly sandwich she'd made him.

Normally, the woman never called the cops when Tyrell went at her, and even if the cops showed she would stand by her man just as her mother did. But when officers from North Charleston PD took the call from a neighbor that they were at it again, Mindy couldn't hide the massive swelling over a broken orbital bone and Tyrell was booked. The judge gave him nine months.

Charlie kept his distance from the rest of the population, including Tyrell, on his first day in lockup. He wanted to get to know his battle space and who the players were in his particular pod, as the inmates called it. There were fifty or sixty inmates locked into Pod-3 as far as Charlie could tell. He strolled the perimeter of the social area, a wide-open space with stuffed chairs and couches that had a couple of televisions on wall mounts and a small stack of books that, by Bowman's estimation, were ignored. He traded between circling   and slouching in one of the chairs as he watched the inmates amble around the open area, most kept to themselves. No one wanted to make any overly loud or boisterous movements—that's how you attracted attention. No one wants to attract attention in jail.

There were a couple of groups outside the majority of poor bastards who just wanted to do their time and get out. Two or three guys would move as a group or play cards or dominos at one of the tables. If you weren't simply trying to hide from everyone, there was always safety in numbers.

Bowman recognized a few faces, a couple of the guys he'd stopped on the street, or seen their mug shots when narcotics was looking for them. He didn't find anyone that first day that he'd put away, but given some of the looks he received and the quiet whispering that followed him everywhere he went, he knew most everybody knew who he was.

So much for keeping a low profile.

And then there were the guards. There were two stationed inside Pod-3, and six more that made random patrols. They strolled through every now and then like they owned the place, like you have to when you work in an enclosed space where the bad guys outnumber you twenty-to-one. Every one of them who made their way through the pod took a moment to glare at him.

Charlie was the new attraction, like a circus freak whose tent was Pod-3. They'd point and talk about him as they made their rounds; some would scoff, while others just shook their heads. Bowman figured there'd be no back up coming from the badges inside the Charleston County Jail when the time came.

Once he got a feel for the place and the players roaming the pod, Charlie kept his eye on Steve Tyrell.. For a guy bad enough to beat up on his girlfriend over a cold hot pocket, he sure didn't adjust well to prison life. Tyrell was not a big guy by any means. Maybe five-eight and a hundred and sixty pounds, if he'd just been pulled out of the mud. He spent most of his time inside sitting in one of the stuffed chairs as far away from the other inmates as he could. He walked with his shoulders hunched. He darted his eyes around as if he thought one of the inmates was going to drop from the upper-level railing and drive a shiv into him. Tyrell reminded Bowman of a cockroach scurrying around the floor with the lights on. He wasn't quite sure what to do, he just knew he needed a place to hide.

In a place like this, populated by predators. They had keyed in on him as he skittered this way and that around the pod. He was an antelope in the midst of wolves, and they sensed his weakness. Bowman waited and watched as though it was a National Geographic documentary.

* * *

The incident, as the guards liked to call it, came the third day of Charlie's confinement. He had posted himself near the library of worn, tattered paperbacks where he could keep an eye on most of the communal area. He had left his cell as soon as the door unlocked so he could get out early and watch the population as it woke for the day.

Tyrell had stayed inside his own cell, hiding, until one of the roving guards spied him trying to lay low and kicked him out. Bowman watched the man shuffle along the upper level, where the majority of the cells were, as he made his way toward the stairs. The man's head was low, his greasy hair hung over his face, and his shoulders caved in around his chest. He looked like he was headed for the gas chamber rather than a dull day of afternoon talk shows and boredom.

When he got to the main floor, Tyrell found his perch as far away from the other inmates as possible, just like he had every day. Bowman scanned the room as Tyrell sat down to try to hide in plain sight. He wasn't the only one watching Tyrell as the wounded animal squirming on the African plain. Two guys, one black, one Hispanic, had tracked him to his seat. They were playing checkers twenty feet from where Tyrell had landed. Charlie watched them whisper back and forth to each other while glancing and nodding in the little man's direction. When one of them got up with the checker board in hand and started to walk in Tyrell's direction, Charlie put his book down.

***

Steve Tyrell *was* hiding in plain sight. When he was seventeen he got busted for stealing a car and spent two months in the Mecklenburg County Jail because no one would pay his bond. Things didn't go well for him then. He was a small guy and he knew it. He wasn't strong or big and he wasn't good in a fair fight. But in the time since his first arrest twenty years ago as a car thief, he'd proven himself. Taken lives when needed, he didn't care who or why, but that was with a gun and more often than not from the shadows. There were no guns in the can. Tyrell might not have been the smartest dude in the clink, but he was smart enough to know that this was not his environment. He was at the bottom of the food chain in jail. He knew he had to stay quiet and low to get out of there in one piece. And it was all because of that bitch.

Steve was at his spot, hunched over in a stuffed chair as far away from the rest of the inmates as he could and still be in the pod. He'd tried to stay in his cell as long as he could, but they'd eventually flushed him out and into the jungle. The pod was crowded with men dressed in orange jumpsuits shuffling lazily around the public area. Steve fidgeted in his seat as he buried his head in the *People* magazine someone had left in the chair. He wasn't reading a word of it. He didn't read that great to begin with, but regardless, the last thing he cared about was how many different hair styles Justin Bieber had sported in the last year, fuckin pansy.

Instead, Steve soothed himself, thinking of the payback that whore had coming to her when he got out. He would get out sooner or later, nobody did real time for slapping around the old lady. He would do his time, stay low in this den of jackals, then get back on the street. And when he got out he was heading straight for his bitch. She would let him back in, like she always did. She was a fuckin doormat, and he was gonna stomp his boots on that fucking doormat; she would never see it coming.

He was going to come home cool, maybe even bring the bitch some flowers. He would apologize, talk real nice, then he would take her out to dinner. Maybe he would take her to the boss' place, he had the money, it was stashed in his truck and she knew better than to go near his truck. Steve was gonna wine and dine the old girl, get her dessert, then they were going out. She liked the beach. They would go to the beach out near Folly. After the sun went down they would walk and talk and hold hands, just like old times. They would walk to the end of the path and look at the lighthouse, maybe even get it on in the sand dunes. It would be the night of her life. Then they would walk back to his truck.

At the truck he would hold the door for her and as soon as she turned her back he was gonna whack her across the head with his most prized possession, the .38 Detective Special that was stashed with the cash in his truck. He would thump her over the head, just enough to soften her up. Then he would tie her up at her hands and feet and drive to Wadmalaw Island.

Wadmalaw was just far enough out of the way for no one to notice him. There were some old dirt roads out there that ran along the marsh. Remote places where he could take his time teaching that bitch her final lesson. He had a hammer in his truck bed, it was old and rusted but it would work. Tyrell smiled without knowing it and licked his thin lips as he thought about the look on her face when he laid into her.

First, he would smash her knee caps. The pain would wash away any lagging dizziness from when he hit her in the truck. Steve wanted her awake for what he had for her. Tyrell was going to work her body with the hammer, smashing ribs, and beat her liver and kidneys.

The bitch was going to suffer for sending him to this shithole. He was going to use the hammer on her body, but he would save her face for his bare hands. Gloves, don't forget the gloves, he told himself. They would come looking for him after she was gone and he couldn't have any bruised knuckles that would give him away. Tyrell could feel her bones crunching under his fists as he beat her senseless. But he would have to be careful. Tyrell didn't want to knock her out; that would be too easy.

For the end he would drag her to the marsh, to a little creek where no one ever went, or would ever see. He would choke her then. She would look in his eyes as he did it. How did such a great night go so wrong, she would ask herself as he strangled her. What happened?

Tyrell shivered a little in his seat thinking about her broken and bleeding body writhing underneath him. When it was over he would drag her into the water and tie her to a cinder block. The crabs would do the rest. He would be satisfied and the crabs would eat good. Within a week there would be nothing left of that stupid whore but bones that no one would ever find. Tyrell sighed and slumped in his chair in a brief moment of peace just as a checkerboard came flying over his lap.

"Motherfucker!"

The pure instincts of fight or flight had Steve Tyrell out of the overstuffed chair and on his feet before all the checkers hit the concrete. He found himself staring down two guys he didn't recognize. They were both taller than he was, with tight muscles around their arms and shoulders. They scowled, thick eyebrows crunched, lips pursed.

"What you do that for, punk?" the first one barked. His bald head gleamed under the incandescent lights.

"Bitch thinks he's funny," the other one, with short dreads dancing around his cranium answered.

Tyrell hadn't realized it but he'd already retreated five paces from the chair he'd been sitting in. He looked at the two men, knowing the confrontation was going to come to blows. This was the playbook while locked up. Everyone gets tested to see what they had. Those who failed lost everything in an instant. His insides were quivering like a Jell-O mold fresh out of the fridge.

"I didn't do shit, asshole, and you know it!" Tyrell shot back. He hoped his voice didn't crack. He directed his words at the smooth-domed Mexican since he was the smaller of the two. These guys were younger than he was, maybe in on their first beef. Tyrell knew they had chosen him as an example. To make their name in the cell block, so to speak.

"What? Punk." The guy with the smooth head closed the gap on him, tried to tower over him. Tyrell stood his ground, let the guy close the distance, and swung a wild haymaker at him. There wasn't much to the punch that a guy raised on the street couldn't handle, and Tyrell knew it. He swung the punch more for pride than anything else. He knew if he went down without a fight he was done for.

His antagonist with the bald head side-stepped Tyrell's attack and leaped back in with a jab that froze Tyrell in his tracks. The strike took him right under the beak-like point of his nose at the pressure point where his nose met his upper palette. The shock of the impact sent an electronic short through his system that paralyzed Tyrell for just a split second. His eyes began to water, blurring his vision; he saw two forms in orange closing on him through the distorted, swimming colors.

They swarmed him and bounced him off the concrete floor. Before Tyrell could get his hands up to protect his face, the bald one had already pummeled him with his fists. He tasted blood. He got his hands over his face and just as he put up his defense, the Mexican turned his attention to Tyrell's abdomen and began raining blows down on his ribs and stomach. A shot to the diaphragm left Tyrell choking, trying to suck wind. He tried to move, to squirm or roll, but the man was straddling him, holding him down with his hips as he beat him savagely. Tyrell tried to curl into a ball as the beating continued but that just opened another part of him up to punishment. He looked like a frog on a hot plate trying to protect himself from the bald criminal using him to build his jailhouse name.

***

Charlie had watched the two predators close in on the oblivious Steve Tyrell and watched them initiate the confrontation. When the yelling started he shot a lazy look toward the corrections officers minding the desk. The guy, balding with a mustache even a child predator wouldn't sport, was at least sixty pounds overweight. He had his nose buried in a magazine with a monster truck on the cover. Charlie knew the little bitch was well aware of the trouble, but the fat bastard didn't want to take the chance of having his ass kicked, too.

Charlie let the two men get Tyrell to the ground before he started their way. Truth was, he needed Tyrell to take an ass-kicking and the more he took, the better it was for Charlie. It also didn't hurt to let the two pricks dishing out the pain wear themselves out a little bit before he got there. Less work for him.

He decided to move when he saw blood spurt from Tyrell's nose. The guy with the baby-dreads had his back to him and was too fixated on the beating his buddy was handing out to notice Charlie sliding up behind him. Charlie grabbed a handful of stinking, greasy black hair and ripped the man's head back while with his free arm, driving his fist into the side of his neck, igniting the brachial nerve like a Christmas tree. The man was at Charlie's mercy as he swept his leg and drove his skull into the concrete with a wet pop that reminded him of a cue ball hitting the floor.

The ground-and-pounder straddling Tyrell noticed his friend fall. He paused his assault and straightened to look toward his friend. This tee'd himself up nicely. His chin rose, eyes wide and confused, just as Charlie tried to kick a field goal with his head. The man flew backward with the momentum before crashing to the floor. Before Charlie turned away he noted the guy was kicking limply like a dog having a bad dream. Charlie wanted to chuckle, recalling the look on the guy's face but there was no time for that, he was in role.

He walked away from the three men without even looking at Tyrell. Just as he turned he caught eyes with the CO and threw him a wink. He heard Tyrell scramble to his feet, mumbling through split lips and bloody gums.

Tyrell gave chase as Bowman continued walking without acknowledging the little man. He heard him huffing and puffing and trying to clear bloody snot from his smashed nose.

"You're that cop, right?" Tyrell asked.

"Not anymore," Charlie responded, still walking away.

"Man, I owe you one."

Bowman spun on his heel and planted his face less than an inch from the one eye Tyrell had that wasn't swollen shut. "No shit, asshole," he hissed. "You fuckin owe me big." Tyrell flinched and moved back. Charlie advanced to maintain the distance on the back-peddling redneck. "Without me they would still be wearin' your ass out right now. And tonight you would be blowing those animals through bloody gums so don't think for a second that you owe me any less than your fuckin life."

Tyrell stuttered, "Uh-uh-huh." He wouldn't look Charlie in the face. "I know," he finally whispered.

"Right." Charlie left the man bleeding and alone in Pod 3.

Chapter Twelve

With three months to browbeat a dumb redneck into believing he couldn't survive a day without him, Charlie had Steve Tyrell right where he wanted him by the time they were released from the Charleston County Jail. They weren't out two days before Tyrell was calling him.

"Hey, man, I need some backup."

"What's it pay?"

"I can get you three bills."

"Fair enough."

They met at a West Ashley dive bar called Ms. Jeans. It was a hole with a much different clientele than Charlie once appreciated at Sammy's. In the dank, rotting bar, Charlie sipped on a lukewarm PBR and kept his head low while he waited for Tyrell, who was twenty minutes late. Charlie scanned the room every now and then, seeing a face he recognized here and there. He had grown his hair out and had a curly mess hidden under a grimy old gamecock's hat and his beard was out a quarter of an inch. Charlie Bowman looked nothing like the cop he once was but that didn't keep him from trying to lay low while he was slumming.

Milligan had done some recon prior to meeting with Tyrell. Ms. Jeans was an old Dixie Mafia stronghold and judging by the biker colors and tattoos sported by most of the twenty or so patrons in the place, it still was. The girl behind the bar, who Charlie figured was at one time relatively hot, was showing the telltale graying skin and dead eyes of a steady meth user. She asked him if he wanted another beer and he nodded. As she set another warm beer down in front of him with a clank, Tyrell slid onto the barstool next to him.

"Hey," he whispered, eyes darting around the room "You ready?"

"Where we goin?" Charlie asked without looking at him.

"I'll tell you when we get there," Tyrell answered. "Let's go."

***

Twenty minutes later, Tyrell pulled the old shit box Chevy he was driving into a warehouse adjacent to the Port of Charleston. The place looked like it could crumble around them at any moment. Charlie took in the wet, gloomy, amber light cast by the halogen lights affixed to the cavernous ceiling. The ancient truck splashed through puddles on the concrete floor as they approached a group of four or five men standing next to a long, metal container box like one would find on a ship. The thought of what the container held made Charlie's stomach turn.

Tyrell put the truck in park, and whispered, "Let me do the talking."

Charlie didn't answer; he was too busy gauging the attention his presence had drawn. He wasn't a full five feet from the truck before a gleaming chrome revolver was in his face.

"What the fuck?" Charlie yelled, putting his hands up. "Tyrell?" The man holding the gun was Billy Hopkins. At least that was how the background dossier identified him. Charlie felt like he knew Hopkins already, given how much he had read about him. Charlie didn't like him anymore now that he was meeting the man in the flesh.

"What the fuck is this, Stevie?" the man barked, keeping his eyes on Charlie.

"Whoa, whoa, whoa! It's cool, Hopkins, damn! He's cool."

"Fuck he is, you dumb shit! This fucker's a cop!"

"I'm not a fuckin cop! Get that thing out of my face!" Charlie ordered.

Hopkin's eyes lit up like searchlights during a

81

break out at a mental institution. "Fuck you say? Huh?" He closed in on Charlie, who held his ground. "You're a fuckin dead man."

For a second, Charlie thought the piece of shit was actually going to shoot him. The idea pissed him off. He had to control himself. He put his hands down, getting ready to charge Hopkins. If he was going to die, he was going down on the advance. "Tyrell! What is this?"

Steve Tyrell stepped in between Hopkins and Charlie while the two glared at each other. He got face-to-face with Hopkins. "This dude's cool, man. I swear, he had my back inside. Did some pretty nasty shit to some East Side Rollers, too. He's not a cop anymore; he did time, for Christ sake."

"That doesn't mean you bring the son of a bitch here, you dumb shit."

"Just give him a chance, Hopkins. Come on, man."

Hopkins looked from Charlie to Tyrell then back to Charlie, silent for a long moment. Charlie watched the man's eyes. He could tell the bastard really and truly wanted to shoot him. He wondered what was holding him back. Clearly Tyrell had more juice than he or Milligan figured. Finally, Hopkins lowered the gun and got in his face.

"Get in the fuckin box truck and stay there. Keep your fucking eyes forward." Then he turned to Tyrell, "You're lucky we need your scrawny ass or I'd have both of you pricks fed to the fuckin gators by now."

***

Charlie figured that since the prick hadn't shot him he would count that as a win. He took his seat in the box truck like he was told and looked ahead down the dark corridor of the dungeon-like warehouse while they loaded what he could only figure was a couple of dozen desperate and broken women into the back of the truck. He'd known that the operation was trading in human slaves, but it made him sick despite the fact he'd had months to prepare himself for it. Actually being a part of it, and not doing anything to help these women ate at his soul. It only took fifteen minutes or so before Tyrell hopped in the truck and they were on the road.

Charlie sat in silence as Tyrell piloted the truck through the streets and finally onto I-26 heading west.

Before he could say anything, Tyrell started laughing. "Shit," he giggled, "I knew Hopkins wouldn't shoot you."

Charlie arched an eyebrow and shot him a sideways glance. "He wanted to shoot you, too, ya know."

Tyrell clicked his teeth. "That angry fucker knows better. Anything happens to me and my uncle would be down here in an hour, mowing down the whole operation."

"Your uncle?"

Tyrell nodded. "He distributes the girls out of North Carolina. Has a couple of trucking companies that run the girls all over the country. Without him, Hopkins and Westchase'd be nowhere."

"Who's Westchase?"

Tyrell paused for a moment and Charlie wondered if he was pushing too far. He watched the wheels turn behind Tyrell's dull eyes for a moment, then Tyrell said, "He's the importer. Old money, he owns a couple of shipping companies and has the girls brought in from mostly Asia. But every now and then there will be a delivery from South America or maybe even Eastern Europe. Westchase is into everything and has the whole town wired. That man has everybody; we've never been messed with once."

"Sounds like a pretty good deal," Charlie observed.

"Keeps me in the green."

"So we are transporting illegals. Is that what all this is at the end of the day?"

Tyrell nodded. "For the most part. They show up here and we move them out. My uncle keeps them moving out to the highest bidder. Simple as that."

"Huh." This is going to be easier than I thought, Charlie thought.

Three hours later they pulled into a barn on an expansive, secluded farm outside of Highpoint, North Carolina. This time there wasn't nearly the suspicion from Hammer's men when they saw Charlie tagging along with Steve Tyrell. He watched as the box truck door slid up on rollers and a dirty, scared mob of women huddled together like a bait ball slowly started shuffling out the back of the truck. The men running the operation here mostly worked in silence.

Charlie saw Tyrell talking to a man maybe sixty years old in jeans, flannel shirt, and old work boots to the right of the gaping barn door.

Tyrell waved him over. "This is Benny Hammer, my uncle."

"I heard what you did for our boy in the clink. Much obliged," Hammer said.

"Don't mention it," Charlie responded.

The drop off made Charlie Bowman's blood run cold. He'd never seen human beings herded like cattle. The women looked vacant and lost. They shambled along at the direction of the handful of men directing them into various stalls within the old barn. The men sorted them by categories he didn't understand. To him they all looked the same, like grimy, shocked zombies. Streaks of dirt and whatever other detritus clung to their skin like stripes on a zebra, their hair matted and clumped.

Charlie Bowman was used to the smell of dead bodies, was familiar with the various stages of hygiene people found acceptable for themselves. But he had never smelled the sticky, foul stench of these women. He found himself struggling to hide his disgust. He felt the gun in the small of his back calling to him, begging him to kill every one of the evil sons of bitches handling these poor souls no better than livestock in a slaughterhouse.

The drop only took twenty minutes and ten of that was Tyrell and Hammer haggling over the quality of the delivery. The old man looked them over with the eye of a judge at a cattle auction. Charlie listened as they studied the women from the stalls' doors. Every now and then the old man would bark at one broken human or another. Turn this way or that, look his way or away from him. He even told one to hold out her dirt blackened hands. They all looked Asian of some sort. He doubted any one of them spoke a lick of English.

Charlie was happy to have the barn in their rearview mirror when they were back on the road. Though no matter what he did, he couldn't get the stink out of his nasal passages.

The next three months went like that, except Charlie was allowed to the pick up without Hopkins shoving a gun in his face, though every time the man looked at him, Charlie could feel a seething rage burning through him.

***

Unfortunately for Charlie and Milligan, the organization kept him at arm's length. Sure, he was part of the running of women from Charleston to Tyrell's contacts in North Carolina, but he seemed to have been compartmentalized. Whenever he tried to strike up a conversation with one of the other men working the warehouse, they would silence him. He wondered if it was his background as a cop. Maybe he'd put a few of their relatives away at some point. He did notice a couple of them wearing t-shirts bearing the local longshoremen's union. He pushed that information on to Milligan to run down; however, outside of that small sliver of information he'd gotten nowhere.

At around the six-month mark of running the delivery truck, he and Tyrell were running up I-26 outside of Columbia in the middle of the night when a state trooper flashed his blue lights and pulled them over. Charlie was driving at the time.

Tyrell started flipping out at the sight of the blue light flashing around the box truck. "Just drive, man!" he yelled, bouncing in his seat. "Just go!"

Charlie smirked. "You think we're outrunning a Police Interceptor engine in this piece of shit, you have another think coming," he growled.

"Fuck!" Tyrell panicked.

"Just let me handle it."

Charlie calmly retrieved his license from his wallet and with a withering look, convinced Tyrell to get the registration and insurance card out of the glove compartment. When Tyrell opened it, Charlie could see the chrome-plated barrel of a revolver catch the cabin light.

He said under his breath, "Leave that thing where it is."

He watched the silhouette of the statie through the rearview mirror. Judging by the amount of fidgeting in the driver's seat and how long he took to approach them Charlie figured he was a newer cop. He watched as the lanky young man climbed out of his unit, adjusted his required Smokey the Bear hat and walked toward the box truck, pausing for a second to touch the rear bumper.

At least he remembered to do that, Charlie thought, recalling his FTO making him do that every time he pulled a car over. "If you end up dead, kid, at least we'll have your fingerprints on the trunk to make sure we catch the right guy." He had found it funny at the time. Charlie took a deep breath as the man came up to his window.

"License and registration, sir," he said in a long, rural South Carolina drawl.

"Fuck," Tyrell spat under his breath.

Charlie saw the state trooper's eyebrow crease slightly as he looked at the passenger seat. He sized up Steve Tyrell for a moment before moving on with his canned spiel.

"Sir, my name is Trooper Oleander. The reason I pulled you over this morning is because I was using radar and recorded your speed at eighty-three miles an hour in a seventy-mile-an-hour zone. Do you understand this, sir?"

Charlie wanted to laugh but he kept a stoic countenance, saving one eye for Tyrell and the other for Trooper Oleander. They beat a nine-point approach for traffic stops into new cops' brains in the academy, even more so for state troopers who do traffic stops day in and day out.

Oleander hit the high points but butchered the delivery, his voice wavering just a bit as he tried to remember the words more than monitor the two subjects he had in front of him. Charlie wasn't here to Monday-morning quarterback anybody but he was finding this exchange a little entertaining.

"Yes, sir. Sorry about that," he responded calmly.

"Why you traveling so fast this morning, sir?"

Charlie went to answer, but before he could mount a back story of having a rental van, and moving from Charleston to Charlotte for a new job, Tyrell belted out, "Damn it! Come on," like he was a crackhead whose dealer was taking too long to retrieve a rock out of the crack of his ass.

Charlie just looked at him. The scrawny redneck's knees bounced on the floorboards. He looked like he could vibrate into a dozen different pieces at any minute. The little shit was losing it for real. "Chill, dude," he muttered.

"Step out of the car, sir."

Shit.

Charlie looked at Trooper Oleander and sighed. It wasn't his fault; he was just following his instincts; even a blind, deaf, three-legged dog could follow the signs Tyrell was laying down. The driver's side door creaked on rusty hinges as he slid out of the seat.

Oleander motioned for him to move to the back of the vehicle and followed Charlie as he slowly walked to the space between his rear bumper and Oleander's Crown Victoria.

Charlie couldn't let the trooper call in his identification. He hadn't given up his career as a cop, his reputation, or do a turn in prison to let the operation end here on the side of the road. He watched out of the corner of his eye as Oleander followed him. He cringed a little bit as he watched the young trooper take his eyes off him while sorting through the vehicle documents.

His eyes would shift from Charlie to the papers in his hands, then back to Charlie. When Charlie reached the gap between the truck and the police car he saw Oleander take his eyes off him. Charlie was on him. Oleander tried to issue an order but Charlie punched him in the throat, cutting off his air.

Oleander's hands went to his throat reflexively and he stumbled backward trying to get away from the threat. Charlie closed on him, punching the man again, this time across the bridge of the nose, and followed up with an uppercut to the chin. As Oleander reeled, Charlie grabbed the back of the man's head and slammed him down as he drove his knee up into his face. Charlie felt Oleander's bone crunch against his knee and he let the unconscious trooper drop to the pavement.

He took a quick look up and down the Interstate and saw the route was clear of traffic. He dragged the statie off to the shoulder next to his cruiser.

"Sorry about this, pal," he mumbled. Then he grabbed the officer's shoulder microphone that was tethered to his radio and pressed the transmit key, "Signal Forty-six," he said calmly. "Officer down, I-26 just past exit one zero two." He wiped the mike on his shirt to try to clean off any fingerprints and dropped it on the unconscious man's chest.

He was rising from a crouch when he heard scuffling behind him and turned to see Tyrell with his revolver coming around the back of the box truck. The scrawny little shit's eyes were alight as he took aim at the fallen cop. Charlie swiped the weapon from his hands and backhanded him with the solid metal in one fluid motion. Charlie could hear Oleander's dispatch calling for him while other units reported over the air they were headed in their direction.

"What the fuck!" Tyrell cried, holding the side of his face.

"Get in the truck, dumbshit," Charlie growled.

Tyrell started to protest but went silent when he looked at Charlie.

"This place is going to be swarming with blood-thirsty uniforms in a minute. You really want to be hunted by that bunch? Get in the truck!"

Charlie got off the Interstate at the next exit and using an old atlas Tyrell found wedged between the passenger seat and the floor, they navigated back roads to get to the drop point at the Hammer farm. The old man was not happy to hear about the close call. He was even less happy to hear Tyrell's version of events.

"The son of a bitch wouldn't let me take out the cop!" he barked, jabbing a finger at Charlie who, for his part, was counting the number of men Hammer had handling the drop. He counted six that he could see, not including Hammer and Tyrell. Five of the men had varying weapons from AR-15s to shotguns and a couple of handguns that Charlie could make out in the low light coming from the barn. All eyes were on him and Hammer.

Hammer stared at him and Charlie had to admit the old man was intimidating. He had the weathered look of experience that Charlie learned to recognize over the years, first in Iraq and later when he brushed up against affiliated bikers, gangbangers, and ex-cons who filtered in and out of Charleston.

That kind of look, that untouchable air of confidence, and a pragmatic stoicism in the eyes was rare. But you knew it when you saw it. Charlie reminded himself that if he survived the next five minutes he was going to push Milligan to figure out where this flesh-trader came from.

All Milligan had on Hammer was the basic background. The man had never done time, never been charged with anything. On paper the old guy was totally clean, just a small-time rural farmer. Hammer's eyes told another story. There was a danger there that could only be built on a long experience of violence.

The old man seemed to look through him for seconds that stretched excruciatingly slowly. Hammer looked at Tyrell and grimaced. "Next time, son, you should keep your mouth shut and do what this man says. He may very well have saved your life tonight." Charlie could see that the man put up with the scrawny little redneck more than he wanted him around.

"Get rid of that truck. Take one of the beaters out of the field back to South Carolina." Then Hammer left the two men for the barn where the load was being sorted. He needed to appraise his new stock. Hammer's men followed him, and Charlie and Tyrell were alone next to the box truck.

Tyrell took a beat-up old Ford from Hammer's farm and Charlie followed him in the box truck as they wound through a series of old dirt roads until they were so far in the Carolina backwoods Charlie was hopelessly lost. He wiped down the inside of the cab before Tyrell doused the compartment and the rear box with gasoline from a can they kept as a spare strapped to the rear bumper. Charlie found a box of old matches in the truck and struck a bundle then tossed them into the cab. With a flash of heat and a deep *whoosh*, the cab flared to light. As he passed the rear cargo area he struck another couple of the sticks and tossed them into the pooling fuel. The truck was engulfed in flames as they pulled away.

Chapter Thirteen

Tyrell didn't speak to Bowman the entire four-hour drive back to Charleston. The small man stewed in the torn and rat-eaten passenger seat as Bowman drove them home.

He couldn't even look at the son of a bitch. Bowman had made him look like an asshole, like some dumb kid, in front of Hammer. Tyrell was not some dumbshit off the street, he told himself, he was the linchpin to the entire operation. Without him those assholes in Charleston wouldn't have anybody to get the girls out into the market. Tyrell had an army of long-haul truckers through Hammer. Without Steve Tyrell, no one would be making any money. And this fucker Bowman was fucking it all up.

His mind whirled at all the shit Bowman had done to him. Sure, he might have stuck up for him in jail, kept the fools in lock up from getting to him, but when he thought about it, Tyrell probably could have held his own. Sure, he wasn't the biggest guy but he was ambushed. The way he saw it, in a fair fight he could hold his own. And besides, he'd gotten Bowman back in the money less than a week out of the joint; he'd taken care of him, paid him back plenty.

He should have shot the son of a bitch *and* the cop—that would have solved all his problems. Taken both of those fuckers out and left the pig and the ex-pig bleeding together. Then he wouldn't have to put up with his shit anymore. Tyrell thought for a minute about taking him out right there, but a little tremor crept up his spine at the thought of something going wrong. Bowman was fast, and he always seemed one step ahead of him. It infuriated him. He was stuck with the asshole. Shit.

As they passed by a billboard for a technical college Tyrell caught the smiling countenance of a redhead.

He immediately thought of his old lady. He hadn't even thought of that bitch in the months since he'd gotten out. She would love this, he cursed, flushing with hate. If not for that bitch none of this shit would be going on. He realized he still had a score to settle with that whore. Suddenly he felt warm. The thought of dealing with that bitch actually lifted the anger he was drowning in. He smiled just a bit. He might see what she was up to when they got back.

***

After they'd gotten back to the warehouse, Bowman watched as Tyrell dove out of the beat-up old truck and stormed off for his own rust bucket. Charlie's eyes followed him slowly as he made his way to the Jeep Milligan had bought him. It wasn't much more than a piece of shit he could call his own, but after the drive they'd just made in the barnyard special from Hammer, he was happy to see it.

Charlie watched Tyrell from the driver's seat of the Jeep. The little shit was pissed. It made him want to laugh, but the tension Tyrell carried made him wonder. The little shit might be going to try to screw him with Hopkins.

As Tyrell pulled off, Charlie sighed, realizing he wasn't getting any sleep today and pulled out behind Tyrell.

Charlie tailed Tyrell to the crumbling brick apartment he rented in West Ashley. When Tyrell parked the old, beat-up pickup truck outside the apartment, Charlie noticed the man was deep into a phone conversation with someone. His head was bowed and his free hand full of jingling keys as he tried to drive home whatever point he was trying to make.

Tyrell was really working the phone as he mounted the steps to his apartment and even paused before entering the building to concentrate on the conversation. He wasn't acting like the pissed off, brooding little prick who'd left him without a word at the warehouse.

"Who are you talking to?" Charlie asked himself as the man disappeared inside the apartment.

After an hour or so Charlie figured he was in for the long haul. He didn't know how he was going to stay awake to keep an eye on his partner in crime, but his instincts told him he had to see this through. The little bastard was a dumbshit, but a conniving dumbshit.

Charlie would be damned if he let himself be blindsided by the little prick. He was fading in the driver's seat of his Jeep and was just about to call into Milligan and try to explain why he'd knocked a state trooper cold on the side of the Interstate the night before, when the door to Tyrell's place was thrown open.

To Charlie's surprise, Tyrell was fresh. He wore a clean pair of blue jeans. He didn't think Tyrell owned any clean clothes. His greasy, red-brown hair was slicked back in an almost-topknot, and he wore a relatively clean Iron Maiden t-shirt. It even looked like he'd shaved. Bowman's interest was piqued as his partner jumped in his truck and tore out of his parking spot. The call to Milligan would have to wait.

Tyrell drove to a Home Depot off Highway 17 and when he came out Charlie could see a wide circular imprint on the inside of a flimsy plastic shopping bag. Duct tape? A loop of rope hung out of the top of the bag and he could see the end of a box under his arm. As Tyrell passed through Charlie's field of view he could see the box contained heavy duty trash bags. Unless Tyrell was planning on cleaning out his truck, which Charlie knew would never happen, things were getting more interesting.

Tyrell's next stop was at a café near the Citadel Mall. Charlie positioned himself across the street so he could blend in with a larger parking lot outside the mall that was full of cars. He was a good bit of distance between him and his target but he could still see Tyrell well enough as he walked toward the restaurant. He entered and disappeared.

By this time it was going on ten in the morning and he was getting close to missing his check-in threshold with Milligan. Any time he went on a run with Tyrell into North Carolina Milligan required him to check in within six hours of the drop. He dreaded calling. The man was not going to be happy to hear of the night's events and Charlie still wasn't sure how he was going to spin it to him. Before he got a chance, his phone vibrated, with a text message. The phone number was unknown but he knew who it was. The text message only read "9-1-1!"

Charlie sighed and punched in Milligan's number. Charlie kept one eye on the café as he listened to Milligan rage. He wondered how Milligan had possibly connected him to the assault on the trooper. Maybe they'd gotten curious when he used the radio to get the trooper some back up, but really? Who knew how Milligan got half the intel he carried with him? Sometimes the agent seemed omniscient.

Regardless, Charlie could barely get a word in edgewise. Milligan screamed for him to come in, threatened to close down the operation, and warned him that the prosecutor he liaised with during the operation had threatened to send him back to prison "for real this time."

"Keith, I saved that kid's life and by doing so saved this operation." Charlie finally said. "Tyrell wanted to kill him, and would have if I hadn't stopped him. The little bastard called me out at the drop and tried to get me killed. Luckily, his uncle had a better business mind.

"As it is, Tyrell is still pissed at me and I'm not sure where we stand, which from my point of view makes things a little hectic. Not in the sense that you people in the rear echelon are having to field phone calls from pissed off state troopers, but in the sense that I could get shot in the back the next time I step outside that shithole apartment you've got me living in." Charlie let the words hang over the phone for a moment. He could sense that he had Milligan stumped.

Charlie continued. "Now if the prosecutor wants to cut the operation because she got a little heat, your call. But given the fact the only way into this group was by ruining my career and name, I'm guessing she and you will be able to weather the storm. Besides, I beat the shit out of an old black guy to get this gig. Are you guys really going to cry when I beat the hell out of a young white guy with a badge to keep this thing going?"

Another moment of silence and Charlie rolled his eyes. At the end of the day he would have no problem going back to the land of productive citizenry. But, there were women out there being traded like cattle and, so far as they knew, there was only one distribution point. There were more women out there living as slaves, and Charlie couldn't have that.   Finally, Charlie heard a chuckle on the other end of the line. "Yeah, but the old black guy knew the beating was coming. He got paid to take a dive."

Charlie had to laugh, too. "Well, drop the trooper a couple of g's. He took it like a man."

"Right. Well, lay low and try not to commit any more felonies in the next few days."

Charlie sat up in the driver's seat as he saw the door to the café swing open. Tyrell was holding the door open for a chunky redhead to exit.

"No problem," he responded to Milligan and cut the connection. "You've got to be kidding me," he whispered.

Tyrell had mentioned his "old lady" several times while he and Bowman were locked up together. Like any other jackass that ends up looking at the world through iron bars, he blamed her for getting him thrown in jail. He went on and on about how he would get even, how the bitch would pay for what she did.

Charlie always listened and usually berated him for

being just dumb enough to let her get him locked up again. Eventually, Tyrell stopped talking ranting about the woman. Bowman couldn't remember the last time he mentioned the girl. Charlie remembered her name was Sherry something.

One thing was for sure, Sherry didn't live up to Tyrell's description of her, though it wasn't Sherry's fault. The description began and ended with the terms "smokin' hot" and "huge rack." Charlie could see from his vantage point across the street that the huge rack description was apt. But that was only because her chest was proportional to her stomach. Sherry was a big girl, with a massive bouffant hair style that reminded him of a truck-stop waitress from the '60s.

Tyrell and Sherry wandered slowly across the parking lot. Though Charlie couldn't hear what was being said, Tyrell was trying really hard to sell something. Sherry gripped a giant handbag, holding it close to her stomach. Her head was down, looking at the ground as she walked while Tyrell talked animatedly next to her. Charlie strained to get a better look at the couple as they made their way across the parking lot.

Tyrel was gesturing with his right hand in a wavy motion in front of him. His palm was up, his arm raising and lowering as he made his point. He seemed to have a perma-smile plastered across his thin lips as he spoke. His eyes were softer than last he'd seen the man. It looked to Charlie that he was trying to mend fences with the old girl.

"Huh," Charlie commented to the cabin of his truck.

Charlie watched as Tyrell steered Sherry toward his truck. She allowed him to herd her around to the passenger-side door where they paused. Tyrell, still laying out his case for her, took her hand. She finally looked at him and the two embraced. She lay her head on his shoulder and he tried to wrap his wiry arms around her back.

Charlie wanted to vomit. He was debating the

merits of continuing his surveillance when he caught the briefest of looks from Steve Tyrell. It was very subtle, but Charlie knew what he saw. Tyrell looked around the parking lot like he was checking for witnesses. It was the same check he did every time they approached the warehouse, or turned off the road heading to the Hammer farm. Tyrell was scheming something. Charlie recalled the earlier stop at Home Depot.

"No way."

Charlie tailed the couple for the remainder of the day. Tyrell was a perfect gentleman. Opening doors, taking his girl shopping; they even went to a movie. Charlie dosed himself with five-hour energy shots, coffee, and food, to keep himself going. When night fell he was tucked away in a parking spot at the marina bordering California Dreaming, a restaurant just across the Ashley River from downtown Charleston. He was usually pretty good as a night hawk, however, as what he could only imagine was a very awkward romantic dinner for two stretched into an hour and a half, he started slipping. After he caught himself dozing off twice, he decided he had to get out and stretch his legs, get the blood flowing.

Dropping out of the Jeep, he realized he could smell himself even over the usual nighttime Charleston breeze which carried a mix of plough mud and ocean winds. He couldn't remember how long he'd been without sleep but his gut told him he had to see this through.

Tyrell was up to something. He'd seen him smiling like he'd just won the lottery as he doted on the girl. The woman who had sent him to jail. Charlie recalled all the plans Tyrell had for taking revenge on the woman. He wondered if the shitty little weasel actually had the balls to go through with it.

As Charlie meandered around the marina, he looked over the assorted boats and yachts moored in the various slips. Everything from chartered sport fishing boats to full-out yachts with full-time crews populated the docks. They gleamed in the moonlight, almost mocking him. He felt so far removed from the life they represented.

After that first meeting with Milligan, then again after the briefing he'd received when he came on board with the operation, he hadn't given much thought to consequences. He'd committed social suicide, even driven away his best friend by picking a fight with him outside the department where he had sullied his badge and embarrassed his fellow cops.

He was a convicted felon, living in a ramshackle apartment, driving a piece of shit old Jeep. And on top of that, he stunk like the methheads and crack addicts he despised and once took off the street. Charlie caught his reflection in one of the mirrored cabin doors of a fifty-foot sport fisher and stopped short. His hair was scraggly and hung in thick curls at his shoulders. He hadn't shaved in a week. The jeans he wore showed grease stains and were ripped, and a dog wouldn't use the t-shirt he was wearing for bedding.

"Fuckin lowlife," he breathed.

Charlie hadn't considered the total cost when Milligan convinced him to join his little crusade. All he saw was the excitement. The challenge of being the guy to get the job done. That was probably how Milligan had hooked him so easy, knowing Charlie would jump at the chance to be the white night for a bunch of people he'd never met. He wondered how far Milligan had dug into his background before approaching him. Did he know about the family?

The scars across Charlie's back itched as the memories of his childhood managed to creep into his mind. His mother's quiet whimpers whispered through his ears like a soft morning breeze. The whites of his father's eyes that final night when his mother decided not to take it anymore. The man's eyes had flashed just as the anger turned to shock and surprise. The smell of cordite, the man's final gasps...

The demons tried to pry open the doors he had sealed shut long ago. Charlie slammed them shut once more and moved on from the twisted version of himself he saw in the reflection. It didn't matter now, he told himself, he was in it to the end either way.

Charlie made a lap around the marina, always keeping a view of Tyrell's truck, and slowly found his way back to the Jeep. It was another twenty minutes before Tyrell and the girl exited the restaurant. They were holding hands. Sherry was beaming as she let herself be led by Tyrell. Charlie noticed the lazy swaying in Sherry's steps as they crossed the parking lot; she was hammered. Tyrell opened the passenger-side door for her and helped her inside. As he rounded the nose of the vehicle Charlie could see that look again. Tyrell's façade slipped under the lights of the parking lot. The gentleman's smile retreated to a sneer as he scanned the parking lot looking for potential witnesses.

Charlie followed Tyrell's truck to the end of the beach road. He thought he might vomit when the romantic reunion continued with a stroll along Folly Beach. The two love birds wandered the trail out to where the old Morris Island lighthouse, long ago separated from the island by beach erosion. The lighthouse stood as its own spit of land in the waters of the north end of Folly. Whether Tyrell had made a perfect counter surveillance choice or was just laying it on in the hopes of getting some later in the evening Charlie didn't know. The fact remained that Bowman couldn't possibly follow the couple to the secluded trailhead without being seen by Tyrell. Once he realized where Tyrell was heading, he pulled off at the last public parking area along the beach and waited.

Again fighting sleep, he downed yet another five-hour energy drink and sipped on a Mountain Dew while he waited for Tyrell's truck to reappear. Maybe the guy was just trying to get back with the old lady, Bowman thought. He sure was putting a lot of work into the evening. It added up: the café, the shopping, the dinner, and now a romantic walk along the beach. Who knows, they could be banging in the sand at that moment. But there was that stop at Home Depot before the wining and dining had started. And there was the strange vibe he got from Tyrell when Sherry wasn't looking.

Back in jail, after Charlie had stood up for the little shit a couple of times Tyrell had started to get brave. Charlie remembered coming out of his cell one morning and spotting Tyrell from the upper deck of the pod. Charlie knew the tool box didn't know he was watching. He was one of the least self-aware individuals Bowman had ever met.

Bowman had watched him from his perch while Tyrell scoped out a kid who'd been locked up the night before. Charlie didn't know what he'd done, but it must have been relatively serious or the kid was relatively unlucky; he couldn't have been more than seventeen. The kid was pale and stringy. He looked like he lived on a steady diet of heroin and Wild Irish Rose. He carried himself like a field mouse dropped in a snake pen, obviously terrified. Bowman chuckled as he watched Tyrell size up his prey. It would have been the battle of the bean poles if Charlie hadn't stopped him from making the move. That's where Charlie saw that look—Tyrell's predatory sneer. Tyrell was scheming, planning something that was to the detriment of someone, and Charlie couldn't help but think it was Sherry.

If the two did screw in the sand dunes it was a quickie. Twenty minutes after the truck disappeared up the coast road Charlie saw the headlights return. He stayed in his spot with his headlights on using the glare to keep Tyrell from getting a good look at him as he passed. As Tyrell passed by he had a good view of the cab and Tyrell, but there was no Sherry? A jolt sped through his body. Whether it was from the caffeine and other assorted uppers running through his system or from the adrenaline dump from the thought that Tyrell might have made a move on her, Charlie couldn't say. He took a couple of deep breaths. There were far too many variables to consider. For all Charlie knew, Sherry could be blowing him in the cab, a little highway head as gratitude for a night out. Charlie's heart pounded in his chest as he pulled onto the road.

Charlie tried to keep his distance as Tyrell left Folly Island, but as the night went on there were fewer cars on the road. There were a couple of times he had to sandbag his speed down to ten or more miles an hour under the speed limit to keep a safe distance from Tyrell's truck.

At times, though, Charlie couldn't keep his distance and ended up right on top of Tyrell at a stoplight on Folly Road before leaving the island, and, again, at a stop sign before leaving the beach. When he was on Tyrell's bumper, he tried to see into the cab. Just to see the top of the girl's head would have lowered his blood pressure but he saw no sign of her.

Charlie was a hundred yards or so back from Tyrell's truck as the two headed back toward the peninsula on Folly Road when suddenly Tyrell's truck swerved. It jumped across the lane for just a moment before Tyrell got the vehicle back under control. Taking a chance, Charlie tried to close on the truck. He got to within about thirty yards and through the flash of oncoming traffic lights illuminating the cab of Tyrell's truck he caught sight of two people in the cab. Charlie sighed, maybe he did just get a blow job from the girl. Then in another flash of light from oncoming traffic the passenger's shadow suddenly darted to the right slamming into the passenger-side window.

"Uh-oh."

When Tyrell reached the intersection at Folly and Ft. Johnson Road he surprised Charlie by making a sudden left onto Riverbank Road which curved around behind a shopping center. Bowman was caught off guard and had to pass by the light before darting across traffic and cutting through the shopping center parking lot to get back on the trail.

By the time he reached Riverbank Road, Tyrell's taillights, or at least the two red dots Charlie hoped were Tyrell's taillights, were the better part of a mile down the dark back road; the man was flying. Charlie hoped the old Jeep had enough left in it to keep up and punched the gas. He got up to ninety miles an hour on the unlit, curving road which was cloaked in old cypress and oak trees. Moss-shrouded limbs stretched over the top of the road to form a tunnel of sorts. His headlights barely penetrated the darkness as he raced down the road, trying to catch his quarry.

"Damn," he said to himself as a surprise curve brought him to within inches of driving head on into a four-foot-wide oak tree.

Charlie was still a quarter-mile behind Tyrell when he saw him hang a left on Maybank Highway. He was heading for John's Island. Charlie arrived at the light a minute later and blew through the red to make the left. Once on John's Island there were any number of backwoods swamp roads for Tyrell and the girl to disappear into. He had to push his proximity to Tyrell more than he would like. He was finally able to get back in control of the surveillance and took up position a couple hundred yards off his bumper as Tyrell crossed over onto the island and caught a red light at Maybank and River Road.

A little voice in the back of Charlie's head told him he needed to call Milligan. His sense that Tyrell was going off the rails was paying off. But the last thing Bowman wanted was agent huffing and puffing in his ear about procedure and back up. Milligan was a good guy, but he was a fed, and feds couldn't help but complicate things; it was in their nature.

He would let this play out a little longer.

Tyrell crossed Johns Island and continued onto the Island of Wadmalaw. Charlie had to give him a wide berth since they were the only two on the winding moss-and-oak-covered road. Charlie's instincts had begun screaming at him that things had gone sideways. He didn't know of any contacts or property that Tyrell had on the islands, and Milligan had done a thorough background on him before inserting Bowman into the operation.

Tyrell turned off the paved road onto a dirt path when they neared some of the most remote swamps accessible by vehicle, leaving Charlie at a crossroads. There was no way for him to continue without being spotted. Charlie passed by and watched the red taillights that shown in the almost complete darkness like the eyes of a demon disappearing down the road. He continued for another two hundred yards and pulled a U-turn. Charlie cut his lights and pulled to a stop on the side of the road. It was a long shot that he would find the couple or be able to catch up to them, period. But things had taken a turn for the weird and he had to continue his tail. Grabbing a compact flashlight from the glove compartment and three extra magazines for the Kimber on his hip, he shut off the Jeep engine and took off at a trot.

When he had been on deployment in Iraq, he and Stills had volunteered for long-range reconnaissance a couple of times. There are varying levels of darkness that he'd been exposed to in his life but the desert nights in Iraq were nothing compared to the middle of the night in a cypress swamp. Jogging down the dirt path where he'd last seen Tyrell's truck was an exercise in balance and guesswork. He didn't want to use the flashlight and give away his position, but he could barely see his hand in front of his face. He stumbled over and over again on tree roots and ruts in the dirt and danced to catch himself. Charlie continued on tenuously, hoping that he wouldn't stumble into some quicksand or any other number of hazards while he fumbled around in the dark.

It was almost impossible to judge distance in the pitch-black humidity and constant cloud of insects that had come to accompany him. He guessed he was maybe three-quarters of a mile in when in the distance he caught a glimpse of a red light peeking at him through the dense underbrush. He retrieved the pistol from the small of his back and slowed to a creep. Since he couldn't see anything underfoot, he tried to slide step his way along so as not to crunch a wayward branch underfoot.

Gnats and mosquitos attacked him like a tourist throng at a Las Vegas buffet, enjoying the free meal while he focused on the target rather than their relentless attack. He found a tree about fifteen yards off the rear of the truck and took up position. He waited silently, listening for sounds of movement over the constant droning of insects permeating the night. There was no movement either in the cab or outside. The taillights dim glow surrounding the truck. He thought he could see Tyrell's silhouette in the driver's seat, backlit by the lights of the dashboard, but he couldn't be sure. He waited for what he guessed was close to fifteen minutes or so at his perch without seeing any sign of the two he'd spent the day following. Deciding he had to confirm they were gone, he left his cover and, in a crouch, approached the vehicle.

He circled around to avoid being illuminated in the truck lights. He slid along the truck bed until he was just behind the driver's window. He paused a moment to listen once more before moving, then he popped up at the window and shined the light on the inside.

Tyrell's remaining eye stared at him through the smeared glass. The right side of his face was flattened against the grimy window, a tendril of bloody drool slid down from his chin along the pane.

Charlie leapt backward and stumbled on a tree root, almost losing his footing. When he gathered himself back up, he focused and saw the handle of a screwdriver sticking out of Tyrell's left eye socket.

He had his gun up, trained on the cab of the truck. It had barreled into a wide cypress tree. Steam rose from the engine block, creating a cloud in the night. His light shown on the passenger side of the vehicle where he saw Sherry's curly red hair. She was leaning on the window, her face outside his view. When he made his way around to her door he was surprised again when she stirred. She looked up at him and he could see thick mascara running down her cheeks to the duct tape covering her mouth.

Against his better judgment Charlie opened the passenger side door which ground and shrieked on its bent hinges.

"I won't hurt you," he told her and gently removed the duct tape over her mouth.

He panned the flashlight over her and noted massive swelling on the side of her face and jaw. Duct tape was wrapped tightly around her wrists, and her hands sat in her lap in strange contrast to the spirit-wrenching fear in her eyes. Her body position, bound in the seat of the truck, looked so calm. Charlie saw blood spatter on her hands and wondered how many times she had stabbed Tyrell with the screwdriver before planting it in his eye.

She didn't seem panicked and Charlie watched her to make sure she wasn't going into shock. Sherry was quiet, her only movement to shimmy her wide hips so that she could drape her legs over the side of the seat, facing Charlie and the swamp rather than the dead man sitting next to her.

The two of them watched each other for a long moment. Charlie kept an eye on her while she stared blankly into the night.

Finally, without looking up at him, her vacant eyes still examining the pine needles and mud beneath her, she said quietly, "My momma told me some men were just no good. 'Some men just plain needed killin', she said." Sherry looked up at Charlie. She seemed to have more light in her eyes, maybe it was confidence or adrenaline. He had no idea.

"Got a smoke?" she asked.

Charlie was able to call in and brief Milligan after he was sure Sherry wouldn't fall out or go into shock. Bowman was fairly certain that his call to Milligan was one of the worst of all the ways a person can be woken up in the wee hours of the night. The man, who was normally so sure of himself, so in control of the situation, stammered and stuttered as Charlie filled him in. Finally he seemed to get his wits about him. "You get out of there. I'll call it into the PD."

Charlie didn't argue and Sherry was strangely thrilled about telling her story to the police. Her chipper attitude about the homicide she'd just committed baffled him, but then again, who knew what the dead man in the driver's seat had put her through? The sirens of police cars racing down the old country roads grew, The cigarette she'd found in Tyrell's glove compartment burned a white tendril through the air as she waved him off.

"I won't bring you into it," she told him.

"I appreciate that," he said as he slipped back into the darkness.

Chapter Fourteen

I t took Charlie a while to get to sleep given all the caffeine and power shots he'd consumed during the previous day's adventure. Finally, as the sun was coming up, he was able to shut his eyes. He slept like a baby, not a care in the world for his former partner in crime. He must have slept for a good while—when the loud banging on his front door shook him out of his slumber, he noticed the fading light coming through his window. He'd slept the entire day.

He answered the door, wearing a somewhat fresh pair of jeans and the Kimber in his hand hidden behind the door. Hopkins glowered at him as he pulled the door open.

"Get your shit. You're coming with us." When Charlie saw the two towering goons to either side of Hopkins he realized that he should have been a little more careful in answering the door.

Charlie did what he was told and after throwing on a t-shirt and grabbing a Charleston Stingray's ball cap, he was taken downtown in Hopkins' tall Ford F-150. They stopped at the corner of East Bay and Broad Streets where some of Charleston's oldest buildings lined the streets like a living museum. Charlie fell in behind Hopkins and ignored the two hulking men flanking him. Hopkins led him through a secluded alley to a private entrance at the back of one of the older white-stone buildings.

Charlie calculated it was going on six o'clock as they entered the building and took an antique brass elevator up to the sixth floor. Charlie hadn't known what to expect when the old bell rang and the well-oiled doors slid silently open. Maybe an office, maybe some tricked-out bad guy's lair. The fact that Hopkins had brought him downtown had confused him to begin with. He was intrigued that they were upstairs in one of Charleston's most exclusive office buildings. He had gathered that once they stopped in the lower end of the peninsula that they weren't planning on killing him.

Not that Charlie had much respect for Hopkins as an intelligent criminal. The man was a short-fused thug, well-muscled and powerfully built. Hopkins relied on his physical power to handle himself. Charlie had seen Hopkins in action several times during their transfers. He would slap women around to send a message to the others to keep them in line. He knocked out one of the hired hands when he was on the phone during a load out. Hopkins was big on bowing up to people, and intimidating everyone he came across. Charlie had yet to see the man employ any intellect while conducting business.

So Charlie was fairly certain he wasn't going to be ambushed in the next few minutes. However, when the elevator doors slid open, the sight he saw was nothing he could have guessed at in a hundred years. They were on the sixth floor of an eight-story building.

As Charlie entered the swirling mass of people moving throughout the ballroom-like room full of heavy oak bar areas, gambling tables, and a huge, plush smoking lounge, he was amazed. The hall, which was the only way he could think to describe it, took up the last two stories of the building. A rail and walkway lined the upper deck. Doors led at intervals to what Charlie could only figure were private rooms, based on the variety of lingerie-trimmed women leaning over the rail fielding catcalls from suited old men sipping brandy and smoking cigars. If it weren't for the modern dress and amenities he was surrounded by, he would have thought he had stumbled into an Old West cathouse.

Hopkins strolled through the throng of men and some women here and there and Charlie followed. They cut a path through the crowd like a boat hull. Charlie scanned the place for familiar faces as he went and ducked his head at the last second as the chief of police, along with one of the leading city councilmen, passed by. Holy shit, he thought, what was this place?

Hopkins crossed the main floor, weaving through the gaming tables with everything from roulette to craps to blackjack available to the patrons, and entered a mirrored glass door. Charlie followed, trailed by the two bruisers, into an office. Plush like the rest of the sixth floor, the room was decorated in rich colors of maroon and gold with heavy leather furniture adjacent to an expansive antique desk that looked like it must have taken a crane to get the piece in the building. Behind the desk sat a plump little man with a baby face trimmed in a helmet of shining brown hair. He was wearing a light tan suit. He was writing on some document.

Hopkins stopped in front of the couch and plopped down onto the supple leather with a sigh.

Charlie scanned the room for a moment then caught Hopkins watching him. The fat man behind the desk was still working and since he wasn't in the military or police department anymore, he didn't see the need to stand on ceremony. He sagged down in a chair opposite Hopkins and threw an arm over the side. The chair was huge; he felt like a little kid sitting in grandpa's recliner. The material enveloped him as the leather warmed to his body heat. The damn thing was more inviting than his own bed.

Hopkins watched him with the same "eat shit and die" look he always seemed to have. Why couldn't this guy have had a badass ex-girlfriend like Tyrell did? Charlie thought. Hopkins arched an eyebrow when Charlie slouched deeper into the chair and made himself comfortable. Charlie didn't try to hide his satisfaction from the man.

Finally, the fat man dropped his Mont Blanc ink pen to the desk and sat back in his chair. He took in Charlie and Hopkins lounging on his furniture, and said, "Well, hell, boys, just make yourselves at home."

Charlie loved the sarcasm but he felt like the guy was trying to do some kind of Boss Hogg impression. He wondered if it was possible for a fat little kid to grow up wanting to be Boss Hogg rather than Bo or Luke. He looked at Hopkins for a quick moment and thought maybe he was supposed to be Roscoe.

The little fat man was looking at Charlie, sizing him up, with some kind of grin on his face that made him look constipated. Charlie stared back at him with the same look he used to give dipshit officers when he was a Marine.

The little man shifted his eyes and looked down at his little sausage fingers quickly, he rose and came around the desk. "Is this him, Billy?"

"Yup," Hopkins said.

The fat man stood before Charlie and stuck out his hand. Charlie didn't bother to rise but he did shake the guy's hand. The lack of respect seemed to make him stutter from side to side a little bit. He danced on his toes for a quick moment before sitting in the chair opposite him. He looked even more ridiculous in the overstuffed chair than Charlie thought he did himself.

"So, Mr. Bowman. I'm Rutledge Westchase." Westchase. With man's pompous manner Bowman felt he should ask for an autograph.   "Nice to meet you. You can call me Charlie."

"Of course." Westchase grinned. "I can imagine you are wondering why I've asked you here."

"Nobody asked me to come here. Hopkins and Big and Little Eniss over there—"Charlie gestured to the two standing off to the side—"sort of made it compulsory."

Westchase kept smiling. "Well, I meant no disrespect."

"None taken. So what's up, Rut?"

Westchase coughed. "When's the last time you heard from your partner, Steven Tyrell?"

That was fast, Charlie thought, but given that the

chief of police was getting hammered in Westchase's casino as they spoke, it wasn't much of a surprise. The intel did give Charlie pause, however; he and Milligan were going to have to up their game. Who knew how many local law enforcement types were in this guy's pocket? "Ah, I guess yesterday, after the run." Charlie shrugged, "He seemed like he was in kind of a rush. Why?"

"Mr. Tyrell is dead."

"Huh?" Charlie asked, feigning surprise.

"His old lady shanked him in the eye," Hopkins blurted.

Charlie looked at the man, keeping his expression neutral. "No kidding."

"Nope."

There was an awkward pause hanging over the office as Charlie held Hopkins' probing stare. He was going to have to do something about that guy, Charlie warned himself.

Apparently Westchase was not comfortable with long silences. He cleared his throat. "Yes, unfortunately, Mr. Tyrell is no longer with us. I asked to speak to you today because Tyrell was our link to our friends in North Carolina who further distribute our overseas product. This has left us in somewhat of a pickle, I'm afraid."

"You can't just call Hammer?" Charlie asked.

"Mr. Hammer is not one for open communication. It seems he takes his privacy very seriously, and takes tall measures to ensure he is linked to the operation here only as is absolutely necessary. I'm afraid Tyrell was that tenuous link, which leaves us without a distribution node."

"So what do you need me for? Sounds like I'm out of a job."

"Not so, Mr. Bowman. As he did with my man Hopkins here, I must imagine Tyrell vouched for you with Hammer. I was hoping you would be willing to run our next scheduled shipment to Hammer in the hopes that he would continue our business together."

"Right, you're hoping that I can keep things going. But in the event he kills my ass you've not lost a whole bunch."

Westchase squirmed in his seat and stuttered. Finally, he said, "That's not how I see it at all."

Bowman shifted his eyes to Hopkins, whose face told him that that was exactly what he was thinking. Charlie acted like he was thinking it over for a moment. "What kind of money are we talkin'?"

"Your normal share plus another thousand."

"Add whatever Tyrell's take was to that and we got a deal." Charlie couldn't make it too easy on him.

"Deal," Westchase answered.

***

It was a week later when Charlie got the call from Hopkins telling him about the next shipment. It was regularly scheduled. The movement of the women from ship to distribution through Hammer was as predictable as the tide. Charlie and Milligan had strategized, tried to come up with a way to provide some kind of back up for Charlie as he delivered his cargo to Hammer.

The problem was that the farm was so remote that providing him a tail that deep into the country would no doubt blow his cover and collapse the entire operation. Charlie had to convince Milligan to let him go through with the drop. To his credit as a handler, Milligan gave Charlie the out. Told him they could pull him right then and just tell the Assistant United States Attorney that the operation had gotten too hot.

Probably should have taken the deal, Charlie told himself as he wound his way through the backwoods of North Carolina. Charlie retrieved his Colt from the glove compartment of the new box truck he was driving before making the last turnoff that would lead to Hammer's farm. He also retrieved two extra magazines. He press-checked the handgun and slid it inside the front of his pants. The magazines went into his front left pocket. Charlie knew the additional rounds would not do him any good if Hammer didn't accept Westchase's deal, but it made him feel better.

The big old barn in the rear of Hammer' property was lit with the usual halogen light stands. Charlie counted at least twelve rednecks with various firearms as he pulled into the structure. He took a deep, then jumped out the driver's-side door like it was any other run.

At first it didn't seem like anybody noticed anything was different. Charlie nodded to a couple of guys wearing plaid, button-down shirts, jeans, and shit-kickers, and wandered around the front of the truck, looking for Hammer. He'd made it about fifteen feet from the truck when he heard,

"Where's Tyrell?"

Charlie turned slowly to see another backwoods hired hand. This guy was Hammer's foreman. He had long, oily brown hair done up in a ponytail, and his beard hung a couple of inches off his chin. Even in the spotty light Charlie could see pieces of what he could only imagine was dinner hanging in the tangled brown mess. The man had a Remington twelve gauge leveled at Charlie's gut.

"You didn't hear?" Charlie asked calmly. "Tyrell's dead."

That got everybody's attention, suddenly every gun on the farm was swinging in Charlie's direction. He didn't move, didn't react to the ramped up aggression. Ponytail seemed at a loss for words. Silence hung over the open space of the barn for a long moment.

A quick count told Charlie that he didn't have enough rounds for the amount of angry country boys surrounding him at that moment. He would have needed to have brought a grenade launcher and a M-60 to have felt remotely safe around this bunch. Charlie was about to ask about Hammer when the man stepped from the shadows.

"What do you mean, Steve's dead?"

Charlie looked at the old man, trying to figure out how to play it. With Westchase and Hopkins it was relatively easy, he played mercenary; worked the money angle. Hammer was another story. The man was far and away cagier than Westchase and Hopkins combined. Whereas it seemed like the operation in Charleston was just in it for the money, Hammer was a working man. Regardless of the fact he was a human flesh trader, this was his way of life, this was what put food on his family's table. Hammer was staring at him and for the first time Charlie noticed the revolver in the man's hand.

"I'm not really sure, sir. I just got a call from bosses in Charleston and they asked me if I knew the way up here and I did. When I asked about Tyrell they said he was dead. They didn't say much more than that."

Hammer expression didn't even twitch. "That so?"

"Yes, sir."

"How do I know you didn't kill him? Or those city-dwellers in Charleston didn't kill him?"

Charlie wanted to run. Hammer was a blank wall. There was no telltale emotion running through him. He wasn't shifting his feet or looking around. The man gave none of the signs Charlie looked for when he'd been in uniform confronting someone. This man scared him, and the worst part was he'd put his head in the noose himself. He wondered if he would live long enough to tell Milligan he should have taken his advice. Charlie shrugged. "You don't, but I didn't kill the man. He got me this job."

Hammer didn't respond. For what seemed an eternity the old man just watched him, like a hunter watching a buck, waiting for it to turn broadside. The circle of well-armed country boys watched him too, but that felt more like they were a pack of coyotes watching a calf with a broken leg, ready to pounce. They were younger; Charlie could see the rage and pure blood lust coursing through them. These guys just wanted a reason to cut loose.

Finally, Hammer looked around his collection of thugs then back at Charlie. "Well, I don't see how even a dumb ass convict such as yourself would be stupid enough to come here if you had killed our kin."

Charlie breathed for what felt like the first time in an hour.

"Clear the truck out, boys," Hammer announced to the group, which quickly dispersed to go about their business.

Charlie could feel the wave of disappointment coming from the group. He looked up at Hammer, who had turned his back on him.

"You get back to Charleston, Charlie, tell them city-slickers we don't take kindly to our kind being killed. We'll find out if there was foul play."

"Yes, sir," Charlie responded doing everything but salute the man who had literally allowed him to live another day. He hopped back into his vehicle and counted the seconds until he finally heard the smack on the back of the truck, signaling the transfer was done. The heavy paw hitting metal sounded like freedom. It took all the self-control he could muster to keep from spinning the back tires as he left the old barn.

Chapter Fifteen

Westchase blew off Hammer's message when Charlie told him. The baby-faced rich boy was sure that Hammer was ruled by greed same as the rest of the world and wouldn't do anything to mess with the cash cow. Charlie wasn't so sure and was largely only concerned to the point that he didn't want to be caught in the crossfire if things went bad between the two groups. He could care less if the whole bunch of assholes killed themselves, as long as he didn't take a bullet for one of these bottom-feeders, Especially Westchase. Charlie couldn't put a finger on it, but the mere look of the man-made Charlie want to beat him to within an inch of his life. Charlie found that funny, especially given the fact that Charlie's adventure into "Indian Country," as Westchase called it, seemed to have paid off.

They were at the club off Broad Street when Charlie related the drop to Westchase and Hopkins. Westchase listened on the edge of his desk like a seven year old watching the end of *Shane*. The man did everything but clap when Charlie was able to drive away from the old man's barn. Hopkins just watched him the way he always did. The man was constantly looking for that one crack, the one slip that would give him the excuse he needed to put a bullet in him. Charlie was disgusted when Westchase decided to parade him around the whorehouse and gambling den like a shiny new toy. It was right after Charlie got done telling them about the meeting with Hammer.

Westchase slapped his leg in joy and proclaimed, "Well, damn, Charlie, I'm buying you a drink."

The crime boss guided Charlie through the cloud of suits, mostly red-faced old men who'd had too much to drink. He nodded good naturedly nodded as he passed through the crowd, acknowledging a few men here and

117

there like a Caesar among his people. Charlie kept his eyes open as they went, hoping his former chief or anyone else from his old life had not been in the mood to party that night. He had no idea how he would handle coming face-to-face with the old man if he saw him.

Charlie was wracking his brain trying to game plan when Westchase slapped a hand on his shoulder. "Ha, Tom!" he said, directing Charlie to the right.

Charlie watched helplessly as he was brought up next to the very man he'd been praying he wouldn't see. Police Chief Tom Herrington held a sweating tumbler holding three fingers of whiskey in his hand. When he turned, his politician's exterior dissolved on seeing Bowman.

"Westchase," he said, in greeting to Charlie's employer. The chief looked over Bowman and scowled; there was nothing but disgust reserved for Charlie Bowman.

Charlie knew that would be the case with anyone from the department. He thought he was prepared to accept his dishonor, but when it was right in his face he was stung. Part of his life had been amputated without any form of sedative. On the upside, Charlie figured that that much undisguised hate had to mean the man was not in on the operation, so at least Charlie's cover, if not his good name, was still intact.

"Chief," Westchase continued, oblivious to the tension between the two men, "I seem to have picked up one of your strays," he said, motioning to Charlie.

The Chief made a point of looking his former subordinate up and down, then glowered. "You can keep him."

"Have a great night, Chief," Westchase responded, plastic smile plastered over his always shining face and continued on, ushering Charlie toward the bar.   "He doesn't seem too fond of you," he commented as the two stopped in front of the massive, curving oak bar.

"He has no reason to be," Charlie returned.

"What'll ya have, Charlie?" Westchase asked.

"Pappy Van Winkle, double," Charlie told the waiting server.

"Good stuff," Westchase said, giving the server a nod, "bit too bitey for my taste, though. I'll have a scotch, Evan, thank you."

The drinks appeared less than a minute later and Charlie took a slow sip from his. The rare whiskey bit him on the front end but smoothed out quickly. Charlie savored the way it stung his throat and heated him from within as it went down.

"So, you did good today. What else can I do for you? How about a girl? We have only the best to offer."

"I never pay for it, Westchase," Charlie retorted.

Westchase laughed. "Everybody pays for it, Charlie, one way or another."

Charlie looked at his employer with not a shred of emotion or empathy on his face. He didn't respond to the man's comment. He just stared at him. He knew instantly it made Westchase nervous. That satisfied him even more than the expensive whiskey filling his glass.

Westchase lasted less than ten seconds in the fog of uncomfortable silence. He started to speak again, no doubt to brag about himself or the operation, but was interrupted when Hopkins appeared from out of the crowd. Hopkins didn't speak but Westchase caught the cue.

"Well, drink up, Charlie; we've got some business to attend to."

Charlie cringed at the idea of wasting such fine spirits but threw back the remainder of the whiskey and followed the two as they wound their way through the crowd once again. Instead of returning to Westchase's office, they entered a service door that led to an old cargo elevator. Hopkins hit the down button and the three rode in silence until the old box came to a grinding halt at the bottom floor. Charlie was surprised when they stepped out into a dank, dimly lit basement. He didn't know Charleston had basements. Westchase noticed him looking around the structure.

"I know, right?" he said, coughing slightly. He put a silk handkerchief up to his mouth and nose to protect himself from the smell of mildew and age that hung in the dark place. "There are not a lot of basements in Charleston. We're actually a decent bit below sea level at the moment, pumps have to run constantly to keep us from drowning down here."

Before Charlie could make Westchase believe he gave a shit, Hopkins stated, "This way."

Charlie fell in behind the two and watched them as they crossed an open floor toward a lighted room on the other side of the massive basement. Westchase seemed excited, He had a spring in his step. Hopkins strode in the same stiff, stick-up-his ass manner he always did. Always trying so hard to be a badass, Charlie observed. He couldn't wait for the day to come when he slapped a set of handcuffs on the prick.

As they neared the room, Charlie started to pick up muffled tones coming from the single lighted doorway. It was one voice and, as it became clearer, desperate. It sounded as if whoever it was, was trying to talk his way out of something.

Before walking through the door, Hopkins grumbled, "I knew we should have ball-gagged this son of a bitch."

Inside, Charlie took in the gloomy scene. The two heavies that always seemed to hover around Hopkins were standing to either side of a white-haired and pale man in his sixties. He was tied to a chair with his hands behind him. He wore the slacks, shirt, and tie of an expensive suit. The tie was loose and first button was undone, relieving the roll of fat under his chin. The man's tailored jacket was in a heap on the floor.

Before Westchase or Hopkins could speak, the man blabbered, "Please! I need my pills!"

Hopkins and Westchase grinned as one of the men guarding the bound man held up a pill bottle and tossed it to Hopkins. Hopkins caught the bottle with his left hand and shook the contents, which rattled in his hand.

He read the label. "Nitra . . . nitro . . . shit, I don't know what these things are."

"Please, they're for my—" The man didn't finish his plea but instead vomited all over his expensive pants and tailored shirt.

Everyone jumped back a step, trying to avoid any splash-back from the man's stomach contents.

Charlie saw the man's eyes bulging, his skin was red as a beet, and he sweated through his clothes. Whatever this guy had done to piss off the dynamic duo Charlie found himself stuck with, it must have been something good.

"Paul, you went to the cops. You tried to throw me under the bus. Take down my entire outfit to save your own ass."

"Wha—?"

Paul was out of it after the gut dump all over himself. He slouched to one side, head hanging limply. The only real proof that he was still conscious was the look of pure anguish across his features.

"How did you think I wouldn't hear about that?"

Paul shook his head weakly and tried to say something but wheezed instead, out of breath.

"I'm *everywhere*, you piece of shit!" Westchase was getting mad now. He leaned in closer to his prisoner. "For a defense attorney, you sure are a dumbshit."

Westchase gestured to Hopkins, who produced a small .32 caliber automatic from his pocket. With a grin, he held it out to Charlie.

Now things were starting to make sense. Charlie quashed his surprise and looked down at the gun. He looked up at Westchase and Hopkins; both were staring at him. "I've got my own, thanks."

"Take the gun, Charlie," Westchase demanded.

"You want me to kill him?"

Westchase looked like a kid on Christmas morning, anticipating a thrill. Hopkins was trying to read him, pushing him to see where he stood. "If you're gonna be with us, you have to be with us."

Charlie took a step back. "Bullshit. I drive a truck for you people. I'm not a hit man. From what I can gather, he's your problem, not mine."

Hopkins shifted the gun in his hand and pointed it at Charlie's chest.

"You better point that thing someplace else, motherfucker!"

Westchase stepped closer to Hopkins; apparently things were going off script. When Hopkins' attention was interrupted, Charlie closed the gap between the two of them, batted away the peashooter and with the edge of his hand smashed the side of Hopkins' neck. The brachial stun was one of the few pressure points Charlie had found use for in the police academy. The nerve running along the brachial artery in the side of the neck acted kind of like a breaker for the entire body. Charlie had perfected the strike during his time on the street to the point he could take a subject out in one punch if it was available. Hopkins had made himself available. When he crumbled, Charlie breathed a sigh of smooth satisfaction as he freed his Colt and drew down on the two bruisers who shadowed the tied-up old man.

Hopkins was out cold on the concrete floor. Westchase had instinctively put his hands up like a little 'bitch, and the two bruisers just glowered at him. The old man had fallen silent, hanging limp in the chair.

"What the fuck is this?"

"Easy, Charlie," Westchase said.

"I'm not your bitch! And I'm not your boy. I drive a truck for you, that's our deal. You have a problem with that, you can go fuck yourself. Don't ever think you fuckin' control me." Charlie wondered if he was laying it on a little thick, but the fact was that he was in uncharted waters.

By law, he should be calling for back up and rescuing the dumb shit tied to the chair. But they still had no idea the extent of the trafficking scam Westchase was running. If the operation were to close down now there was no way to know how many women around the country were living like slaves. If they were going to rescue them, the op had to continue.

One of the men guarding the old man took a step toward Charlie.

Charlie flashed his weapon toward the man's face. "Don't do it, shitbag," he growled. To both men, Charlie ordered, "Turn around and bury your heads in that wall. Do it now!" They did as they were told and Charlie turned his attention back to Westchase. "He still alive?" Charlie asked, gesturing toward the old man.

Westchase shrugged.

"Check his pulse."

Westchase danced on his toes for a second, trying to convince himself to touch the man, get his fingers dirty. It was as if he'd never seen a dead body before. Some criminal mastermind Charlie thought. When he finally reached out for the man's wrist he looked squeamish, as though he might throw up all over his own expensively tailored suit. The little man paused for a moment, then recoiled and felt the wrist again. After he felt for a sign of life the third time Westchase looked at him like a child who'd mistakenly crushed a bug under his shoe.

Charlie grimaced. "Looks like you're a murderer,

my friend. Nice to know you can get your hands dirty when you have to." With that Charlie backed out of the room. Just as he was about to leave, he looked at Westchase. "I would think long and hard about how our relationship progresses from here. Anymore goons show up at my door for an unexpected meeting and you're going to have to hold a job fair."

Chapter Sixteen

C harlie had no idea how to proceed. He ducked into a bar up East Bay Street as soon as he was clear of the building. He ordered a double of Maker's Mark and called Milligan. When Milligan picked him up, Charlie could see he was still trying to process the information Charlie had reported.

"You're done," Milligan finally said. "You're done. I'm pulling you out."

Charlie started to protest but was silenced by a wave from the older agent. "Don't start, Charlie, this is why we have handlers when we do undercover operations. You can't see that this is going bad; you're too close to it."

"But I just got in with Westchase. I finally meet the head of the snake and we call it quits?"

"You threatened his life in front of his people. That does not mean you two are buddies now."

"We're closer than we were two days ago. Besides, these assholes need me now that I'm the only link to North Carolina."

"It doesn't matter how valuable you are to them, you rock the boat and you embarrass them. They are going to try to kill you. If not Westchase then this Hopkins prick, and he's got the pedigree to do it. The son of a bitch has had felonies from rape, to arson, to homicide linked with his name since he was fifteen years old. You're screwing with a bona fide bad guy, Charlie. He won't let this stand."

"I can handle Hopkins, dealt with plenty badder than him before."

Milligan jabbed a finger at Charlie, then spun in the driver's seat of the SUV he was driving and almost veered into oncoming traffic. "There it is, that's the problem! You think you're indestructible out here. You've had a good run with this, pulled out of some tight spots. But even a cat only has nine lives, Charlie. Sooner or later your luck runs out. The trick is knowing when to get out before that happens."

Milligan returned his focus to the road and the two left the Charleston peninsula for West Ashley in silence. It was an uncomfortable ride until Charlie's cell phone rang, breaking the quiet.

After reading the incoming number he answered, brow furrowed, teeth clenched. "Yeah."

He stared straight forward out the windshield as the caller spoke. He was so still and silent, Milligan couldn't get a read on what was going on, and like any investigator working a case, the suspense was killing him.

Charlie listened to the caller for close to a minute before cutting the speaker off. "Listen, Rut, I thought we had a good thing going too, but I'm not your monkey to dance whenever you give the word. I stick to my lane. You guys can go do that Scarface bullshit all you want but leave me out of it. I'm in this to make money, not be some fuckin thug in your gang." He then fell silent as Westchase continued.

It was killing Milligan that he couldn't listen in on the conversation.

Finally Charlie tossed a quick look at Milligan, then back out the windshield. "All right," he said, "but you better tell Hopkins if he comes at me again, I'll break his neck. All right, tomorrow night."

Charlie flipped the phone shut, cutting the conversation off. Milligan grimaced.

***

Milligan conceded and gave Charlie a little more rope. For the next couple of months things went smoothly. Charlie went on two solo runs up to North Carolina without incident, simple drops, on one he didn't even see Hammer, just his ever-present army of gun-toting hillbilly flesh traders. It made him sick every time he dropped off a fresh group of women. Desperate, dirty, and probably half-starved by the time they arrived at the dingy barn only to be distributed again to God knows where. Charlie felt the operation beginning to wear on his soul knowing that he was the one driving these women to whatever fate awaited them.

This grinding on his soul was only added to by his seemingly newfound best friend, Rutledge Westchase. Charlie would have laughed at how easily the little weasel played into his hands if it wasn't for the fact he had to actually humor the piece of shit. It seemed that all he had to do to get on the guy's good side was to threaten him with a gun.

Westchase called Charlie at least once a day, and they met for drinks or to cruise on his sixty-foot yacht off Charleston harbor every third or fourth day. Charlie couldn't tell if the man had daddy issues or if the old adage that if you beat a dog it will love you all the more applied to humans as well, but Charlie had the doughy, rich, human trafficker under his thumb.

Whereas Westchase was Charlie Bowman's sudden true fan, Hopkins still gave him the eat-shit-and-die greeting every time the two saw each other. Charlie knew he was under ever increasing surveillance by the pit bull so he kept himself from pushing too many buttons. Hopkins would seethe whenever Charlie was at the club. Charlie sipped on rare whiskey and mocked Westchase mercilessly while the rich boy kept coming back for more. Westchase had a thing for showing off his women or his cars, or his boat if the chance presented itself. At one point he and Charlie, and Hopkins were walking around Westchase's plush yacht at the city marina and when the plump aristocrat was finished bragging about his prize in detail Charlie simply asked, "Did that come from you daddy's money?"

Charlie had actually thought for a minute that Westchase might have Hopkins shoot him when he'd dropped that line. In the end though Charlie had the rich boy's number. The more he abused him the more Westchase came back for more. Charlie was impressed. It wasn't a self-esteem thing like he'd used when brow beating Tyrell in lock up. That weakling was so scared of Charlie abandoning him to the wolves that the little redneck would have come back to him whimpering if Charlie had started beating him himself.

Westchase was another story. It seemed to Charlie that the man was insulted that Charlie was not as impressed by his toys and his wealth as he should have been. So every time Charlie bashed him when he showed him a sports car, or a yacht, Westchase's next move would be to up the ante and show him his prized horse, or estate. The pure narcissism displayed by the man was fascinating. Charlie was having fun and it seemed to him that Westchase liked the challenge presented by Bowman.

Things leveled off for a time. Charlie quietly let his influence over Westchase grow while not prying too much to make him curious. But Charlie had a job to do. He started working Westchase one evening when the club was relatively quiet. He changed tactics on the man so quickly that Westchase must not have noticed that he was not being treated like an annoying little brother so much as an equal. He was suddenly giving Charlie whatever he wanted.

"So how'd you get into this racquet?" Charlie asked out of the blue.

Westchase grinned over the rim of his scotch. The man was red-faced and sleepy-eyed. Charlie had decided to drink him under the table and start pressing him. For being a baron of ill repute, the little man held his liquor like a sixteen-year-old girl with a six pack of wine coolers.

"My daddy."

Charlie hated how Southerners always referred to their fathers as "Daddy." It creeped him out. He nodded, encouraging Westchase to continue.

"He was a doctor going way back like his daddy before him. Granddad was around during prohibition and the like. He saw there was a market for the vices deprived us by the government and opened a series of speakeasies around town. After prohibition, the booze started flowing but the gambling and the women were still illegal. Granddad just made things available to the finer folks in town. It grew from there. Daddy had a heart attack, in this very room by the way, five years ago. I've been running things ever since."

"Huh, so you guys always brought chicks in from overseas?"

Westchase grinned again. It reminded Charlie of a twisted version of the Cheshire cat. "That was my baby. Met these boys in Prague while I was vacationing a while back. One thing led to another and bam!" He slapped the overstuffed arm of his easy chair. "Instant money."

Charlie was grinning himself now. He looked at the gaming floor to study the faces of tonight's patrons. Charleston's elite and most respected were always in attendance, though tonight Charlie didn't recognize anyone. "So how have you not gotten pinched? When I was on the street I never even heard about this place. This would be the bust of a lifetime to any cop on the street. How do you do it?"

This brought out a hiccup-riddled, wheezing laugh from Westchase. He leaned up in his chair and gestured clumsily with his glass, some of his drink sloshing into his lap. He was so drunk he didn't even notice. "Look out there. I've got everybody from the chief of the fire department to congressman passing through my doors on any given night. You saw the police chief yourself, which was hilarious, by the way."

"I bet," Charlie commented.

Westchase giggled. "Anyway, none of those folks want this place to fold. This is their own private playground. Men like this come here for two reasons: To get away from the wife, and to do it quietly. Everybody here has the same to lose, so no one is going to talk. No one wants this to end. That's been the bedrock of this place since my grand-dad was running things. He knew to market to these people. Not only are they where the money is but they got the most to lose. Simple."

"Simple." That summed it up, Charlie couldn't argue. He sat quiet for a minute watching the doughy drunk revel in how brilliant he thought he was. "So what's the name of this place anyway?"

The man could barely keep his eyes open. "This place has no name," he said lazily. "If it had a name, people could find it. We're just a ghost."

***

It was going on 1:45 AM that night when Charlie left Westchase drooling on himself at his club. It was a good first step in breaking into how the organization was set up.. He wasn't able to get the names of his overseas contacts but he did get a good history of how long his organization had been in business. That scared him. Westchase, as weak as he seemed, had a generational criminal enterprise surrounding him. He wasn't kidding when he talked about the officials and policymakers that filled his gaming tables and bought his whores. It explained a lot as to how that operation had stayed under the radar for so long. The simple fact was that the radar was turned off when it came to Westchase and his cronies.

***

Sammy grimaced as he struggled with a garbage bag full of empty beer bottles. Half carrying, half dragging as the bottles banged against one another, he limped through the back door of his bar into the semi-dark patio. The old man hobbled over to the recycling bin and with a wheeze hefted the refuse over the side. As the bag of glass tumbled and fell to the metal floor with a resounding crash, he spun on his fake leg and in one smooth motion pulled his aged .45 caliber Colt 1911 and drew a bead on the shadowed bench opposite the door.

"Easy, old man," Charlie said.

Sammy didn't relax one twitch. He'd been robbed … rather, an attempt had been made around fifteen years ago. Some fool looking for some quick cash had pulled the same move, lurking in the shadows. Anthony Garrow. Sammy remembered the name clear as day. The dumb son of a bitch was carried off to the morgue with two slugs bisecting his aorta.

"Charlie?" Sammy asked.

Charlie slid off the bench and into the cone of light from the lamp over the door, "It's me."

"You dumb son of a bitch!" Sammy bellowed, dropping the gun. "You almost got a face full of lead." The two shook hands as Sammy took in the young, former officer who'd once been a fixture at his bar. He saw the look on Charlie's face. "You look like you could use a drink."

Two minutes later Sammy slapped three fingers of Jameson down in front of Charlie and leaned back on the liquor rack. "I knew that was bullshit the whole time," he said plainly.

Charlie looked from the drink to his friend. "How?"

"You're stupid, boy, but not that stupid. I've seen the dumbshits that'd get caught beating an old man in public come and go for fifty years, and as thick as you may be, as much of a hot head as you may be, you ain't one of them."

Charlie chuckled.

"So who you working for? FBI, DEA?"

"ICE."

Sammy nodded. "Huh. Whachu into?"

Charlie looked at him.

"Okay, don't tell me. But something's on your mind."

Charlie sighed. "I'm under, way under, and I'm beginning to realize my targets are really connected."

"Life on the ledge is getting a little tense, huh?"

"You could say that."

"Your handler dirty?"

Charlie shook his head. "No, he's good."

"Then what?"

"These guys I'm going up against have their claws into everything. I'm not sure how far in they are. I need an insurance policy." Charlie produced a tiny micro SD card. He held it out in the palm of his hand for Sammy to inspect.

"What the hell is that, then?" the barman whispered.

"This holds all the recordings I've gotten over the last year. I need a safe place to keep it."

Sammy reached out slowly and took the small storage device into his ungainly cracked and dried sausage fingers. He stared at it like Charlie had just shown him a piece of alien technology. "It's pretty small, Charlie; how much stuff could you possibly keep on here?"

"You need to get out more, Sammy." Charlie chuckled as he headed out of the small courtyard

"Wise ass," Sammy breathed. Before Charlie disappeared into the shadows he stopped him, "Does Stillwater know what you're doing, son?"

Charlie shook his head. He wouldn't look directly at the old man. "No."

"He's your partner, Charlie. If you need backup, he needs to know about it."

Charlie didn't answer his friend. He slipped into the darkness without another word.

Chapter Seventeen

The next month's shipment went off without a hitch. Charlie pulled up in the box truck like always and did a walk around, inspecting the tires while a new throng of women were ushered into the back of the truck. Charlie didn't look at them as they moved past; he couldn't.

Hopkins was keeping his distance, or at least seemed to be. Apparently, Charlie had sent the right message during their last encounter and Westchase's hired muscle had decided to lay off, for now, anyway. Charlie was back in the cab before the transfer was done. He waited for the signaling slap on the back of the truck and pulled out of the old warehouse to start his route.

He made good time up to North Carolina. The trip was smooth, no cops, no problems. Charlie had begun to relax until he pulled off the Interstate for the last leg up to Hammer's farm. As was his custom he pulled up to the back-country farm and backed the truck up to the graying barn. He hopped out of the cab as the transfer started. He looked around for Hammer in the darkness, lit sparsely by halogen lights around the truck and the immediate area outside the entrance. The usual clan of well-armed hillbillies milled about, watching him as well as the women. He squinted through the lights until he finally caught sight of Hammer leaning against an old Dodge pickup, a cane helping to prop him up.

"What happened, Mr. Hammer?" he asked, feigning concern.

Hammer huffed. "Damn steer got a lucky shot at me the other day. Blew my damn knee out."

"Ouch."

"Uh-huh. How goes our friends to the south?"

Charlie shrugged. "Same as always. They're sons of bitches, but they keep me employed."

Hammer chuckled slightly.

"Speaking of which," Charlie said suddenly dipping his eyes toward the mud, "I don't suppose you have any work up here in between shipments, do you?" It was time to see if he could push this operation forward a little bit. He hadn't discussed trying to branch out with Milligan, but Charlie needed to get some progress, he felt stove-piped between Westchase and Hammer.

Hammer looked at him tiredly, but didn't say a word.

Charlie was trying to be humble, which was a challenge for him. "I just mean that these shipments only come about once or twice a month, so I could use some extra work if you have anything."

Hammer was about to answer him when someone suddenly yelled from the barn, "What is this?"

They started in that direction only to be greeted by one of Hammer's men, who sported a greasy ponytail, jeans, and a wife beater. He was dragging one of the females with him. The girl was a mess, long black hair stringy and matted, her face hidden. Charlie could see her hands, blackened by grime.

"What is it, Jeh?"

"This bitch is pregnant," the man said, throwing the girl to the ground.

Charlie's heart leapt into his throat.

Hammer, slow and steady, lowered himself to look over the girl. He separated the flaps of a torn and stained jacket the girl was wearing to reveal a distinct bump in the woman's mid-section. Charlie studied the girl, too. She was rocking slowly, hands in a steeple at her lips. A jade cross trimmed in gold hung from her hands.

Hammer sighed. "We're not running a daycare center here, Charlie."

"Dumb bastards," Charlie breathed.

"Take care of it," Hammer ordered in Jeh's direction.

Charlie watched as the man blanched.

Jeh started stutter-stepping, shotgun in hand. He looked from the girl—no, not the girl, to the bulge in the girl's mid-section—then back to Hammer. "Uh." He looked from Hammer to the girl again. "Uh."

"Did I not make myself clear?" Hammer hissed.

"Uh …."

Others were watching now, likewise fascinated by whatever was about to come next. Charlie was in the same boat; however, aside from the standoff over the defective product at their feet, Charlie salivated over the intelligence this girl had. She was his—

"I'll take care of it," he said smoothly. All eyes were suddenly on him . . . again.

The fear and relief washing over Jeh's face was palpable.

Hammer's brow furrowed as he looked from his employee to Charlie. Charlie didn't give him a chance to argue. "This is a Charleston problem, not yours. Let me handle it. I'll get rid of the problem on the road so no traces get back to either camp."

"That is only part of the issue, Charlie," Hammer said, his eyes on Jeh.

"I get that and I'm not trying to get in the way of you and your people. I'm just thinking that we don't need to drop a body where we do business. Kind of a 'don't shit where you eat' kind of thing."

Hammer turned on him. "You seem pretty okay with this. Either you've got a dark side or there's something else at play here."

Charlie stiffened, took a step forward, and looked Hammer in the eye. "Trust me, this ain't my cup of tea." He looked at the girl. "But a job's a job and believe me, Charleston will pay me for it. It's business," he said slowly.

Hammer studied him for a long moment, in the way Charlie hated. He tried to stay frosty. Finally, Hammer turned and faster than any seventy year old man should be capable of, laid Jeh out with a single right cross to the jaw. "Better get a move on, Charlie," he said with his back turned to him. "Seems you've got business to attend to."

***

Charlie skipped the Interstate and stuck to the back roads, trying to catch anyone Hammer may have sent to follow him. He was an hour and a half away from the farm when he finally called Westchase.

"What the fuck kind of asshole operation are your people on the other side of the pond running!"

"Whoa, whoa, whoa, what?"

Charlie had woken him up and ambushed him. Westchase back-peddled under the pressure. Good. "I just delivered a goddamned pregnant chick to North Carolina, that's what, Hammer was pissed."

"Shit."

"No, shit! So what am I supposed to do now?"

"What are you talking about?"

"She's in the back of the van; Hammer wouldn't take her. What do we do with her?"

Westchase stuttered, "Don't bring her back here."

"What?"

"We can't have her here, damn it." Westchase's voice raised an octave.

Charlie wanted to laugh. How this guy ever got to be a criminal mastermind was beyond him. "What do I do with her?" There was silence on the phone. Charlie gave it ten seconds. "Hello! You still there?"

"Shit," Westchase hissed. "Get rid of her."

"What do you mean?"

Westchase broke. "I don't care what you do, drop her in a swamp, throw her off a bridge, I don't give a fuck, just don't bring her back here."

Charlie was silent. Then, "You son of a bitch. This is gonna cost you big. You know I don't like this shit."

"Name it, Charlie," Westchase said flatly.

Charlie reveled in the man's defeat. "Five K."

"You got it."

"It's done, then." Charlie left Westchase hanging and clicked the phone off. "Mark that," he said into the device, leaving himself a note on the recorder in his phone that saved every word he said.

His next call was to Milligan to figure out what to really do with this chick. He sure as hell didn't speak whatever language from wherever she came from, and this chick was a walking encyclopedia of this whole mess. She had to be.

***

It was another two hours before Charlie met Milligan off a dirt road outside of Santee, South Carolina. They parked bumper to bumper and met in between the cars. Charlie shook his hand and the two started walking toward the rear of the box truck

"This is big," Milligan said.

"Hell, yes, it is."

. There were two males and a female who had parked behind Milligan. They looked like feds; Charlie figured they were ICE out of Milligan's office as he looked them over.

"They're Marshals," Milligan said, noticing Charlie's look. "The chief deputy is a buddy of mine. He vouched for them. I told them not to talk or even look at you so do me a favor and do the same."

"No problem."

Charlie cracked the latch at the rear of the truck and pulled the door up slowly. Milligan shined a flashlight into the dark confines. The girl was huddled in a corner all the way in the front. Her head was buried in her arms.

Charlie felt his stomach roil as he took in the pitiful scene. How many girls has he transported like so many cattle to the slaughter? Milligan would remind him that it was for the greater good. That when this was over they would find and free all these women. Charlie knew in his head that he was right. That to identify the entire organization took time and rescuing one truckload of women wouldn't matter a damn in the long run. But neither of them knew what waited for these girls at their destination. There was no way Charlie could know what he was delivering these women into. He started to feel nauseous.

Milligan, ever vigilant, noticed Charlie's stress level, and said, "Come on," pulling Charlie away while the female marshal leapt into the box and started trying to speak to the girl in Mandarin.

"What?"

"This shit's getting to you; I can see it."

"I'm good. Let's just hope this chick gives us what we need."

"Let's hope."

To change the subject, Charlie said, "I do have some good news." He held up his phone and played the conversation he'd had with Westchase. When the recording finished, he was beaming from ear to ear.

Milligan stared at him. "Are you fucking kidding me?"

Charlie was caught off guard. "What?"

"You seem to think this is some kind of a game."

"No, I don't."

"You're taunting your adversary."

"These guys are fucking morons. It's like beating up the slow kid on the playground."

Milligan closed in on him. "That's it right there. You are getting cocky. You're complacent and you think you're better than Westchase and his men. That kind of thinking will get you killed."

Milligan turned as the Marshals helped the sniffling, weak and desperate woman from the back of the truck. The Marshals brought her to the car and secured her in the backseat.

The knowledge that Westchase, Hammer, and the lot of them were getting rich off women like this boiled Milligan's blood. He turned his attention back to Bowman. "Look, Charlie, you've been able to pull yourself out of some pretty ugly situations so far by thinking fast. You're good, there's no denying it. But you have to remember you're a fucking mouse dropped into the viper pit. No matter how badass you think .you are, you are outnumbered and they have the advantage every time you meet. You need to get your head right before you see Westchase again. I hear of any hot dog shit like what you pulled tonight and this is over. Other than that, good job. Now go get some sleep."

***

Walter Chatsworth stared straight ahead, eyes boring into the blue oval Ford emblem in the center of his steering wheel. The family's Ford Aerostar sat anonymously in a Harris Teeter parking lot off East Bay Street. Old-timers, stay-at-home moms, and others on their lunch break flowed in and out of the store. Cars pulled in and out of the parking lot, and still Chatsworth stared at the steering wheel, oblivious to the world around him.

The manila folder and pages within it sat heavy on his lap. Such a small thing, though it felt like an anchor around his neck.

Walter's life—the lefts, rights, and sweeping curves he'd taken that led him to this point replayed themselves with startling clarity. Things hadn't started out that bad. He came on duty as a new Customs and Border Protection officer at the ports around Charleston and did his job. He was good at what he did, not great—it was hard to be great when the majority of the time he was just another face among dozens of other uniformed officers. But he got high marks on his performance evaluations, and his bosses seemed to like him. Life progressed. He met Jenny and they got married a year later. Two years after that came Dylan, their first son, who was followed in what seemed an instant by Ashley. Suddenly his base pay wasn't cutting it and the little starter home he and Jenny bought in Summerville was as cramped as a bus station locker.

Walter did what anyone else would do. He worked harder. A supervisor's position came open and he applied. To his surprise he was promoted, then promoted again. A few years went by and he was asked to take over a desk in the immigration office and he took the opportunity to move up, just like anyone else would do. He replaced Steve Kerrick, a guy who'd been around for years, sifting through and approving visa applications. Kerrick had finally decided to retire.

Steve showed Walter the ropes, how paper flowed, who to help, who to avoid, the ins and outs of office life. Walter listened and learned and was a good student. Then Steve showed him the benefits to his newfound position. Turned out, Steve had been granted access to some of the more exclusive executive locations in Charleston. Walter found it hard to think of himself as an executive when Steve said it, but he was, so why shouldn't he enjoy the perks, too?

Steve took him to the club, so exclusive it didn't even have a name. Steve introduced him to all the right people, and showed him around. Then Steve introduced Walter to the gaming tables, to black jack and craps, and five card stud. Steve tried to introduce Walter to the girls on the second floor, too, but Walter was a family man and Steve got the point.

But the poker was another story. Walter was never much of a gambler until he became a member of the club, but he really took to the game. And why not? He was doing great, the kids were in private school, Jenny was happy in their suburban four-bed, two-bath ranch, and there was still some extra money every month. Walter began to play., Walter was good at cards, but no one was great. The club offered a line of credit. Walter continued to play.

Then one day a guy named Hopkins called on him. His credit had come due.

Hopkins scared him. He knew where Walter and his family lived, where the kids went to school, even where Jenny went to do Pilates, and he threatened them all. Walter realized he'd been played and was in over his head.

When he asked what he had to do, Hopkins had a simple answer ...too simple. Walter was to keep his eyes out. Hopkins knew what clearances and what kind of information Walter had access to. The safety of him and his family was dependent on information he thought Hopkins might need to know about. There wasn't a lot to think about when put in those terms. Every day since that fateful moment when he knew he was no longer in control of his own life he had hoped and prayed he would never get that visitor, or receive that message that he knew he had to pass.

Then, yesterday morning that life-defining moment came so subtly it scared him. There was a knock at the door and his contact with the U.S. Marshals office came in carrying a file. He hadn't even finished his first cup of coffee and there she was with a visa application in hand for a Thai national—a pregnant Thai national. There were no other details except a picture. Walter studied the dirty and tired face. He gulped down the bile that threatened to escape his gut, and took the forms with a stiff smile and trembling hand.

The unofficial deal Walter's office had with law enforcement agencies throughout the area was simple: He expedited visa/immigration paperwork during rare instances when law enforcement needed to get someone an emergency immigration status. Usually this was either a witness or a victim of some investigation the feds needed time to debrief.

It was easier, and normally safer, to get a person an immigration status than it was to try to keep track of a foreign national in another country, especially if a case depended on that person for court. Instead, snitches or victims like the Thai girl in the Marshals' file would end up sitting in a hotel room or safe house somewhere in solitary confinement until a trial date where she would testify, or do whatever the prosecutor wanted. Walter's position was one of the most sensitive in government. He never realized fully the importance of what he did. He looked down at the file on his lap. Until today he thought.

A sudden smack on the A post of his driver's-side door shook him and he jerked.

"You're kinda jumpy, Walt, you know that?" Hopkins asked, leering at him.

Walt didn't take the bait; he just handed over the file, seeing that Thai girl's face in his mind. But the girl's features did not shine quite so bright as the images of his children. Hopkins took the folder and started fishing through it, taking his time scanning the documents. Walter knew he was drawing it out torture him. "We good now?" Walt asked. He felt like such a weakling, like a guppy in a pond full of pike.

Hopkins didn't answer at first, still drawing out the exchange. Finally, he slapped the file shut and looked around the parking lot. Walter was waiting for Hopkins to release him.

Hopkins dipped his head toward the driver's window and looked at Walter. "This is good, Walt, real good. Don't be a stranger now, ya hear?" Hopkins slapped the A post once more and walked away.

"Son of a bitch," Walter breathed.

Chapter Eighteen
2013

When Charlie woke up he wasn't sure where he was. Whatever sedative he'd been injected with brought him back in a haze; he couldn't focus. He shook his head trying to clear the fog, which set off the ringing clatter of handcuffs against rail of the cot he was lying on. The clanging broke the haze and he tried to sit up, to flee. Fire shot up the left side of his body and he fell back to the cot.

"Do not try to get up. You are bound and injured," he heard a woman say in a thick, soft Asian accent.

He craned his neck around to see his captor. It was the female who'd dosed him and cleaned his wounds before he'd passed out. That memory triggered a second. He looked toward the center of the gloomy cargo hold.

"Your friend is gone. They took him away."

Charlie looked back at the woman who held a syringe in one hand and gauze in the other. She sat down on a stool beside his cot without looking at him.

"What is that?" Charlie asked, trying to inch away from the woman.

She held up the syringe. "It is antibiotic to fight infection."

Charlie laughed through a dry mouth. "Isn't that kinda like swabbing the arm before a lethal injection?"

The woman did not respond. She injected him. The pinch made him jump, which set off a scream from his left side.

He tried to examine himself but all he could see was gauze covering the left side of his hip. He moved his left leg and found that it responded—at least he had that. He turned his attention back to the woman. "I've seen you around, but we haven't met. I'm Charlie."

"I know who you are."

"Oh."

"You are police."

No sense arguing the point now. "Yup."

"You are very stupid man."

"I'm not the one treating the wounds of someone soon to be shot in the head." That got her attention. "Who's stupid now?"

***

Mai Chupak did not take the prisoner's bait. She could care less what fate awaited this man. She knew he would most likely be dead soon, and so be it. Mai knew what was expected of her and would perform as ordered.

Mai had landed in Charleston after a long, winding road from Bangkok. She had been on what she believed was a normal night out with her fiancé when her world flipped upside down and changed forever. They had had a wonderful dinner by candlelight and wandered the gardens afterward, holding hands and chatting as she always did with Xu.

Xu was the love of her life and she'd known it from the moment they met. Their first date lasted twelve hours and was filled with conversation like two long-lost friends finally reunited. They were inseparable after that. That night they had walked and talked like always, discussing the most boring of things, given that it was their last night on Earth together. Mai now wished she had thought of some way to get more out of that moment.

Xu was a programmer and she was a nurse, her stories regularly ended with Xu being disgusted by the various damage she witnessed on the human body. He normally told her about the pranks and games he and his friends at work played on each other rather than the work he did. There were times that she was not sure he really had a job at all.

They were strolling through the streets, into each other and oblivious to the world around them when suddenly a pop seared the air followed by the squealing of tires. Xu's hand fell away from hers and she watched him fall forward. Before she could try to catch him, she was grabbed from behind and lifted off her feet. She remembered the fear, the sudden surge of adrenaline. She tried to kick but her feet only found open air. She could not strike her attacker as her arms were pinned to her side. A hood was thrown over her head. Mai's last sight before the hood was of Xu lying on the street in a pool of blood, not moving. She was thrown hard against the interior of a vehicle. It stunned her, but she continued to fight until she was bashed in the head and everything turned black.

When she awoke, she soon grasped she was inside a box of some kind. A low thrum underscored a constant moan of whimpering and shuffling. The place stank of body odor, feces, and feet. Her head swam and her vision took time to clear. When she was finally coherent enough to take in her surroundings she realized she was not alone. At least thirty other women were locked in with her. Most had their head bowed between their knees as they rested against the walls of the container. No one talked. Mai wanted to move, to fight, to do anything, but her entire body ached and she went dizzy when she tried to move too fast.

She sat, watching the others around her. The stench was almost overpowering and she fought to keep from gagging during those first hours in captivity. She refused to identify the worst of the smell until one poor woman stood up and shuffled to a bucket in the rear corner of the container and squatted unceremoniously.

Mai's heart sank. This could not be, she told herself.

The isolation got to her maybe a day or two into her captivity. The thought of Xu and the idea that something horrible had happened to him filled her with such panic that she struggled to breathe and couldn't stop shaking. She estimated that they were three or four days into their journey before the first of the women spoke. Mai did not join them. They were Vietnamese as far as she could tell. She did not speak their language well, but understood them enough.

They told her story, kidnapped from the street of whatever city they called home. Eventually a few of the others joined in and they all told the same tale. They'd been captured off the street. The question of why repeated itself in Mai's mind; she couldn't help but keep an eye on the heavy metal door that was the only way out of the dank, stinking hole.

Mai jumped when a sudden blow horn reverberated. She had realized the gentle swaying throughout their voyage and the constant drone emanating from seemingly everywhere. The resounding horn was the first real tangible evidence she understood to make her believe she was on a ship of some kind. . The signal spurred the woman to steel herself. She was not like the other girls where she came from. Her parents had died at an early age during an uprising and she'd been raised by her grandfather. Grandfather taught her to be a lady in the best way he could, but he also taught her the steep lessons he had not taught her mother. Honor above all else was his motto. He would beat it into her while teaching her to defend herself.

"Honor above all else," she repeated in the dark, smothering hell, all the while keeping watch on that door. They were transferred to a truck. She could feel it in her stomach when the crane picked up their container, then felt the rumble of the tires as the truck pulled off.

Mai was perfectly alert then. She hadn't eaten since waking up in that hell. Her legs and back were stiff and in constant pain from the cramped conditions and she was a filthy mess after so much time without bathing.. But she was alert and ready. She knew that door would have to open at some point and when it did she would strike whatever was on the other side.

When the truck stopped, she tensed, watching the heavy metal doors, along with all the other scared, pitiful faces surrounding her. Then she heard muffled voices; there were men outside. She knew they were speaking English but it was so low and her comprehension was weak enough that she didn't know what they were saying. It didn't matter. Suddenly someone was fumbling with the door. A heavy slam, then a crack and she saw light for the first time in what felt to be an eternity. She steadied herself for her attack. When the door slipped wide she had started to lunge forward when she was hit and knocked into the side of the container as a flood of panicked women went berserk. They all seemed to try to scatter, to do anything to escape the trailer's suffocating dark conditions.

Mai regained her footing just as a fire hose let loose on them. The water cannon hammered the fleeing women, knocking them backward in a tumbling mass of bodies. Mai was buried under a pile of filthy bodies and a river of freezing water that soaked her to the core.

They were screaming, some were pleading for them to stop in whatever native tongue they spoke, Vietnamese, Thai, Tagalog, the Philippine dialect. When the water stopped, Mai was shivering, freezing like all the others. Then the door slammed shut and some of them openly started weeping. Mai tried to get her bearings. The fear that she had missed her only chance to escape threatened to paralyze her. They sat in darkness, dripping wet for several minutes until a defeated silence settled over the container.

Finally there was a banging on the container and a man shouted, "Ladies! I'm going to open this door again and you will slowly exit in a calm, orderly fashion. Otherwise, it will not be a water hose we shoot into this container."

Mai doubted that even half of the women in the

container understood the English orders. But she was certain they got the message.

When the door swung open she saw Billy Hopkins for the first time.

***

"You do not fear death?" she asked Charlie while changing the bandage on his hip.

"Terrified," Charlie answered.

Mai stopped what she was doing and looked at him.

"But I'll be damned if I let those sons of bitches know that."

Charlie was relieved when she smiled at him. She wasn't a huge fan of these guys, either, he told himself.

Chapter Nineteen

Alex Stillwater was sitting on the hood of his car, ear bud in one ear, staring intently at his phone. Around him Sammy's bar looked like a disturbed ant hill. Patrolman lingered around the outside of the yellow tape as the public began to gather in small wads of gossiping civilians. A crime scene unit from SLED, the South Carolina State Law Enforcement Division, worked inside the tape with militaristic efficiency decked out from head to toe in protective white Tyvek suits. One team of two snapped pictures around the outside of the building, while another roamed the ground looking for impression marks or any other telltale signs from the assailants who had done battle with Sammy and Alex merely an hour ago.

The crime scene unit supervisor surveyed the interior of the bar, doing a preliminary walkthrough. He watched the technician begin the process of documenting what had happened there. He would get a feel of how best to conduct the examination of the scene from photos, to sketches, to evidence collection in a place considered a second home to most, if not every line officer the Charleston Police Department on the job for the last thirty years and set the rest of his team to work. It was surreal. Stillwater felt the buzz around him, knew what was going down but didn't lift an eye or ear to the activity.

When Sammy had handed him that chip, he had been under such a dump of adrenaline that he hadn't given it a thought. The old man bled out in front of him, covering him in blood. Once Stills realized the old man was gone, he'd shoved the chip in his shirt pocket and moved on, clearing the building, disarming the man he'd killed, and calling in the incident.

It wasn't until after the first two patrol cars arrived and he'd handed the scene over to them that he finally was able to breathe again. He leaned against his hood, the fight replaying itself over and over in his shocked mind. He didn't know when he'd snapped out of it but his first thought went to the tiny disk in his pocket. Looking the micro SD card over, he knew it was evidence in Sammy's murder and that he should have it in an evidence bag to be handed over, but Sammy told him Charlie was involved. He jammed the card in the slot on his phone and started listening through an earbud.

Stillwater didn't know it was possible to have so many conflicting emotions at the same time but within three minutes of the first track he felt pissed, guilty, and terrified all at once. Charlie had a way of doing that to people, so he shouldn't have been surprised.

"Sammy, if anything goes down I need you to get this to Stills. He's the only guy I can trust with this. You need to remember that, too. These guys are everywhere. Stills, I hope to God you never listen to this. If you do I'm in some deep shit . . . even deeper than usual."

"Asshole," Stillwater breathed as he listened to the recording. "What have you done?"

"What's who done?"

Stills looked up to see Captain Robertson heading his way. Shit. "Huh?" The commander of the Patrol Division had managed to sneak up on him. Stills paused the recording, ripped the earbud out of his ear, and slid his phone in his pocket as he stood. "What's that, Captain?"

"You were mumbling something."

"I didn't realize."

Robertson grimaced. "You know how this works, Alex; I need your statement, then you go on leave. What were you doing here anyway?"

Alex fought the urge to stutter. "Erica left her phone here last night. I knew Sammy was an early riser so I figured I'd try to catch him on the way in."

"And?"

"And what?"

Robertson rolled his eyes. "The shooting you just survived. How about that?"

Alex paused for a moment and suppressed a grin. If there was one thing being a cop taught you the first day out of the academy, it was to never talk to cops. "I'm going to wait for my attorney before giving my statement, Captain, you know?"

Robertson sighed. "I know, don't blame you. Anyway, once the state guys are done with you here, you can head for the station, get this going."

"Right."

Robertson headed off toward his own vehicle, then stopped. "You okay, Stills?"

Stillwater smiled. "Yeah, Captain, thanks."

Robertson continued on. "Well, you did good. Sorry about Sammy; I know you guys were pretty close."

Alex nodded, the memory of Sammy slumped against the bar, struggling to speak while he drowned in his own blood replayed in his mind.

The captain pulled away and Alex turned the recording back on. As he listened, he took stock of the scene and put an eye on Phillips and Clements, the two Homicide detectives who caught the call. They were talking with the Crime Scene Unit Supervisor. He heard a name through the ear bud, Westchase, then another, Hopkins. Charlie must have been talking to his handler. He said "Keith," and he could tell they were discussing the case, but even with a transcript of the conversation it would've been difficult to figure out what they were talking about. Two guys already familiar with the small details of what they were talking about didn't have to say most things out loud. Either way, Stills had a couple of names. It was a start.

The state agents hadn't asked to interview him yet, so Alex sat down in his driver seat and signed on to his laptop. The dash-mounted computer was not something that was common in a detective's car, but Alex had requested the device. The laptop was linked into the department's database, the National Crime Information Center (NCIC), and the state database. He liked having the intel on hand when he was away from his desk. He logged in and started searching. The only names he'd been able to figure out so far were Westchase and Hopkins, no first names, no identifiers. He searched wanted files, the active case directory, and the archives that were available electronically and came away with nothing.

While he searched, he kept the recording running through his ear bud. The tracks—Stills had no idea how many tracks were on the small chip—played automatically from one to the next. He started to pick up more names, like Milligan, who he figured was Charlie's handler, and Tyrell. Tyrell didn't sound familiar to him, but he and Milligan were talking about Tyrell getting him set up in some job. Alex could not believe Charlie had thrown his career away to go undercover as a fed. The guy did jail time, for Christ's sake! There was so much about this that felt like a movie. He had to focus to remain on task.

Tyrell was a bust. He wasn't getting anywhere with the databases, and the state agents hadn't shown yet. The more Charlie talked in his ear the more Alex began to stir. He was just sitting there while his oldest friend was God-knows-where, in God-knows-what circumstances. He didn't even know if he was still alive. Then he heard a name that froze him in his tracks. Police Chief Garrett.

"The chief was there," Charlie said. "Chief Garrett looked me in the eye while drinking in this guy's club. Christ, Keith."

Alex had to rewind the recording and listen again.

"What have you gotten yourself into, Charlie?" He took another look at the front door of Sammy's bar. The crime scene unit was at full stride by this point. No one was even looking at him. Alex slipped the Crown Victoria into gear. They know how to find me, he thought.

***

Though it was still early, Stills figured Mac would be up and moving by now. Alex had gotten nowhere with the records check on the little bit of info he had from the recordings. But if there was anyone on the Charleston Peninsula that would know who Charlie was messing with it would be Mac Thorn. Mac was a coke dealer for a time, a fence for stolen goods for a time, and even ran an investment fraud racket for a time before Alex put him away six months ago for the fraud and an eight ball he'd had floating around the interior of his BMW.

Mac was out on bond awaiting trial on the fraud charge and Alex had held off on charging him with the cocaine. Mac had a past, including an arrest for distribution of cocaine several years back. If Alex were to drop the coke on him Mac would still be sitting in county waiting for trial. Instead, the cocaine was sitting in evidence and Mac was sitting on a hook.

Alex stopped in front of the old, brick two-story row house on Water Street, a Mercedes Benz parked in the driveway. Before going in he swung around the corner to a vacant lot and changed his clothes. The feel of blood sticking to him and crusting around the hairs on his arms made him want to jump out of his own skin. He dipped into a go-bag he kept in his trunk and found a polo shirt and a pair of jeans. He quickly changed in the front seat of his car and used his soiled clothes to try and remove as much of Sammy's blood as he could.

The blood, staining his hands red-orange, enraged him. He would find whoever did this to Sammy and they would pay.

It was going on nine-thirty in the morning so Stillwater had to knock five or six times before a skinny white guy with a bright bald head, goatee, and dual pierced ears with gold hoops answered the door. When Mac opened the door, Stills chuckled as recognition fell over Mac's groggy features.

"Shit," he grumbled, then walked inside.

"Mac," Stillwater said in greeting.

"It's a little early, isn't it, Detective?"

"Sure is, Pal. You should've seen how my day started."

"Coffee?"

"Sure." Stillwater followed Mac into the kitchen.

The home was immaculate. Expensive, plush leather furniture covered the living room, a gigantic flat-screen television hung from the wall. Stills was no art aficionado but even he could tell there were tens of thousands of dollars in oil paintings hung throughout. Mac started the coffee pot and Alex took a seat on a bar stool, then leaned his arms on a custom slate countertop.

"What is the scam this time, Mac?"

Mac looked up from filling the filter basket and must have noticed Stills looking around the professional-level kitchen. Now it was Mac's turn to chuckle. "Needed a place to crash, man. Your fault."

Stillwater then noticed a couple of pictures littered here and there. They all had a woman featured in them. She seemed maybe late fifties or early sixties. Some of them had her with a twenty-something female, others with a twenty-something male.

"Renting yourself out now, huh?"

Mac cocked his head. "I wouldn't say that. She gets what she wants; I get what I want. Besides, she keeps it tight for a chick approaching senior citizen-hood. Don't hate, man."

"I'm not. Good on ya."

"It beats slinging powder all night long. I'll tell you the pay is good in that gig but the hours blow."

"You don't have to tell me."

Mac set a cup of coffee down in front of Stillwater

and leaned against the other side of the counter. "So what did you interrupt my beauty sleep for? You want something?"

Stills took a sip and set the cup back down. "You're the most connected guy I know so I figure you're the guy to talk to. You know a guy named Westchase, runs around with a guy named Hopkins?"

Mac stopped mid-sip and looked at Stillwater like he'd just kicked his dog.

"Tell me about them."

Mac put the coffee down and his face turned serious. "The fact you have never heard of these guys until now should tell you all you need to know."

"Not helping."

Mac crossed his arms. "Look, I don't know much about these two; they run in some pretty heavy circles. I know they are into some shit, some real shit, but I don't know the particulars. We never ran in the same parties."

"What do you know about them?"

Mac cringed. "Ahhh, shit. I know that they are like ghosts when it comes to you guys. Everything around them is fuzzy. They are supposed to be running this town as far as any type of shit you can think of, chicks, dope, gambling, and they're never so much as pulled over for speeding. It's like they're Bigfoot or something. Everybody's seen them but no one can prove they exist."

"Where can I find them?"

"I don't think you can, that's exactly what I mean. I don't think these guys are a part of your universe, dude."

"These guys just came into my orbit, Mac. Where?" Stills' voice grew cold.

Mac looked at him for a moment; he got the message, "Look, Stillwater, you did right by me by holding that powder off my sheet. But let me tell you, man, these guys have too much clout; you can't get close."

"That's not what I asked you."

Mac cringed again. "I know."

Alex continued to stare at Mac.

"Okay, Westchase is old money from what I hear, and he runs an off-the-books executives' club or some shit down on Broad Street."

"Broad Street?" Very few times in Stillwater's career had crime and Broad Street ever intersected.

"Yeah, it's like he has some secret place down there. I don't even know where it is."

"That's it?"

"Yeah." Mac was wide-eyed, hands gesturing like Stillwater just wasn't getting what he was saying.

"What about this Hopkins guy?"

"Supposedly muscle or something, never met either one of them but Hopkins is the guy people are scared of. Westchase is just supposed to be some rich dude, like a sugar daddy or something."

Stillwater studied his source for another moment. "All right," he finally said. "Thanks for the coffee."

"So are we good now, you know, with the whole coke thing?" Mac asked as Stills exited.

Stills didn't answer him.

Alex let himself out. As he took the first step toward the street he saw them. Water Street was a relatively quiet, affluent street in downtown Charleston, especially at ten-thirty in the morning on a weekday. There were three vehicles parked down the block that hadn't been there when he went into Mac's place. Though that in and of itself was not overly troubling, the fact that each SUV had at least two occupants wearing sunglasses was a big red flag.

He continued toward his Crown Victoria. There were two black SUVs up the block and one farther down the block toward where Stillwater would be exiting. They had him boxed in. Stills retrieved his keys from his back pocket and shook out the jumbled mass as he fumbled for his key fob. He kept his head down as he stepped into the street and rounded the rear of his car. He bolted when he got to the driver's side door. Cutting perpendicular across the street, Stills sprinted in between two of the long, narrow row houses. He jumped a fence on the other side of the yard he was cutting through and as he landed he heard car doors slamming and men yelling.

He was outnumbered but he had the initiative, and if there was any place on the peninsula you wanted to run it was south of Broad Street. Many of these old houses had fences, gardens, fountains, and some had old brick cubby holes that had been preserved for historic importance.

Stills hopped two more fences, listening for his pursuers as he went. He didn't charge across the backyards to the next street because he knew there would be someone assigned to box him in. Instead, huffing and puffing now after jumping fences, continued to stay within the boundaries of the yards, only darting from one to the next when he thought the coast was clear.

Stillwater heard them yelling, issuing commands to one another while they searched. Whoever they were, running through back yards was not their bread and butter. These guys were as loud as an Occupy Wall Street camp on a Saturday night. He crouched behind a row of bushes as he heard one of his pursuers coming. Creeping just inside a thin spot within the vegetation he heard the man breathing as he jogged his way. Stillwater remained still until he felt the man's feet on the ground next to him, then leaped from the brush and jabbed the man in the throat. The man gagged and fell to his knees. A Glock semi-auto hand gun hit the ground at Stills' feet. He grabbed it as the man fumbled to get up.

"No, no, no," Stills whispered as he kicked the man in the side of the head, dropping him back to the dirt path. Before moving on, he looked the guy over. He wore jeans, hiking boots, and a polo shirt with the tail out to cover a leather holster. Stills patted the man's back pocket and felt a wallet. He pulled folded leather out of the man's jeans and whistled to himself as he realized they were FBI credentials. That was not what he'd expected.

Stillwater needed to know what was going on. Bowman warned him not to trust anyone, being chased by the FBI did not make sense, but then again nothing Stillwater had experienced so far this morning made any sense. He was in the dark. He needed intelligence. He heard voices closing in on him. They weren't yelling at each other anymore but he could still hear the men talking on their radios, trying to contain him.

There was no way Stillwater was getting out of the area by crossing through yards to the next street over, and Charlie didn't have the time to allow him to lay low. Stillwater crept around another two yards and stole a glimpse back at Water Street. He found the intelligence he was looking for.

Chapter Twenty

Matt Helmsley stutter-stepped as he waited by the SUV. Matt was the youngest agent on the squad by several years and as such spent more time as a gopher for the older agents than he did in the field. His radio crackled with the guys barking at each other as they hunted through the back yards for their target. Matt tried to remain professional, tried to act like it didn't bother him being left like a valet while the rest of the guys were off doing what real cops do but his resolve faltered.

"Come on," he mumbled, straining to see around bushes and trees to get a glimpse of the guy. He danced on his feet, the nervous energy getting to him. He felt jittery like he was holding onto a live wire rather than a walkie-talkie. The SUV was still running and the driver's side door was open to the direction of the action. Then his cell phone rang and he swore. Oh God, he thought. He remembered the pushups and the embarrassment his classmates at Quantico suffered when their custom ringtones sounded out when they were on the range or sitting in class. Silencing a cell phone was rule number one in the field. Helmsley jumped and strained to find the offending device singing from the cab of the vehicle. He finally found it buried under paperwork cluttering the center console and shut it off.

Matt started to back out of the cab so he could return to his post when suddenly he felt a tug on his belt at the small of his back, followed by a knee in his ass.

"Sh—!" he tried to scream as he was catapulted into the cab of the SUV. Landing head first, his arms tangled in the dashboard and center console until he found himself face down toward the floorboard, neck cranked, looking into the eyes of his assailant. The man was pushing a gun into his throat.

"Not a word, asshole," he said, slamming the driver's side door.

***

Al Farraday was on the back side of a house three doors down from Matt's SUV when he heard a sudden squeal of tires. The sound was frantic, a high-pitched whine that held until the unseen vehicle gained traction. Farraday took off at a sprint, hitting the street just in time to see the stolen government vehicle disappear around the corner onto Cumberland Street. Matt Helmsley was nowhere to be found.

***

Stillwater stood near the marsh looking over the surprising find taken from the pockets of the man he'd just kidnapped; FBI credentials. The kid's badge case still had a shine to it. It wasn't warped and bent from years of being sat on and tossed around, and it wasn't loaded up with receipts and credit cards. The holograms were intact. Stillwater couldn't find issue with the authenticity of the cards; even the tiny little gold badge looked legit.

What the hell have I gotten myself into? He wondered.

He could see the marsh by looking through the off-kilter doorway of the old, dilapidated boathouse, past the man shackled and handcuffed at the end of the dock . It was not easy to find someplace quiet and out of the way in the middle of the day in Charleston, South Carolina, but Alex remembered some of the old spots from his time creeping through the city as a patrol officer. The marsh was always so peaceful and calm, and expansive; the tall grasses surrounding the city just watched the world go by.

The old covered dock creaked and snapped in argument to his walking on its old boards. Matt Helmsley watched him through wide eyes as he approached. Stillwater had duct-taped his mouth and bound his hands behind his back in the man's own handcuffs. On his ankles were a pair of heavy shackles he'd found in the back of the SUV. The man was young and scared and Alex didn't blame him. He had plenty of reason to be scared. Alex stopped in front of him and made a point of looking down into the deep water slip below.

"One of my oldest friends was killed this morning and another is missing in action," he said slowly to make sure the kid was listening. "I have questions. I'm going to remove the tape. You answer me when I ask and that's all. You don't scream, you don't make a peep other than what I want to hear. You utter anything other than the answer to the questions I ask, and you learn to swim without the benefit of your arms or legs. You get me?"

Helmsley did not respond.

"It's important we are on the same page here."

Helmsley slowly nodded.

"Good." Stillwater ripped the tape off the man's face, eliciting a cringe and a grunt. "Why were you and your boys following me?"

Helmsley studied Stillwater for a second. "We're looking for two agents from our task force. You are a target."

"Bullshit." Alex grabbed him by the arm and turned him toward the water.

"Whoa, whoa, whoa!"

Alex pulled him back to center.

"You're Alex Stillwater!"

Alex didn't answer.

"You're an associate of Agent Bowman's. We're trying to recover Agent Bowman and Agent Milligan. They failed to report in last night."

Alex stepped back for a moment to consider what he was saying. The problem was that anyone on the bad guys' payroll would have all this info, especially if they'd worked Charlie around enough that he would talk—though I would hate to run into the son of a bitch that could make Bowman do anything, Stillwater thought.

"What do you know about a guy named Westchase

and another one named Hopkins?"

Helmsley was getting pissed. "You don't seem to get it, I am an F-B-I agent."

Stills grinned. "Just because I haven't dropped you in the drink yet, doesn't mean I'm not going to. Westchase, Hopkins, go."

Helmsley sighed once more. Maybe he thought he was getting somewhere with Stillwater. The young agent was about to speak when the sudden crack of a rifle shattered the relative quiet of the old boat dock. Stillwater watched Helmsley suddenly crumple in front of him. Spinning on his heel and ducking for cover, Stills saw he was twenty feet from a bulky black man sporting what looked like an SKS rifle.

Alex started shooting before he had a clean bead on the guy. Watching over his front sight he noted bullets stitching the old, off-kilter boathouse doorway before catching the man in the kneecap. The guy yelled as he hit the ground then tried to bring the powerful assault rifle to bear. Alex fired five more times into the ample target box of the man's abdomen until he slumped over and fell limp at an unnatural angle.

Stopping at the doorway, he quick-peeked up the slope away from the boathouse and caught sight of another man carrying an SKS; however, this one was smart enough to flee. The man scrambled up the hill toward an old SUV, his weapon shuffling from side to side as he ran.

Alex propped the back of his hand against the aging doorjamb for support before firing. He needed to be very careful with this one. Alex's first shot caught the man in the center of the calf.

With a scream, the man fell. His momentum carried him back down the slope away from his vehicle.

Alex was on the move before the man came to a stop. He curved around to his target's flank before he was able to get his bearings. The man cried and rolled himself into a sitting position, SKS all but forgotten in his lap. To Alex the man looked like a rabbit whose only tactic when frightened is to sit still and hope the threat doesn't see it. Without losing a step, Alex was on the man just as he turned his way. His target's eyes were wide as a Frisbee when he saw Alex closing, gun in hand. In one smooth motion Alex buffaloed him, slamming the hot slide of his Glock model 22 into the man's temple. The man's shocked expression went slack and he crumpled to the dirt, unconscious.

Chapter Twenty-One

Matt Helmsley hadn't so much heard the shot as felt it. Just a heavy, sudden thud and he was on his back, teetering precariously on a rotting dock above disgusting brown water. He tried to get up but it felt like his right shoulder was pinned to the wood somehow. When he rolled to his right he heard his bones grating together. He bit his cheek against a torrent of pain and clenched his eyes shut.

Get up! He told himself. Who knew how long that son of a bitch was going to leave him be? Who knew if the bastard was still alive? Maybe the asshole that shot him made the second shot count, right through Stillwater's head, and was going to finish the job he started by putting a bullet through his other shoulder. The searing pain caused spots in his vision as he rose to his knees. His shoulder felt unnaturally heavy, as if it were sagging off his body. He had a mental picture of pieces of meat hanging where his shoulder had been. When he looked, he saw the hole through his shirt. He tried to touch the wound with his manacled hands and stopped. It felt like a railroad spike was being punched through his deltoid at the slightest movement of his right arm. He was bleeding pretty good but there was no spurting or gushing from what he could see.

Helmsley stumbled from the lopsided boathouse, shuffling dumbly on bound legs into the sun and felt the pressing heat of midday Charleston fall on him. He looked around tentatively and stopped when he noticed the body. He must be in some sort of shock, Helmsley figured; there was no way under normal circumstances he wouldn't have seen a dead man before he got within ten paces of the corpse. He studied the man for a second. Could see the bullet holes stitching his yellow shirt. His eyes were open and he looked like he was staring lazily across the marsh.

164

Helmsley suddenly felt numb. This was the first time he'd seen a dead man. The eyes were so blank, so slack.

"Never seen a dead body before?"

Helmsley almost lost consciousness as he jumped at the sudden sound. A wave of excruciating pain shot through him, almost buckling his knees. Stillwater was suddenly at his side. He tried to recoil from his captor but with his hands and feet still cuffed he knew there was no point. He didn't answer him.

"It's okay," Stillwater said. "As far as I'm concerned, he validated your story." He tossed Helmsley his credentials back and moved to unlock the handcuffs.

"So that's all it took, huh?" Helmsley was suddenly exhausted as he was able to step out of the metal rings that had been shaving off layers of his skin.

Stillwater grabbed his wrists, and another shockwave of pain blew through Helmsley weakening his knees. "Well, it's been a weird morning," the detective said.

Now Helmsley was getting mad. He wanted to lash out and pound on Stillwater but the throbbing in his shoulder kept him in place. Well, that, and he suddenly felt bile rising in his stomach.

Stillwater ripped the short sleeve off Helmsley's shirt and inspected his wound. "The bullet just took a chunk out of your shoulder; it's not bleeding too badly," he said mechanically.

Helmsley didn't respond and watched as Stillwater turned and walked away. The detachment the man showed him was chilling. He felt like a steak thrown at a tiger that the tiger suddenly tossed away because the handler dropped a filet mignon on top of it. This guy is fucking nuts, Helmsley thought. "What are you gonna do now?"

"I got a new lead," Stillwater said, still showing him his back.

Helmsley sighed. In the last hour he'd been kidnapped and shot, but as he watched the man responsible for it all walk away he suddenly felt the urge to follow him. He didn't want to be left behind. He started to follow. "Where are you going?"

"None of your business."

"Do you know where Agent Bowman is?"

Stillwater didn't respond. He approached an old, beat-up Ford Explorer that he guessed had belonged to the attacker, now dead.

"I'm going with you!" Helmsley demanded, reaching out for Stillwater's back.

The man spun like lightning and hit him in the shoulder. Helmsley saw white for an instant and dropped to the ground.

Stillwater kneeled next to him. "You're wounded. You're out of the game. I respect your heart, but you'll slow me down. If you want to help me you can give me a five-minute head start." He handed him his bureau issue Blackberry. The battery had been removed and was sitting on the outside of the case. Helmsley took the phone in his right hand.

"You're still going to jail," Helmsley said through clenched teeth as he regained his feet.

"I know," Stillwater responded, "but don't try to get in my way until this is over."

As Stillwater passed the government vehicle he dropped the keys in the sand. "Also, I'm borrowing the AR that was in the back."

A minute later Stillwater was gone, taking the Ford Explorer and disappearing in a cloud of dust.

Chapter Twenty-Two

Vander Thompkins squirmed against the entire roll of
duct tape securing him to the base of a tree. He was
planted on the ground in a sitting position. His calf
throbbed and his temples thundered. He remembered
getting shot but he could not for the life of him remember
how he got ...here? He was in the woods somewhere. Short
palms and sweet grass surrounded him. The heat of the
afternoon sun was suffocating, only adding to his dizziness.

"I was just about to wake you up. We got things to
discuss."

The voice was calm. Thompkins froze. Whoever it
was, was behind him, behind the tree.

"Who dat?" he barked.

Footsteps on crumbling pine needles signaled his
captor's approach. "I'm the guy you and your buddy just
tried to kill. What was his name again?"

"Leonard, and fuck you."

"Well, A: Leonard is room temperature, and, B:
'Vander,'"—Stillwater was reading the license he found in
the man's wallet—"you have only a matter of minutes to
decide if you live or die."

"Man, you better let me go, you got—"

Alex planted his foot on the man's calf and ground
it into the dirt.

Vander howled and fought; he struggled against the
tape, breathing heavily.

"Did you notice I didn't bother to gag you?"

The question seemed out of left field; it brought
Vander up short. He looked up at the madman who had
kidnapped him. His eyes were . . . nothing . . . brown.
There was no crazy, wide-eyed stare, or squinting like Clint
Eastwood in one of his westerns; there was just ... nothing.

"You can scream all you want, Vander. No one will
hear you out here."

The guy looked him right in the eye as he said it. He was so matter-of-fact, so business-like. Vander felt his bladder let go. His captor must have seen darkness spreading over his jeans because he chuckled as he stood up straight and looked around the woods.

"Now, Vander, I could beat the living shit out of you. I could grab a knife and start cutting on you. You tried to kill me, either way you'd be getting off easy in the end. But." He paused and produced a small jar of honey he'd picked up at a roadside farmer's market as they were heading out of town. The jar was shaped like a cartoon bear; its smile mocked him. He must have been staring at the bear for too long, "Vander!" the guy snapped his fingers.

"What, man, you're a cop! You can't do this."

"Some things are bigger than the law, Vander. I've got questions. You answer me straight and you might get to a hospital before they have to amputate that leg. You don't answer me and I have an army of friends who will convince you to talk." The cop pointed in the direction of a little mound of sand maybe twenty feet away.

"Fuck dat."

The cop, just said, "Okay," and flipped the top off the bear. "Who sent you and your boy, Vander?" he asked as he hovered over him.

Vander didn't respond. If this guy didn't do him, the other guys would. He looked at the honey and the sordid grin on this crazy cop's face. Suddenly honey was oozing down his forehead.

"All I need is the name, Vander, and we'll get you some help."

The sticky stream of amber fluid clung to him; Vander felt tendrils of it sliding into his ears and over his eyebrows. "No, man."

"Come on, I don't hold it against you that you took the job. A man's gotta eat. But there are bigger things at play today. I need the name."

The honey fell from the bear down his abdomen to his waist and down his injured leg. The honey pooled around his wound.

Vander said nothing.

"You know, honey is supposed to be a powerful antibiotic," the cop stated as the honey filled the wound and continued toward his ankle.

Thompkins' eyes grew wide and he took in a gulp of air when the slithering brown stream dribbled off his boot onto the sweet grass and sand. "You can't do this," he said, his voice wavering.

"All I need is the name of the guy that sent you after me," the cop told him without stopping the flow of the honey. "I know he's more connected than you are; he's the one I want, not you."

Thompkins didn't respond. He watched the madman step slowly toward that mound of sand. He was merely a couple feet away when Thompkins felt that lurch in his gut. He knew what was coming, anybody who grew up in the South knew what an army of hungry fire ants would do to a person—not to mention a guy covered in honey. And as Vander watched the man slowly creep up on the anthill, he knew this cop was insane and there was no way he was going to stop.

Vander wondered what he had gotten himself into. This started out as just another job. Lenny had called him around nine and told him they had a special. That they weren't going to the Hall for work today. He and Len had done this kind of work time and again over the years. They usually meet at the same old dive in the neck, get some coffee and wait. Then a suit shows up and gives them the package. Usually, it's just an envelope with two grand inside, one for him and one for Lenny. Along with the money is a picture with a name and address written on it.

He should have known as soon as they saw the

address. It wasn't a house, or some schmuck's work. It was a bar, the one bar in the peninsula that everyone knew not to fuck with. They were told they would find their mark there, and they did. Vander almost shit himself when he saw this crazy bastard leaning against a cop car. A fuckin cop, come on, he'd told Lenny. But they'd taken the cash, the deal was done and they knew not to go back on the suits at the Hall. But this ....

This was some out-of-the-box shit. No two thousand dollars was going to get him out of this. Even if Vander did try to buy his way out, the dull look in this fucker's eyes told him there was no way. This guy was cold. He wasn't enjoying himself. Lenny had a thing for beatin' on people. Vander always took the specials, as they called it when they were hired out for muscle work, as a little extra scratch but Lenny got off on it. Not this guy, he was like the fuckin Terminator.

Vander saw the anthill start to stir as the honey hit the first grain of sand.

The cop was looking at him.

"I just need a name, Vander; I got no interest in you."

Vander knew he wasn't lying. Nothing this guy said had been a lie, which made it all the more freaky. When the cop stomped on the hill and the little demons started going crazy his mind was made up.

"No!" he screamed, "I'll tell you, I'll tell you! Shit!"

**

Stillwater hid his relief with a chuckle when Thompkins finally broke. He raced the ants back to his captive while the man twisted and fought against his bonds. Thompkins screamed like a lobster thrown in a pot as he watched the dark fog of insects racing his way. Stillwater slipped an auto knife from his pocket and cut the duct tape holding the man to the tree and pulled him up. Thompkins broke from him and Alex didn't fight it as he hobbled away on his damaged leg.

A half hour later the two were driving over the intercoastal waterway toward James Island. Thompkins leaned against the door frame, eyes vacant as he stared out the windshield.

"You're sure this is where I'll find him?"

"Yeah, man," Thompkins said tiredly. "He always do lunch at the country club."

"Hell of a thing," Alex commented, "you union boys, those of you not smuggling cocaine or moonlighting as contract killers, work your asses off. And this guy sits here spending your dues money on caviar and steak."

Vander didn't respond.

"How did you guys come to work with this outfit I'm chasing?"

Vander shrugged his shoulders but kept his head pinned to the door frame. He looked like a little kid who'd been told he couldn't have any ice cream. "Thas jus' the way it always been," he said, "My daddy was a longshoreman, his daddy was a longshoreman, an' we always was in somethin' dirty."

"Huh."

Stillwater arrived at the Charleston Country Club, one of the most exclusive establishments in the city, and in an area known for golf, that was saying something. He circled the parking lot and Thompkins pointed out a black Mercedes with a vanity license plate that read: LCL 427.

"That's it." Thompkins pointed with a shaky hand.

Alex could tell the man was in shock. Had probably had lost a fair amount of blood by that point, too. He didn't give it a second thought.

Retrieving his phone he pulled up the picture he'd taken from the Internet. "This the guy?"

"That's him."

Stillwater left the country club parking lot and

drove three blocks over into a residential neighborhood. "Get out."

There was absolutely no fight left in Vander Thompkins. Without comment, he slowly opened the creaky, rusted passenger door and stumbled out on the street.

Before he closed the door, Stillwater stopped him. "Vander?"

The beaten man turned toward him.

"I ever see or hear about you again I finish what I started. Next time I feed you to the sharks. Hear me?"

Thompkins looked him in the eye and nodded.

"Good, now go get yourself looked at."

Alex looked himself over in the cloudy rearview mirror of Thompkins' truck and noted the sweat stains and dirt patches covering his face and the grime coating his button down shirt. He brushed himself off and tidied himself up as much as possible. The country club was a black-tie establishment. He was going for Larry Wineman, President of Local Longshoreman Union 427. He took one last look in the mirror and moved out.

Stillwater parked toward the rear of the parking lot since the old beater he was driving stuck out like a sore thumb in a lot populated with German and Italian luxury vehicles. He was three rows from the entrance and was already ducking the valet who was looking at him sideways when he pulled up short as his phone vibrated in his pocket. He fished his phone out of his pocket then arched an eyebrow when he read the text.

"Do not enter that building" was the short message.

Alex spun and scanned the parking lot. Then, he saw them. Must be slipping, he told himself as he looked over the firepower these men were bringing to bear. He recognized two of them immediately as the agents who had chased him down on Water Street. The look on their faces was grim; those boys wanted to shoot him. Not that he could blame them.

He still had his weapon holstered in the small of his back, but knew he wouldn't draw. He might be out of bounds, and the rest of his career and freedom might be on the edge of a cliff, but there were some boundaries even he wouldn't cross.

He scanned the area for a way out, to make a run for it, but saw that they were ready for him. There were agents coming from all sides with long guns and Tasers all trained on him. He put his hands up, then with one hand reached outside the truck and opened the door. He kept both hands up as he slid out of the driver's seat. An agent with a smudged, button-down shirt and a nasty contusion over his right eye came at him head on.

"This is over Stillwater," he heard a female say. Keeping his hands over his head he pivoted to see a short, almost tiny brunette walking toward him, unarmed. She was dressed in a crisp, black business suit. Her modest heels snapped on the ground with each step.

Alex was just about to ask her who the hell she was when his attention was drawn to the valet stand.

"You will burn for this!" Larry Wineman, handcuffed with an agent on each arm, snapped. "Call my lawyer!" he yelled to anyone who would listen.

The petite brunette brought Alex's attention back to her. "You're coming with us."

He glanced back at Wineman, then down at the female agent. "Sure am."

Chapter Twenty-Three

Charlie was strangely calm.

Tied to a gurney, which was tied to a ring bolted to a metal floor, he tried to ignore the constant hum of pain. He had to find himself a way out. He figured there were long odds on him being able to free himself, even if he did have use of both arms.

The bullet in his hip made moving an exercise in torment. Even the slightest twitch made him see stars. The painkillers Mai had given him while she cleaned the wound only took the edge off; he had to grit his teeth when a wave of nausea-inducing pain sporadically drove through his body. He didn't know how long he'd been lying there with his pseudo nurse/jailer. He might have lost consciousness a time or two; he couldn't be sure.

Every now and then he'd look toward the chair where they had executed Milligan and grimaced, heaviness in his chest. Milligan had his quirks, but he was a good man. He didn't deserve that. Charlie knew it was his own ego that had landed him there. Milligan had warned him time and again that he was pushing it too far, and now it had cost him …cost both of them. Charlie just hoped he had the opportunity to even the score. When he heard the screech of metal on metal echo through the cargo bay, he looked at Mai, who was sitting quietly with her head down. She looked like a soldier on deployment, trying to get a moment's rest whenever she could.

"Hey there. Any chance you could give me one of those scalpels you got over there? Just for sport?"

She looked up at him but did not respond.

He smiled and lifted his head off the bed. "Worth a shot."

That got him the faintest of a smirk.

Heavy boots tramping on the metal deck signaled they were coming.

He turned to face them as much as he could. Great, the two thugs he'd threatened with a gun over the dead guy at the club. They eyed him. He could tell they were looking forward to whatever was to come. He had a split second before it began. He closed his eyes, took a breath, and thought about Keith Milligan. Then he screamed.

They cut the zip tie, yanked him off the gurney and ripped the IV in his arm from the vein. The pressure on his wound felt like his pelvis was getting crushed in a vice. They didn't say a word, just dragged him to the metal chair bolted to the floor in the middle of the cargo bay—Milligan's chair. They threw him down and strapped his hands behind his back with a couple fresh zip ties. His vision blinked in and out against the firing nerves in his hip that threatened to overload his system and knock him unconscious. He heaved for breath, head bowed and exhausted, when they finally let go of him.

***

He didn't look up as Hopkins entered. "How's your leg?" he heard from behind him. He listened as the man's boots banged against steel deck plates, but he didn't answer. He heard the man stop in front of him and then his head was yanked up by the hair until he was looking in Hopkins' eyes, wide, all amped up with nostrils flaring.

"Whatsa'matter? No wiseass bullshit from you now?" Hopkins threw Charlie's head down. "I wish I had shot you months ago."

Charlie remained silent.

"Look at me!" Hopkins roared.

Charlie raised his head. He saw that Hopkins had a revolver in the front of his pants, and a case file in his hand.

Hopkins held up the file. "You know what this is? This is how we got you. You shoulda known we were everywhere. An organization like this does not survive as long as it has without having eyes and ears where we need them." Hopkins pulled a photo out of the file and held it up.

It was the pregnant girl he and Milligan had transferred to the U.S. Marshals.

Charlie shook his head but did not say anything.

"You were sold out by your own people, hero. You got your boss killed. How much of his blood has soaked into your clothes from that chair? You know, I'm going to ask the next guy the same question about you."

Hopkins backhanded him and Charlie tasted blood but didn't respond.

"I told Westchase from the moment you showed up you were a rat, but that bloated fuck didn't listen to me. That rich boy never did."

Did. Charlie marked the wording.   Hopkins grabbed another metal chair that rested against a bulkhead and dragged it over to where Charlie was bound. He sat down and leaned into him. "Charlie, I would love to take you apart piece by piece but I have a lot going on today, and I promised you to someone else. So tell me where your stash is. I know you had back up, you wouldn't trust everything with that bumbling idiot, Milligan. You tell me where it is and I will put you down quick and quiet. I won't let Hammer have you."

Charlie felt himself stiffen as he heard the name. He soon noticed that Hopkins noted his response also..

"That's right, I don't even want to think of what that hillbilly fuck has planned for you. You finish this now, give me what I need, and it's all over. Otherwise you disappear into the mountains with those inbred sons of bitches, and you disappear so deep that not even the Tenth Mountain Division could find you."

Charlie didn't respond.

Hopkins was not a patient man, his nostrils flared and he dropped the file. He swung up from the chair and, grabbing it by the back, smashed it against Charlie's side.

Lightning shot through his body and Charlie screamed. He couldn't breathe, he couldn't focus, the pain had overloaded his system to the point his body was shutting down on him. He struggled to remain conscious. He wasn't gonna give this fucker the satisfaction.

Hopkins threw the chair off to the side. "Oh, yeah, there's also this." Hopkins leaned over to Charlie so he could see. When his eyes cleared from the shock of the sudden attack on his wound, he saw the badge. It was a tarnished old City of Charleston badge, number 176. Even as wrecked as his brain was he recognized the number immediately. He'd seen that very same badge a hundred times, night after night hanging over the bar in between an old hickory night stick and a slap jack. "No."

"Sammy was his name, wasn't it? From what I hear, the old bastard put up quite a fight, but in the end he just couldn't hang." Hopkins started to say something else when his phone rang. He answered and listened for a minute. Without saying a word, he closed the phone. "Saved by the bell." Hopkins looked at his two shadows. "Well, maybe not. Don't kill him yet, boys." He walked out of the cargo bay.

Charlie watched him go, then noticed the two men look at each other and turn toward him. He took a deep breath and before the beating began noticed Mai watching passively from her little makeshift medical unit.

Chapter Twenty-Four

Alex tried to get comfortable with his hands handcuffed behind him. He felt like he couldn't breathe, his shoulders ached, his hands were numb. He had never thought about the discomfort associated with being cuffed before. It was driving him crazy, adding to the growing anxiety over where Charlie was, and what had happened to him.

The moment Sammy had said Charlie's name an alarm went off and Alex was on mission. Like a cruise missile launched from a destroyer. But now, strapped in handcuffs, wedged in between two FBI agents who wanted nothing more than to put him away for a millennia out of pure embarrassment, he realized he hadn't talked to the man who'd thrown his career and freedom away in over a year.

Damn, he thought. Alex still remembered the last day they spoke, or fought. In the parking lot behind headquarters. Charlie was the disgraced cop handing in his badge, facing prosecution, and there he was, a newly minted detective moving forward and upward. Alex started getting pissed off as if he were there toe-to-toe with his best friend all over again, only it was worse now. That Helmsley kid had called him Agent Bowman. So all that had been bullshit. Charlie had set the whole thing up, even beating up the old bum? Even the trial? And jail? Alex had been played by his friend.

I'm going to kill him, he thought.

He didn't know why he suddenly fell back in time then, but suddenly he was back in Germany where the both of them had been sent for treatment after the battle in Fallujah. They were bunked together in the medical dorm at Landstuhl. Alex remembered the night, one of the most embarrassing of his life. His leg and hip were bound up really bad after surgery to remove the rounds he had taken so he was confined to quarters. Charlie was more or less able-bodied after the surgeons were able to stitch his neck back together and replace the couple of pints of blood he'd lost. Alex moped around the room moving stiffly when he could no longer sit still. He switched between bad German TV and worse Armed Forces Network commercials about wearing reflective belts while PT'ing in a war zone. Then he would slouch on their miniscule balcony overlooking the base. Charlie had found a way to sneak over the wire and was doing so on a nightly basis.

Alex couldn't forget the night he dove into a bottle of Jameson Charlie had smuggled in for him before smuggling himself off base. Alex was two-thirds through the bottle when Charlie blew through the door like he was being chased by a pack of hyenas. This was almost true, as he *was* being hounded by MPs. When he busted in Alex stayed on the balcony, trying to hide in the tiny confines of their dorm room. He didn't want Charlie to see him falling apart.

"Man, I don't know what it is about German chicks, but damn," Charlie announced.

Alex didn't respond. When Charlie made it to the balcony, he tried to hide but it was no good.

"You all right?" Charlie asked when he finally saw him.

Alex expected mocking, merciless jokes, unending from his friend.

Instead Charlie sagged to the concrete on the other side of the balcony. "Thinking about the fight?" he asked.

Alex looked up. How the hell would he know that?

Charlie nodded slowly. "You don't really think about it at the time, too busy trying to survive, I guess."

Alex knew Charlie was right. The day, that day, had tormented him all night. Like someone had thrown a switch in his memory, making him re-live it moment by moment. Every move he made or didn't make, every instant he could have bought it and didn't. He could even see the pattern on the scarves the enemy wore as they dashed in and out of his line of fire, shooting at him with their AKs. He froze his memory in some of those moments. In one instant he couldn't move, couldn't shift this way or that and he just watched, squirming, paralyzed by his own mind as the jihadis lined him up like a deer in the woods and blew him away. Each moment like that changed just so slightly to the next until he was driving himself mad thinking about all the ways he could have died in that shithole mud-brick hut. Visions of his mom and dad, the rest of his family, gathering up the pieces of him as he was returned to them in a metal coffin under a red, white, and blue flag.

And if that wasn't enough, the deep recesses of his mind took the brief moments of peace he'd managed to acquire, to remind him that he left squad mates over there. Here he was sipping German beer and Jameson whiskey while men who'd depended on him were getting blown up and ambushed by the enemy every day. Who was he to leave them a man down? Who was he to be sitting out on the bench while they bled and died?

"You were pretty jacked up for the first couple days we were here. In and out of surgery, you were unconscious for the better part of a week before they got you put back together. Once they stitched me up I was pretty much just cut loose, left on my own here at the dorm. I had my night a couple of days later. It hasn't gone away yet; I'll feel that bullet sting at times every day. See you laying there in the cloud of dust trying to use a haji for cover." Charlie paused for a moment, "Don't make me do that again, okay?"

Alex scoffed through a stuffed nose but didn't say anything in response. He passed the bottle of whiskey he'd been sipping on to Charlie who took a healthy swig. The two sat in silence the rest of the night, each man wrestling with his own demons.

***

Alex pulled out of his trance and noticed that the small convoy of SUVs passed the turn that would take them from James Island to downtown where the federal offices were.

He studied his captors. They were feds, that was clear enough, but who and what? Some task force, some undercover team? Either way, the bottom line remained the same, he was going to get his friend today somehow? His wrists itched as they started to lose sensation behind his back. He studied the other occupants of the vehicle, and there wasn't a fed made who could stop him. He hoped Wineman was heading to the same place. He was Alex's only lead at the moment. He watched as they drove through West Ashley through a series of side streets until coming to a seemingly empty office park. The two SUVs pulled through a high, rollup door and stopped inside a massive garage.

A couple of minutes later Alex was alone in an interrogation room. He was still handcuffed, though now his hands were in front of him resting on a cheap metal table which matched the metal chair he sat in. The torture device seemed to be built for the specific purpose of aggravating his lower lumbar while at the same time gouging his shoulder blades. There was a one-way mirror to his left and a single door opposite the table where he sat. He didn't see a camera mount in the room but figured it had to be mounted on the other side of the one-way glass.

This seemed like a pretty high-speed operation. He'd seen Wineman dragged off to another side of the building when they'd arrived, which Alex figured to be another interrogation room like this one. He watched as his only lead disappeared before his eyes. The silence and solitude began to get to him as he sat in the quiet room. He tried to keep his focus, tried to come up with a way out so he could go help Charlie but he was coming up short. He felt a knot in his chest at the thought of his old partner in the hands of whatever bad guys he'd been going after, and here he was stuck in a locked room with no way to back up his friend. Alex suddenly felt like a caged animal. Panic threatened to drive him mad and he had to fight to drive it back down.

It wasn't easy to maintain a mission focus when by all rights he was done, like a chess piece swept from the board. The worst part was that technically he'd been taken out by his own people. If they had come at him head on instead of following him like a bush league spy-versus-spy cartoon they might have been ten steps ahead by now. Now Alex was out of the game, with no idea how to get back on the board. He wracked his brain as he studied his surroundings. All avenues of escape included one unbreakable road block: Other cops.

As bungling as these feds had been in chasing him rather than backing up their own undercovers, he could not take them out just to get to Charlie. It wasn't that he particularly gave a shit about the people who had brought him in but there was a line he could not cross. For a moment in that parking lot he had found his gun hand slipping toward his holster. Maybe it was just a natural reaction to a threat, maybe it was something darker, but the bottom line was that Alex couldn't go there, not even for his oldest friend.

The narrow door to the interrogation room slipped open and the brunette he'd met in the parking lot along with one of the agents he'd given the slip to on Water Street entered. They glowered at him. He knew the agent, mid-forties maybe, but built like a brick shithouse, wanted to rip his head off. He couldn't blame him. But he also got more than a little Kick out of it.

The brunette was in business mode. Her brown glossy hair was tightly cropped in a bun on the back of her head. Her crisp business suit trimmed out her fit, well-balanced figure. She had a file in her hand that she dropped on the table before she and the agent sat down.

"Detective Stillwater, I'm Assistant United States Attorney Laura Banefield, and this is Special Agent Al Farraday."

Alex did not respond.

"Do you know why you're here today?"

"Am I under arrest?"

"Damn fuckin right you are," Farraday blurted out, earning him a curt look from Banefield.

She paused for a minute before saying, "That remains to be seen." She went to continue her spiel when Stillwater interrupted her.

"Lawyer."

"Excuse me?"

"I want my lawyer. Unless of course I am not under arrest in which case you will unlock these cuffs and show me the quickest way out of here."

Time stopped as the three of them stared at each other.

Finally, Banefield continued, "Detective, on any other day I would consider what you just said, however today is not any other day. You are an associate of Special Agent Charles Bowman."

He nodded.

"And you realize he is missing."

Alex nodded again.

"I was unaware of you prior to this morning. Then you ran database checks on two of our primary suspects in the same investigation Bowman was working on when he and his control agent went missing. When we looked further, we found that you began your day with a gun fight that resulted in the death of Samuel O'Laughlin. We were on our way to making contact with you when you left the scene of the incident without authorization. We followed you and I think you know the rest."

Stillwater looked at Farraday. "How is Helmsley?"

"Shattered shoulder, and a pretty scar thanks to you," the man growled.

"Not according to him," Banefield retorted.

That caught Alex's attention.

"Agent Helmsley stated that you saved his life. He led us to the scene of your second shooting of the day where the body of a man was found. The weapon in his possession matched the wound Agent Helmsley suffered. This man was also known muscle for a local group associated with our primary suspects."

Alex was again given silent permission to respond, he declined.

Banefield sighed. "At first, Detective, I wanted to know if you were part of the problem or part of the solution. You see the problem with this particular investigation is that the criminal target we have is highly connected to all levels of local politics, industry, and law enforcement.

"You may have noticed that we are not local personnel. I am on assignment from the Arizona District. Agent Farraday leads a Special Operations Group out of the DC field office. Given your behavior this morning and the simple fact that the body count so far shows you are in direct conflict with our subjects, I am willing to believe we are on the same side. Is that—?"

"Give me Wineman."

"Excuse me?"

"You're not going to arrest me. You want to work together, okay. Give me Wineman and let's get to work."

Banefield smiled and looked down at her file. When she met Alex's eyes once more her smile was gone. "You've killed one person that we know of. I get that you two are war buddies, but your scorched-earth policy to find him ends here. We have missing agents, and you are doing nothing constructive here."

Alex noticed her voice waver for a microsecond, and her eyes dipped. "The situation calls for outside-the-box thinking, I get it. Wineman is a high-level union official. A phone book and a pair of pliers won't work on him and it will get us all thrown in jail. None of that will help Charlie. Farraday and his team will work on Wineman." Banefield stood, the discussion was over.

"What am I going to do, then?" Alex suddenly felt like he was on the bench.

"You are going to take a breath and get your shit together."

Alex looked at his hands and noticed the crusted dark chips under his fingernails. He also noted blotches of crimson red on his shirt and pants. Holy shit, he thought, I hadn't even noticed. Was it Helmsley or Sammy's blood he was looking at?

He thought of Sammy; the old man was a warhorse. It both pissed Alex off and made him proud thinking of the way the old man held the fort when the horde crashed the gates. I'm not done yet, Sammy, he silently promised his old friend.

Al Farraday grabbed Alex's cuffs with a yank, snapping him back to reality. He had a key in his hand and malice on his face. He slowly unlocked the shackles. "Helmsley is a young agent," he breathed. "You kidnapped and threatened an FBI agent. I know he lied to me. There's nothing I can do about it if he won't come clean, but I promise you, you will pay for that." Farraday shoved Alex's wrist away. "Keep your shit together, cause I'll be watching."

Alex rubbed his wrists and followed Farraday out of the room into an open space. Part cubicles, part garage, part war room, Alex drifted toward the digital battle board. A six-by-six screen with a hierarchy of photos and bio data related to the group Charlie had infiltrated. He finally got a look at Hopkins and Westchase, and noticed there was a faceless icon representing Bowman. He felt ice sliding down his spine as he realized he was once again back in the game. Instinctively, his right hand slid over an empty holster and he realized they still had his gun. When he turned to chase down Farraday, he came face-to-face with Matthew Helmsley. The man had a scowl that could freeze a volcano. Alex was speechless.

Finally it was Helmsley who spoke. "There are bigger issues going on here today than you and me."

Alex cleared his throat, to say he felt like an asshole didn't quite cut it. "I am glad you're okay."

Helmsley rolled his eyes and walked off. "Come with me; you need some new clothes."

Since the team in place was mostly dedicated to conducting surveillance, there was a pile of clothes on hand for quick changes during operations. After some searching, Alex was able to find a pair of jeans and an old button-down shirt that managed not to make him look like a homeless person. He came out of the restroom where he changed to find Helmsley holding his unloaded service weapon, two magazines, and loose rounds in a plastic bag with his police ID and badge.

Alex took the bag with a grin. "Now what?"

"Now we wait," Helmsley said and walked away.

Helmsley seemed to have no interest in showing him around and Banefield and Farraday were intently watching Wineman as he threatened lawsuits and demanded calls for his lawyer like a malfunctioning jukebox. Stillwater found his phone and ear bud and started listening once again to Charlie's recordings while he poked around the office.

Alex immediately saw that this task force was outfitted to the nines. In addition to the fleet of Suburbans, the operation had two undercover surveillance vehicles. They looked like work vans, one was disguised as an industrial cleaning service van, and the other as a plumber's van. Stillwater was familiar with the automobiles, the police department had one of their own with a telescoping camera and high-tech antenna system built into the rack of PVC pipe on the roof.

After sliding past the toys, Alex found a bank of computers with one lone technician manning what looked like intercepts. The technician was reading a saltwater fishing magazine with his boots up on the desk. Their eyes met briefly as Alex strolled by; Alex saw no recognition in the man's expression.

The tech said, "No joy," before returning to his reading,

"What's the problem?" Alex asked, fishing in the hopes of finding out what the rig actually did.

The tech sighed; apparently he'd told this story before. "Either these guys have dumped their phones or they just aren't talking today. We just got up with emergency wiretaps on both Westchase and Hopkins since the UC went missing."

Alex cringed inwardly. The guy talked like Charlie was a special piece of equipment rather than a cop in trouble. "Only thing we can do is wait and see. Either they start talking or they don't."

Alex looked at his watch. It was almost two in the afternoon. "When did you flip the switch?"

The tech looked at a log sitting on the desk in front of him. "Not long ago; it's only been since noon or so that we've been listening. It's too early to throw in the towel. Bad guys don't always operate right on schedule."

Alex grunted.

Alex left the tech to his reading about tarpon or whatever he was into and completed his circle back to the battle board. He studied the photos of Hopkins and Westchase. They didn't seem right; they came from different strata of society. It didn't sit right with Alex and he couldn't put his finger on why. There was a computer terminal to the right of the big board. Alex looked around for a moment to ensure he was still being ignored and sat down.

He hit the space bar and the screen came to life. It was locked and password protected. Alex grimaced for a second then picked up the keyboard and turned it over. He grinned. The login and password were taped to the bottom of the keyboard, just like his own at the office. He hastily signed in and began searching. There were files on each of the main subjects to include the guy named Hammer in North Carolina, which seemed to be the way station for the girls they smuggled into the country. Alex shuddered at the thought of what these women were put through. From one dark shithole to the next until their final hell which could be slave labor for some big shot in Beverly Hills or being hooked on smack and pimped out on Craigslist until they were eaten up with VD, pregnant, or dead, each option a veritable certainty.

The more Alex listened to the running commentary of this case in his ear bud and read through the files he'd hacked into he began to get it. Charlie was always looking for the next fight, the next bad guy, you got addicted to that sort of thing if you did it long enough. Charlie had found a legitimate fight this time.

Alex was pissed off Charlie had left him in the dark, though.

He was flipping through the documents on the computer when he suddenly went still. In his ear he heard who he figured was Westchase, guiding Charlie through some sort of get together. Alex heard Charlie clear his throat the way he did when he was uncomfortable, when he was really sweating something. He remembered the most obvious instance on the day Alex told him he was proposing to Erica. Shit, Erica! Alex suddenly thought.

He hadn't thought about his wife all day. He just

went to work chasing down Mac and the rest of it! Shit! He fumbled for his phone but stopped just before hitting pause on the recording. Westchase was introducing Charlie to the chief. The grumbling reply, "You can keep him," was low but he knew that voice anywhere. Motherfucker! Charlie wasn't kidding with his caveat at the beginning of the recording.

Alex was suddenly torn between an intolerable urge to storm 180 Lockwood Boulevard or calling his wife to get her out of town. This shit was getting too close. Though Alex had heard Charlie mention the chief in an earlier track, the reality of hearing the chief's voice on a surveillance recording shocked him.

***

The phone rang and rang and when the pause came he knew he wasn't getting anywhere. At the hospital where she was now a surgical tech she could be out of pocket for hours at a time. Alex left as calm a message as he could for her to call him and hung up. Then he noticed he was trembling.

Chapter Twenty-Five

Hopkins squirmed. He never squirmed, never got nervous, never let anyone get to him. But this Hammer guy scared him. The old man sitting next to him in the Jeep Cherokee was the real deal. He didn't even know the guy, but he could see the old man had that quiet darkness that spoke of the unbound ability to commit violence.

Up until about an hour ago Hopkins had thought it was all rumor, just stories he'd picked up from Tyrell before he got killed. The old man, old-school Dixie Mafia and had bodies buried in the hills around his farm. Some of the things Tyrell told him Hammer had done he didn't even want to think about now that he was sitting next to him.

It had taken him three days to call Hammer the first time. It was after he and Bowman got into it at the club. He suspected right from the start that Bowman was a cop, and when he balked at killing Ferris he was sure. He tried to tell Westchase, but that blubbery douche bag didn't care.

Westchase loved having people like Bowman around, like himself, Hopkins admitted. People from the other side, the dark side of society, some novelty for the aristocrat to show off to his upper crust cronies to try and look like a bad ass. Westchase thought having himself and Bowman around gave him some street cred, fat fuck couldn't buy street cred, Hopkins thought.

The money was good, though, and there weren't a lot of options for twice-burnt muscle for hire. Hopkins had gone up for two felonies back in the day, manslaughter and aggravated battery, when he was working for the cartels in Laredo. After he went up the second time he'd had to ditch Texas.

Turned out that the cartel is real serious about their OPSEC (operational security), even more than the damned army was during his conscription with those assholes in green. So Charleston it was, Westchase spotted him after Hopkins knee-capped his last hired hand for trying to buy a stripper out from under him at the Southern Belle. It was fun and Hopkins had all the whores and dope he could ask for. That was all well and good, but you always needed to know when things were going south.

He had put up with Westchase's curiosity over Bowman and saw it for what it was. The little shit had a new toy he wanted to show off. But when Charlie caught him unaware with the gun in that basement he was done—done with Charlie and done with Westchase.

He was out of Westchase's league, even if the rich boy never saw it. His plan was just to kill them both and take over, and he needed Hammer to do it. Once he was able to track Hammer down, then work up the nerve to make the call, things started happening. Hammer wasn't thrilled with the way things worked down here either, and was willing to give him a shot.

Hopkins looked down the street to the nondescript, single-story stucco homes trimmed in well-cropped bushes and flowerbeds. It was the same as any other cookie-cutter neighborhood that had suffocated the geography surrounding Charleston. Boring pastel stucco boxes, cheap construction, and postage stamp yards that suburbanites could call their own.. Places like this disgusted him—real-life docking stations where the worker bees of the city went to recharge between trips to the office. The place had no character.

Regardless, the target house was as bland as they come. He watched as his men, on loan from the local longshoreman union, moved in. The point man, one of his own named Ferris, carried an SKS rifle like the others. Ferris was bold, if not bright. Trying to keep the weapon concealed by his leg, he walked right up to the front door and in one swoop kicked it in, and all hell broke loose. The sound of the Russian weapons left a distinct impression on anyone who ever heard one go off. Kind of like a two stage kah-kah. The weapons were fired in rapid succession. Hopkins thought he may have heard return fire, but his ear didn't have the sensitivity to pick it up.

It seemed like an eternity while the firing continued but he was sure no more than a minute or two had passed. When it was over it hell on earth came to a stop. He wondered how many people had just died. It'd happened so suddenly he wondered if any of them even had a chance to fight back. Another minute passed and he saw Ferris come out the front door. He was followed by the other four longshoremen who'd been hired. As they all moved out, he saw Ferris step to the side and vomit.

Hopkins leaned forward over the steering wheel, confused by the man's reaction—the one guy in his corner he was sure could handle the job. He didn't realize how hard he had been gripping the inside of the Jeep's door until Ferris straightened up and returned to the old, beat-up burner car the assassins had arrived in.

Ferris got into the driver's seat and spun a U-turn in the narrow road, mowing down a small stand of flowers in one of the yards and headed their way. Ferris braked at Hopkins' window and they both rolled down their windows. Ferris held out a necklace. It was a crucifix with a jade inlay. Hopkins noticed the black hair and sticky blood clinging to the jewelry. Ferris didn't look at him.

"It's done," he said, swinging the necklace back into his fist. Ferris pulled away, leaving Hopkins feeling cold.

Hopkins watched his man drive away. Ferris, normally the most fearsome man he could ever remember meeting was pale, almost like a ghost. He was distant and stared out the windshield while he showed his proof. It gave Hopkins pause. Finally, he turned to Hammer, who was sitting next to him.

"Humph," was the old man's only response.

Chapter Twenty-Six

M ai was not at all bothered by the beating the men gave their prisoner. It was not the first time she had watched these men dispense pain on another person. Sometimes it was a stranger she had never seen before, and sometimes it was one of the poor souls who'd arrived in a container from overseas.

They were all strangers to her, but there was a kinship with the women who crossed the ocean in that hellish metal box. They were so scared, so starved, dehydrated, and filthy. Once Hopkins had seen her meager medical skills put to work on some of the girls, she had been conscripted to act as a medic in his army of sadists. On balance, Mai realized her circumstances could have been much worse, the severity of which was only limited by her imagination. She was still tormented only by a single man.

Hopkins kept her as his own slave; just thinking of herself in those terms brought such shame she hardly could stomach the thought. Hopkins always had her on hand to treat those he and his men abused.

He would joke when it came to the women they chose to enjoy before they were sent on to parts unknown. He made jokes about her packaging the women up for sale after his men were done with them. Keeping the product moving after their own version of quality control was the way he worded it.

Hopkins also kept her on hand for his own pleasure. At first she had tried to fight him, and, when given the chance, showed herself by scoring deep gashes across his face, drawing blood.

Unfortunately, the savage outweighed her by almost a hundred pounds, and his proclivity for violence seemed to know no bounds. For her own survival, she had given in. Mai now gave Hopkins what he wanted whenever and wherever he wanted it, if not with any exuberance or spirit. Mai was always watching, though. Studying her enemy, learning every facet of this animal who controlled her. She may have ceded her body in the war, but she had not relinquished her mind or her soul.

Mai caressed the scalpel she had secreted away months ago as she watched Wallace and Higby punch and kick their captive.

In one sense, she pitied the man. If what Hopkins and the others said about him was true, then he was trying to help her. And if what she'd heard was true, he had managed to free the young, pregnant girl from this hell. They continued to beat him and there was nothing she could do.

Mai was sorry she didn't even know the girl's name. They didn't have names when they were freed from the metal box; they were just heads to be counted and moved out. Mai had seen her when she arrived, wide-eyed and trembling. Mai had convinced Hopkins to at least give her an extra ration of the horrible chunks of meat and spare food they handed the arrivals to keep them occupied and alive for transport.

Mai remembered how scared she was that they were simply going to kill that girl and throw her body in the marsh when they saw she was pregnant. Pregnancy was not something to be tolerated in this business. There is no market for that sort of thing. It had caused quite an uproar and Hopkins was furious when he'd seen her. But business must continue and he had her sent to the truck, making her someone else's problem down the line.

That little girl was terrified, she thought.

She looked up as Wallace stepped back from his prisoner, and said to Higby, "Think we might want to call it, not sure he can take much more softening up."

Higby nodded and they walked up the ramp toward the outside. They didn't even bother to look Mai's way as they exited.

Once they were gone Mai took a bowl of water and a towel and approached the prisoner. His head hung over his chest and a mix of blood and sweat dropped from the tendrils of thick, dark hair covering his face. He panted like a dog left in the heat too long. She soaked the towel and pressed it through the matted hair to his cheek.

The man's head shot up.

His left eye was swollen shut and his lips were bulging on the right side of his mouth. He pulled away from the wet cloth on instinct until he realized he was no longer under attack. It took him a moment to focus on her. "I think your pain killers have worn off."

He coughed.

Mai could not hide her smile. "You should just tell them what they want to know."

He pulled away from the cold towel again and looked at her with his one good eye the same way she had seen him look at Hopkins and his men. She paused for a moment. It hurt to see that she was associated in his mind with them.

She stared at him then quietly said, "I am not one of them."

He looked at her with his one good eye. "I know."

"I grow very tired of this. The only reason I am here and not sent along on that vile truck is because they saw me caring for some of the women I was held with. Because I could splint an arm and stop bleeding they saw a use for me." She was fighting tears and it confused her after so long living like she had.   The prisoner did not respond.

"You make Mister Hopkins very angry," she said in an attempt to keep the conversation going.

"I know," he said on a soft breath out.

"Even before this I remember him cursing you. This was before I ever saw you, long ago. He does not like you."

"I know. Give me one of your scalpels and I'll sort it out with him."

"You will not kill him!" Mai snapped.

This time it was the prisoner who shied away from the blaze in her eyes.

"He dies by my hand," she said firmly.

The prisoner looked upon her blankly, she decided he was trying to decide whether or not to trust her. Mai let the silence continue for a long time. He dropped his head again trying to conserve energy, trying to breathe in deep lungfuls of air.

"Is it true that you rescued the pregnant girl?" Mai asked softly.

The bound man nodded slowly.

Mai looked down at her hands, studying the chipped and worn fingernails she used to take such pride in. There was a faint shadowing of blood coating them. "I did not even know her name. So many women come through here, I do not want to know them. I do not want the burden of thinking of what their future holds to weigh on me. I fear what it would do to me if I had a name to go with the face."

"I understand."

Tears welled in her eyes. She was not the same person who'd lived a normal life only a year ago.

The two prisoners, stuck in the bowels of a slowly rotting ship held each other's eyes, each trying to measure the other when the distant echoes of boots on metal deck plates sounded.

Mai looked toward the heavy doors, then back to the prisoner. Instinctively, she produced her scalpel and slashed the restraints at his ankles and wrists and disappeared back toward her corner of the cargo bay. He looked up at her with new life in his bruised and swollen eyes. As the footsteps of the two thugs got closer he nodded slowly in thanks. She returned to her make shift medical station and he bowed his head to wait for his chance.

Chapter Twenty-Seven

A lex couldn't sit still long enough to look through the case files. He'd seen enough to know that he had his targets in Westchase and Hopkins. Both of them were in the wind, and the "task force" didn't have a clue as to where any of their subjects were.

Alex found himself at the double-sided glass, staring through his own vague reflection to the man in a suit seated opposite Al Farraday.

Though Alex was late to the viewing, he could tell that this fight was over before it started. Larry Wineman was the president of the longshoreman union responsible for keeping the Port of Charleston running. The guy was connected and he had the resources of the legion of dockworkers he represented. He was not afraid of a badge. You don't rise through the ranks of the union racket without being willing to bend the law. Wineman wasn't afraid of the law; he had no respect for it whatsoever.

He had managed to get hold of Wineman's rap sheet when he stood next to Banefield. She'd looked at him with a tired, disgusted look, but begrudgingly let him keep the small file they had cobbled together on the man.

Wineman had a series of arrests for assault, possession of stolen goods, and grand theft auto, probably all related to his twenties. Then, as he'd drifted into his thirties, it seemed his wayward days had come to an end, at least that's what the file said. Given the business he ran, it was more likely he'd found himself a good coach who'd taught him how to operate under the radar, to keep his misdeeds quiet. Now, he was at the top of the labor racquet in Charleston. The smug grin on his face as he lounged in his chair, staring back at Farraday told Alex that this lead was dead. Shit.

Alex turned from the window and sighed. They were getting nowhere and every second he stood still was another second ticking off Charlie's clock …if Charlie's clock was still ticking. He looked up to see Banefield staring at him. "What's the plan?" he asked.

She didn't respond at first, just stared at him.

He wondered for a moment if she was re-thinking Helmsley's bullshit story and was about to throw him in jail.

Then she said, "You know anyone at the local?"

Alex tried to think back, if any of his sources had ever had a hook into the union.

Before he could answer her she got in his face. "Part of the reason you are not in jail right now is that Hopkins thinks you have something he needs. That's the only reason I can think of that he's tried to kill you. What is it?"

***

Alex didn't answer but saw the wheels were still turning in her mind.

"What was it Sammy had that got him killed? How did you end up there at the right moment?" She was closing the distance on him as she spoke.

Alex fought the urge to back away.

He was about to defend himself when suddenly the tech manning the wire shouted, "He's up!"

Banefield left him without a blink and was hovering over the tech's shoulder. He flipped a switch and suddenly a voice was playing over the speaker: "Yeah, no." Background noise scratched and crackled around the voice as if the speaker were traveling in a convertible on the freeway. "I went out on the boat last night with some investors. We hit international waters and just stayed overnight. Had some business to get done."

Alex thought he might have heard a little giggle

199

after the statement.

"Westchase," Banefield whispered.

"Hell of a time for a vacation." Was the reply on the other side of the intercepted phone conversation.

"Hopkins," Banefield said, filling in the blanks for Alex.

"We have some shit going down, Rut. Where are you?" Hopkins asked..

"Heading downtown. Gotta get cleaned up. I'm playing golf at five."

"Uh-huh."

"Come on down. We'll talk there."

"Right."

Before the line clicked off Alex was on the move, heading for the garage bay. Suddenly Farraday was on his flank.

"Where are you headed?" he asked.

"Going to get in position at the club. I would have thought you'd be of the same mind." Banefield was right behind Farraday until her phone chimed and she dropped off.

Before they hit the garage bay Farraday grabbed Alex by the shoulder and pun him around. Alex ignored his first instinct to attack the FBI agent but didn't back down as they were nose-to-nose.

Farraday poked a finger in Alex's chest. "You take orders from me on this, I'm in charge. Your Wild West show is over. She thinks you have something to add here while I think you should be in a cell. You—"

"WHAT?!"

Farraday cut off mid-sentence and he and Alex looked at the attorney. She was looking at them, her face suddenly drawn. Her eyes welled up with tears and suddenly Alex's heart sank. He braced himself to hear the worst.

"No," she said. "How?" She paused for a moment.

She needed to compose herself. "I'm coming down there." Banefield shut off her phone. She was motionless. Alex could see that an anvil had been dropped on the woman. No, no, no, he thought, there's no way.

Alex immediately thought back to that last moment they spoke. While being pulled apart by other officers in the back of headquarters. He had hated Charlie then in that moment when both men had their blood up. Alex was so pissed off then. All the times he had stuck up for Charlie, all the times he had put his ass on the line when his hot-head partner went off the rails. And then for Charlie to have the nerve to accuse *him* of stabbing him in the back. Had it been an act? Or had Charlie really thought he had betrayed him?

Alex's mind spun, wondering about all of it. Was the last thing Charlie remembered about him a stupid fight they got in in the back of a police station? Was the man who had saved his life dead? Did he die believing that Alex was on his way, that back up might have been coming? Or did Charlie die thinking he was alone, believing his best friend had cut ties and moved on?

"The safe house was just hit." It was Banefield.

Alex heard the statement but none of it made sense. "What?" Farraday asked. "How?"

Alex watched and listened to the interplay. Relieved, he realized the call wasn't about Charlie. "I'm going to get Westchase," he said and moved off, leaving the stunned task force.

Alex jumped in the truck and didn't look up when Farraday leaped into the passenger seat. He threw the vehicle in gear and pulled out of the garage before the agent was settled. He glanced in his rearview mirror and saw another SUV fell in behind him.

"We had four Marshals and a witness at that safe house." Farraday growled. "A pregnant girl Bowman risked his ass to keep alive long enough to hand her off. She could have been the reason he got caught."

Alex was listening but the information was ancillary to the task at hand. He had a lead, there would be plenty of time to follow other aspects of the operation when they had Charlie and his handler back. Until then, none of it mattered. "We should break out the long guns," he said.

"That's my call," Farraday said. "You are back on the reservation now, got that? We do this right, like cops. You do anything other than what you're told and you will be back in cuffs and this time you don't have some dumb shit agent to lie for you. I will send you to jail for as long as the law will let me."

Alex ignored him.

"Head for Broad Street," Farraday told him.

Chapter Twenty-Eight

Westchase parked in the rear lot behind Broad Street and strolled toward the club. He had woken up with the telltale signs of a hangover but mitigated his day being ruined with a series of bong hits and a shot of whiskey. Whistling a shag tune, he let himself in and wandered up the stairs to the bar.

Rutledge Westchase loved having the club all to himself. Without the noise, the smoke, and the clutter of old men chasing women half their age, fleeing their fears and indulging their impulses. The silence was so peaceful, it enveloped him like a safety blanket. Before heading for the comfort of the plush sofa in his office, he slipped behind the bar and poured himself a scotch, three fingers neat, and decided in that moment that he was on vacation for the rest of the week. He'd earned it.

He had sufficiently impressed the congressmen and senators last night to earn his new port, completely taxpayer-funded, of course. Rule number one is never conduct business with your own money; his daddy had beaten that into him. He had pushed for the new location farther up river from Daniel Island for the last year with campaign contributions and the like, but the politicians had been hesitant to take any more than his money. Westchase understood; in these days of political scandal and sting operations any congressman worth his payoff was not going to jump at the first bucket full of cash tossed at him. He'd groomed these men, showing up at the right functions at the right times, shaking hands with the right people. He'd finally worked up, or paid in enough to earn the trust of these men, and it had all led to last night.

He had hosted four congressman from the committees related to national infrastructure, commerce, and the like. Westchase knew who his targets were and how to push them. Like all of his targets, they had allowed themselves to be pushed sufficiently. Everybody has their price, and for the corrupt, whose price is often known up front, it's just a matter of convincing them to follow their impulses. All it takes is time. Politicians are simple animals.

Rutledge had pulled out all the stops, the women he provided were contracted from a broker who supplied women to the powerful in places like Dubai and Kuwait, places where money flowed such that a perfect ten was simply the starting point. These women were goddesses in both form, skill, and discretion. They knew the game they chose to play and were the pinnacle of the profession. He had a selection of narcotics and other drugs that were suitable to indulge any taste. The heroin was of the highest quality, cocaine straight from the source, the pills were pharmaceutical quality, and the weed was the hybrid product of a British Columbian artist in the subject of hydroponics. It was all there and his targets had chosen to play. That was all he needed to get them on board with his plan.

It was expensive but they were giving him billions of dollars of other people's money, and he stood to make billions without risking a dime of his own capital. Last night was expensive but it was the only juice he needed to put in the game. There was no risk. Each politician had given him their assurance, and he accepted each without question. At the same time, however, Rutledge knew the value of a guarantee. The entire yacht was outfitted with the subtlest state-of-the-art surveillance system money could buy. If someone had second thoughts or tried to go all moral on him he had the leverage he needed to secure their cooperation. There was no risk when Rutledge Westchase planned an operation, and last night the deal had been sealed.

There was no more work to be done. It was time to sit back and watch the machine work. Soon some unknown spit of land would be converted from pristine marsh to concrete and cranes. Ships would come and go, load and off load product and his legitimate fortune would grow exponentially. His trucks would ferry containers here and there and he would sit back and watch the money roll in. Westchase would make his mark in the family history, earn his place and expand his own empire.

He sipped at the golden liquid as he mounted the short chute of stairs to his office. He leaned forward, swung the door open, stepped through, and came face-to-face with Billy Hopkins. The man was perched on the corner of his desk, arms crossed, his usual scowl creasing his features.

Westchase started to greet his man, then he noticed the other two occupants of his office. One was an older man, probably in his seventies. He wore faded jeans, well-worn work boots, a green flannel shirt tucked into his jeans, and a set of striped suspenders stretched over his shoulders. The man's thick coat of shock-white hair sat in a cardinal's peak on the top of his forehead. The old man did not attempt to greet Rutledge or offer him his hand. His expression seemed to be a mix of impatience and anger. Westchase did not know what to make of him, although he found himself instinctively fearing the man, many years his senior. His underling was similarly dressed but had a greasy black ponytail stretching to the middle of his back. Unlike the old man, this man with the ponytail was maybe in his early thirties. His intense blue eyes reminded him of those of a wild animal. He looked ready to pounce at any second.

"What's going on here, Billy?" Westchase asked. He was not often in a situation he did control. The feeling that he was suddenly at a disadvantage swept over him, making him uncomfortable in his own skin. He had a sudden urge to run and urinate at the same time. The buzz he had been fostering throughout the day evaporated as he tried to wrap his mind around what was happening.

"This is Mister Hammer, Rut. He is our main point

of distribution in North Carolina."

Westchase went into businessman mode and immediately approached the man. Hammer's tall white hair did not so much as quiver as he made no reaction to Westchase's advance. He tried to act as if he hadn't noticed the insult. "It's a pleasure to finally meet you, Mister Hammer; with all the business we've done over the years we should have become acquainted long before this."

Hammer finally stood and Westchase shriveled as he realized this senior citizen towered over him. The man had a wide, barrel chest and strong hands. His gruff demeanor did not dissipate as he finally spoke, though he still ignored Rutledge.

"Hopkins, I ain't got all day. Don't waste my time, boy," Hammer said, looking over Westchase to Billy Hopkins.

Rutledge spun and looked to Hopkins, who was still leaning on the desk. "What is this, Billy?" he asked, trying to keep his voice calm. He fought the panic growing inside him. His eyes darted to the door that was now to his left and for a second he wondered if he could flee. When he looked back at Hopkins his subordinate was shaking his head ever so slightly.

"They're here for the money, Rut," Hopkins said, matter of fact.

"What money?"

"And the files, too; we need it all."

"What's happening?" Westchase was folding; even to him that last statement sounded like a plea more than a question.

"Things are changing, Rut," was all he said.

Rutledge looked around the room, trying to make sense of the upside-down version of reality in which he now found himself.

Hammer finally addressed him. "You let yourself be infiltrated. You have put this entire operation at risk. I don't do business with men like that."

Westchase was staring at him blankly.

"Way I see it, I need to better judge the people I do business with to keep this thing goin'. You just don't cut it, mister."

"What?"

Hammer nodded at Hopkins.

Westchase looked at his subordinate with the look of a cow about to be slaughtered.

"You let Bowman in. I told you over and over the guy wasn't right, but you didn't give a shit. You're gonna give a shit now, rich boy."

The man slumped. Like a lightning strike to the soul, he found himself on the brink of losing it all. All his father had built, that his grandfather had started. He was a hair's breadth of losing it all, and to these *backwoods hillbillies*. Fear turned to anger and the wheels in his mind started turning again. He was an Ivy League-trained businessman; people like him did not lose to people like this.

Westchase straightened his shoulders. "I'm sorry you feel that way, Mr. Hammer. I wish you had come to me sooner with your concerns."

"Humph," was the only reply.

"I understand you feel you are owed something for your trouble; however, I don't understand how you plan to continue our operation without me in it. I provide cover both political and otherwise. I lend legitimacy to our front establishments. I keep the wolves at bay while we make money." Westchase was on the offensive now, hoping to open room for negotiation.

Hammer chuckled. "We do things a little different up north, boy. I don't need none of that shit you just said."

The man with the ponytail pulled a handgun from under his flannel shirt.

"Money, files, now," Hammer growled.

"I don't have any of that here," Westchase stated defiantly.

The thug leveled the handgun, an old and weathered revolver.

Westchase stiffened, trying to keep his knees from shaking. He forced himself to refrain from looking at the weapon and focused on Hammer. "I did not say I could not get what you ask," he said simply. "Put your weapon down," he added without looking to the old man's henchman.

Chapter Twenty-Nine

When Alex swung around the lot behind the Broad Street location of Westchase's club, Farraday pointed out the man's Porsche. Alex immediately began to feel it then. That interior vibration he felt whenever he got close to making an arrest or whenever he stacked up with other officers to kick in a door. So much energy building within him with nowhere to go. He could feel it in his chest, tingling in his arms, and the only way to expend this energy was to move.

"Two minutes," Farraday spoke into the microphone hanging from his ear bud.

The team in the following SUV broke off as Alex swung behind the building and took up position around front.

Alex freed his Glock from its holster and press-checked the slide to make sure he had a round chambered. He released the slide which made a *schnick*! as it returned to battery. He could barely sit still. They had finally found the head of the snake, the man responsible for this entire hidden operation, and responsible for his friend's disappearance. He was one step closer to recovering Charlie.

Farraday must have noticed Alex chomping at the bit. "You know, I get why you went off the way you did."

Alex didn't look at the man.

"I don't agree with what you did, but I get it. I would hope for the same from any of my men if the same happened to me."

Alex glanced at him.

"But I need you to remember that we need this asshole to find Bowman. This isn't the guy that you can beat on and get the results you want." Alex did not voice his disagreement but Farraday could see it in his eyes. "We go at him smooth and soft; we give him a chance to see the light."

"And if he doesn't see the light?" Alex asked.

Farraday sighed, he knew what was on the line; they all did. He popped the passenger door to the SUV. "Then we reassess," he muttered. "Let's go."

***

"What the fuck do you mean, it's not here?" Hopkins shouted. He looked hesitantly at Hammer, then charged behind Westchase's desk where a massive painting of his grandfather hung, and ripped it off the wall. The safe behind it was state-of-the-art, Westchase didn't do anything on a budget.

There were only three safecrackers in the world who were known to be able to defeat the security device standing between Hopkins and his payday, and they were all in Europe.. "Open it," he demanded.

"I just told you there is nothing in the safe. I have had some dealings within the recent past; I have no cash on hand other than what's in my wallet." Turning from Hopkins, Rutledge looked at Hammer. "I don't think that is what you came for."

Hammer did not respond.

"Bullshit," Hopkins grabbed Westchase by the lapels and slammed him against the wall. He put his gun to his former boss's head. "Open it."

Westchase grinned and again ignored Hopkins. "I'm a businessman, Hammer. I'll take you to what you want and we can discuss how to mend whatever deficit you believe exists between us to get our operation back on track. But I am not opening this safe. Since my man here seems to answer to you now, call him off."

Hammer stared at the two men for a long moment, his contempt undisguised. He began to speak but was interrupted when Ponytail's phone chirped.

"What?" Ponytail demanded, then listened for a second. "Okay." He looked at Hammer and shook his head almost imperceptibly.

Immediately both men started to leave.

"What? Where are you going?" Hopkins asked. Now the panic was in his voice.

"Cops are here," Ponytail said as he followed Hammer out the office door.

"Shit," Hopkins breathed out, running behind them.

Westchase was suddenly free, but for how long?

He looked around the office, wondering what the damage was going to be if he was caught here. He could usually rely on the local leadership to mitigate any exposure he might have, but now with the recent business with Bowman he wasn't sure. He scanned the club through his office windows and saw Hopkins, Hammer, and the other moron arguing. Ponytail was on the phone; he looked like he was talking options. Westchase was relieved at his sudden release from captivity and sipped at his scotch. Winding slowly around his desk he flopped into his plush chair and started thinking.

***

Alex and Farraday met up with a second team, two FBI agents from his surveillance team who had entered the building from the front. Alex didn't know their names or trust them anymore than he trusted Farraday but he was going to play along. At least until he thought they were slowing him down. He would ditch them the moment he thought they were holding him back.

Intel from Bowman had located the club on the sixth floor of the old office building. The design of the building was such that there was a main corridor of stairs which zig-zagged from floor to floor. The four-man team crested the fourth floor and made their way down the hall to the next set of steps when a shot rang out of the stairwell in front of them.

"Contact front," Alex announced as he scanned for

a target.

"Contact rear!"

Alex heard the warning a millisecond before all hell broke loose.

A hail of gunfire spat at the small team from stairwells to their front and rear. Alex, who was on point, reacted on instinct. He fired as fast as his handgun would cycle toward the muzzle flashes to his front, and charged forward toward a doorway that would lead them out of the ambush. The sound roared in the contained space of the hallway, all the gunfire taking place within a twenty-five-foot circle, and it was him and three FBI Agents caught in the crossfire. He fired at the figures who popped up in the stairwell ahead of him like whack-a-moles, making them duck for precious fractions of a second as he closed in on the door. He didn't know where it led, might be a janitor's closet for all he knew. But to remain in the hallway, on the X marked by his enemy, meant certain death. He could feel the concussion of Farraday's weapon behind him as he moved; he hoped the rest of the team had reacted with him.

Alex kicked the door with all he could muster. The heavy wood gave a fraction of an inch. He followed with his shoulder and muscled his way in. Once through the door, he scanned left and right then broke to the left in an effort to clear as much of the room as he could. The firing continued outside but he heard the rest of the team file in and take up station. The door had led to a small office with a bank of cubicles in the center.

"Smith, Banks, cover the door!" Farraday shouted as he took the right side of the office and began clearing the room. Stillwater and Farraday met at the rear of the office where there was another door. Each was on opposite sides of the frame and with a nod Alex tried the handle. It was locked. As Alex fell back, Farraday stepped out, then smashed in the frame with a heavy boot. The small, single desk was the only item inside. Apiece of the frame bounced off a writing mat that sat on the small desk, then landed on a cheap office chair.

"Clear," they said simultaneously. Then both dove for the floor as rounds split the air between them.

***

Hammer had tapped Jeh on the shoulder and ignited the ambush. His ponytailed nephew was no stranger to guns, and had buried his share of bodies in the North Carolina hill country. Jeh opened up with his handgun and Hammer followed. Hopkins, taking the cue from the others had followed suit. The men he'd left to watch the street below had closed the trap.

The man reacted well, moving instantly, firing on instinct. Hammer had seen the value of men like that in rotting jungles on the far side of the world. Hammer was of the same cloth, kill or be killed. It was plain luck that the four men, well, three and a half, had made it to cover before being cut down.

When the four men disappeared, a sudden lull fell over the hallway. Peering around the now-pockmarked marble façade around the stairwell, Hammer locked eyes with Hank and Bean, who were crouched in the opposite stairwell. With a hand motion Hammer ordered the men out and to fire on the doorway into which the feds had fled. He waited as his two men silently moved into position and he moved with the speed not normally seen in a seventy-plus-year-old man as Hank and Bean started firing blindly into the doorway.

***

Alex and Farraday hugged the tightly carpeted floor as rounds popped through the air all around them. He tried to flatten himself against the floor, feeling the weave of the carpet imprinting on his face as the air around him sizzled. It reminded him of his time in Ramadi, right before he and Bowman had their early checkout during the Battle of Fallujah. The insurgents, as they were called, actually just the Iraqi military no one had bothered to take into custody during the initial invasion, took to firing rockets and mortars at the small Forward Operating Base (FOB) Ar Ramadi. At any given time on any given day the alarm could sound and no matter where you were or what you were doing you either hit the deck or you ran like hell to one of the concrete bunkers that were positioned throughout the small base.

It was maddening to suffer assault that you couldn't confront. The enemy fired on you from miles away and instantly blended back in with the population. It was like being in the middle of a fight but there is nothing you could do but take the other guy's punches over and over and hope he doesn't put your lights out   Alex fought the urge to move, to get up and charge the bastard pulling the trigger. They were in a shitty position and the bad guys had the upper hand. Did he make a wrong move in leading them into that little office? Was there anywhere else he could have taken them? Was it going to be his split-second decision that led to three other cops dying and the loss of any hope of recovering Bowman?

Chapter Thirty

Rutledge Westchase chuckled slightly as he depressed the triggering mechanism that was flush with the wall. A seam suddenly appeared in the rich oak paneling where there had previously been none and a door slid open, revealing his safe room. No one, not even his former associate Billy Hopkins knew about the room, Rutledge's own private last resort. The room had everything he needed from food and water and booze, to a functioning washroom and cable feed. He could hide there for up to seventy-two hours if he saw the need. He slipped inside the room, thinking it was better for him to wait it out a little while where no one would find him . . . just in case those fools were cut off from their exit and retreated back to the club.

The sounds of gunfire made him jump despite himself. At first he didn't believe what he heard. Maybe it was old pipes banging around in the old building. But no, when he heard the return fire his bowels turned to water. They were shooting it out with the police! Right in his own building! Rutledge dove out of the safe room just as the automated door began to slide closed. He wasn't thinking, he just knew he had to get out of there. He had to escape and the safe room would provide him no sanctuary; not if there was a pile of dead cops two floors down. He had no intention of trying to keep himself hidden when cops started crawling over the place with a fine tooth comb. There was no way to find an alibi when you're cowering at ground zero. He had to get out of this place.

"Jesus," he breathed, "No, no-no-no." it was almost a whimper.

Rutledge went to the wall safe and with trembling fingers. He mis-entered the combination twice before he was finally able to wrench the door open. There were stacks of cash and a collection of gold pieces which he unceremoniously dumped out of the safe and into a leather satchel he had hanging off a coat rack behind his desk.

"No-no-no," he whispered to himself.

There was no way to fix this. He knew it in his guts that no matter what was happening downstairs no amount of blackmail or bribes could take the heat off the men's actions downstairs. He could only hope that they were all killed so he could get away. If he could get some distance from this he could come up with a plan, claim it was a burglary or some such. That was for later, he commanded himself. He just had to get out of there.

Rutledge ran out of his office, blowing by the exit as fast as his pudgy body would take him, and sprinted for the service exit. Not many people knew about the service exit. Most of his clientele and his men used the regular entrance to his oasis of vice; not even the girls bothered with it. The stairwell was dank and musty. Dust and cobwebs decorated the rusting and loose handrails as Rutledge bounced through the door and tiptoed down the stairs at more of a controlled fall than a coordinated run.

The firing stopped almost as abruptly as it had started but Rutledge didn't pause to listen for any sort of follow up. All he could think about was the Porsche sitting in its spot at the rear of the building. If he could just get behind the wheel he would be free. He craved for that feeling, seeing the sports car's interior in his mind. He could smell the leather and oil that his detailer used to keep the vehicle's fabric and interior components in mint condition. When he got out he was going straight for the dock, he told himself. Reflexively he retrieved his phone from his pocket and fumbled to activate it. He almost took a nose dive as his attention was away from his footing and he had to leap the last three steps to get to the third floor landing safely. He looked at his phone and swore when he saw he had no bars. Calling the captain aboard his yacht would have to wait.

He was gasping for breath when he finally reached the ground floor. Bile threatened to spew from his stomach. He forced himself to stop behind the final exit in that dark concrete stairwell. He had to compose himself. Had to make this look right. He doubled over, trying to catch his breath. He could feel his heartbeat pounding in his ears. It was so loud he feared for a moment he was having a heart attack. He thought his heart was about to leap from his chest. He heaved in three more deep breaths the last of which he held in for a moment as he reached for the security bar. Flashes of an army of cops with guns pointed at him flashed through his mind.

He was shaking when he pushed on the bar and the door cracked. Light streamed into the dark stairwell and Rutledge Westchase forced himself out into the humid Charleston air.

***

Alex's ears were ringing when the shooting stopped. He looked at Farraday, who was looking toward the door and his two agents. The large black Agent looked at him and Alex saw his eyes scan him to make sure he wasn't injured. They got up slowly and hugged the wall to stay out of the field of fire from the door which now looked more like a buffet for giant termites than a barrier to hide behind.

"Smith! Banks!" Farraday hissed through the dust and smoke that clung in the air.

"Here," was the reply.

When the two men rounded the squared honeycomb of cubicles they came upon the other two members of their team. One man, a black man Alex thought might be Jack Banks, had his hands on the other's calf. Blood seeped from between Bank's fingers as he tried to keep pressure on the wound. Smith's jeans pant from just below his knee to his hiking boot was soaked in crimson. Farraday stripped out of his button-down shirt and started to tie it off around the calf, working around Banks' hands until he could cinch it down as a makeshift tourniquet.

Alex was inching toward the door and trying to keep a look out for threats when Smith screamed "Fuck!" as Farraday increased the pressure.

Farraday did one more study to ensure the tourniquet was secures and came up on the other side of the doorway. "I'm going to call this in, get an ambulance."

"Good," Alex responded and suddenly raced out the door.

"Stillwater!" Farraday shouted.

Gun up, Alex moved as quietly as he could through the corridor now strewn with bits of wood, concrete, and marble from the hell that had been unleashed on the place. It was clear, whoever had ambushed them had made their escape and that pissed him off. Alex hadn't gotten a good look at the shooters but he knew that his best lead of the day had slipped through his fingers. He looked around the hallway. There were only two ways they could have run.

He took off running down the stairs.

***

Westchase didn't give himself time to revel in his luck, such as it was. He moved as calmly as his quaking body would allow toward his convertible sports car. The little bundle of horsepower, gleaming in her champagne finish, called to him. He was getting choked up as he neared his vehicle. So close, he thought. In his mind a door behind him was going to crash open at any second and he was either going to be shot, or dragged away in handcuffs.

"No," he whispered, "No."

He was three feet from the Porsche when his nightmare became reality.

***

Alex paused at the glass door covering the rear entrance, and scanned the lot. It was relatively small, palm trees dotting the tiny asphalt parking area. Alex caught sudden movement across the doorway and ducked back just a bit. His heart leapt into his throat as he recognized Rutledge Westchase's soft features hustling toward a Porsche.

There was no doubt in Stillwater's mind as to who it was. When he was a rookie he and other young cops would be conscripted for warrant roundups. He'd be assigned an area and given a list of BOLO forms with known subjects with outstanding warrants. Alex got very good after a while at memorizing his quarries' faces. Individual aspects about eyes, hairline, jaw, there was always something that jumped out as a defining feature on a given person, an anchor point in his mind that he could key on to identify the subject quickly. The learned skill had earned Stillwater a couple of really good busts in the past.

He had done the same with Westchase. It wasn't so much one defining characteristic with the man so much as an overall trait that was undeniable in Stillwater's eyes. Stillwater could not help but think of the baby mob boss in the movie, *Who Framed Roger Rabbit*. The kid with the stogie, Alex couldn't even key in on what it was that made him equate Rutledge Westchase to a cartoon but it just happened. The man was just . . . soft, as far as Alex could tell.

When Stillwater crashed out the door and drew a bead on the man and ordered him to "Stop!" he saw Westchase jump just like he would expect a cartoon character to do. Kind of a little hop and while in the air a quick paddle of feet, like one of the three stooges. When his feet hit the ground he shot off like a dragster that finally caught the road with its tires. The panic spurred a burst of speed out of the doughy bastard and he galloped for the driver's side of the sports car.

Alex sprinted for the vehicle. Even at a dead run he knew he wasn't going to make it. Westchase made the door and threw himself down in the seat. Alex heard the high whine of the German-made engine a moment later and changed his angle of attack. He cut toward the tight exit of the lot which was framed on either side by an ancient brick wall about six feet tall.

He saw Westchase look at him frantically. Alex growled, he was still a good ten feet from the vehicle. He thought for a second about shooting the tires or trying to hit the engine block but he knew the little .40 rounds he fired would do nothing but splatter against the solid metal of the engine, and that a madman could easily still drive with a shot-out tire. Bearing down, he fought for one last burst of speed. Westchase was passing him. Stillwater threw himself toward the driver's side of the car at the last second. Luckily for him the vehicle's top was down. He cleared the driver's door and caught the top of Westchase's head with his thigh as the rest of him sailed into the passenger seat. The world spun and tumbled as he fought to right himself in the speeding car.

Alex braced himself against the passenger seat headrest and the windshield. Westchase shot out with a weak right-handed swipe that seemed more a warning than a strike meant to do damage. Stillwater batted the weak right hand away and, bracing himself with his hands, kicked Rutledge Westchase in the side of the head. The impact didn't take him out; however, he had such a grip on the steering wheel that as his body shot to the left, his hands yanked the vehicle hard in the same direction. The Porsche caught the edge of the brick wall guarding the lot and spun until the rear fender did the same. The sports car came to a jarring halt and Alex went sailing through the air.

He didn't think, he reacted by curling into a ball and hoped the traffic was light on East Bay Street in the middle of a week day afternoon.

Chapter Thirty-One

Hopkins did all he could to keep up with Hammer and his men. It was clear when the retreat started that he was merely an afterthought, if he was lucky. He followed their lead, sticking close behind Hammer as they exited the building. When Ponytail called a halt in the stairway he thought they were crazy, like they were just waiting to get busted. Then the shooting started.

Hopkins had been in his share of fights over the years. He had his bodies under him, and he didn't give a second look when he dropped someone. But these guys were coordinated and cold. What he thought was cowering in a stairway had turned into a precision ambush. And they'd attacked a team of *cops*.

During his first robbery he had grabbed a hundred bucks from the till and pistol-whipped an old man out in Phoenix. The robbery and the assault were easy, it was the waiting afterward that had scared him. It was the worst week of his life. The old guy that he'd beaten up had later died of a stroke. That wasn't that big a deal to Hopkins, even at seventeen, but it did push the case up the food chain for the cops. What started out as a simple robbery for the young Hopkins had left him as the main target in a murder investigation; at least that was how he saw it.

The news had shown the shop video cameras caught of him, over and over for three days, driving him to paranoia. The video was grainy, and only showed his back. He was wearing a hood and he had a bandana over his face when he did the crime, but still, seeing that video, seeing himself leaping that counter and smacking that old man with the barrel of his cheap Saturday night special had been enough to tell him to find another way. That kind of sweat for a hundred dollars wasn't worth it in his book.

After the third sleepless night he used what was left of the hundred bucks on a taxi to take him to the nearest Army recruiter. He figured he liked to fight, so why not try the army? That was the whole point of an army, right? The recruiter had been more than happy to take him, what with a war on and all. He'd passed their test and gone to basic training with an infantry slot.

Basic training! No one had ever told Billy Hopkins about basic training. Billy didn't take shit off no one. It was one of the only rules his asshole of a foster father, well, his third foster father, had imparted to him. The drill instructors didn't see it his way. Pushups weren't the problem and he could run all day long but they got in his face over dumb shit, pushing him. Who gives a shit about boots, or how tightly a bed was made? Billy Hopkins had tried, in his mind he really had.

Then that drill instructor got in his face over a little stitch of fabric sticking out from his bed. Billy had stomped the man's face into the linoleum floor of the barracks, crushing his nose and actually fracturing a vertebrae. After a few months in the brig, he was stripped of his rank and tossed out of the army with a dishonorable discharge. That incident told Billy Hopkins all he needed to know about the world. They're all against you, so go out and take it all for yourself.

That paradigm served him well over the years. After returning home from the brig he started hitting gas stations again. He leveraged robbery into dealing cocaine and heroin for a while until he got popped by the DEA. He did five years after rolling on everyone he knew in the drug game and then tried the northwest. In Tacoma, Washington he tried the weed game and found that the little plant was a gold mine. It was right around the time medical marijuana was springing up. Little shops all over Washington and California started selling weed in the open.

Luckily for Hopkins, the laws governing marijuana sales at the state and federal levels remained in conflict despite society's acceptance of the marijuana market. Those who ran the medicinal marijuana establishments found themselves having a huge problem. The feds would not allow these distributors to deposit their capital into the banks. According to the federal government, marijuana was still illegal and the proceeds from the sale of marijuana were considered profits of unlawful activity. Thanks to aspects of the Bank Secrecy Act, banks would not take money from the dispensaries. That left fertile ground for the likes of Billy Hopkins.

His first job came as a fluke. He was into the whole medicinal marijuana thing. He got a quack to write him a prescription for chronic back pain and with his medical marijuana card in hand he bought his first legal sack of weed. When he was paying for his score he noticed the owner switching out register trays and the damn things were full of cash. He lingered and watched as the owner took the cash and disappeared into his office. Billy started coming back every week at the same time and noticed the same cash flow. He then stalked the owner after closing time and tracked him to a bar where he followed him in and struck up a conversation.

They became close due to the fact that Hopkins had picked up a few tricks in the art of human behavior, thanks to the Arizona state foster system. You learned to survive, growing up in that life. Competing with however many other kids the foster "parents" could cram into a house to maximize their take from the government, you had to be on their good side if you wanted food, clothes, or a decent place to sleep.

Billy was a veteran of that environment, and since he was never a big kid, he'd needed something other than fear or intimidation to get what he wanted. So he had watched his overseers. The woman—he'd never call that boozed up old bitch his mother—was always complaining to the old man about dishes, and cleaning, and upkeep. One day little Billy picked up a towel and helped her dry dishes, on another day he broke out a broom, and so on. She started to take to the little kid. Not only did Billy start to learn secrets of the house, but there was always a little something extra waiting for him at the end of the day.

Hopkins cultivated that skill of watching and listening. By the time he met that old hippy shop owner whose name he couldn't for the life of him remember, the shop owner didn't stand a chance. That first hit had been a breeze. The shop owner gave him a dissertation on the ins and outs of the Bank Secrecy Act. Because the banks would not accept money resulting from the profit of marijuana dispensaries, these shop owners were running a completely cash business, which left people like his mark sitting on a pile of cash with no way to secure it in banks.

Hopkins had listened to the man over beers and later a couple of joints sitting on the man's porch. The old guy had even shown him where he kept his safe. Hopkins had come back while the old man was at the shop and cleaned him out of almost two hundred thousand dollars.

He hadn't even fled the state after that score. The shop owner had only a fake name to give the cops, and since the old timer was high most of the time Hopkins knew that whatever description he gave the law wasn't going to be looked at with any degree of seriousness. Hopkins was able to pull two more hits just like the first and by the time he lined up his mark for the fourth he was sitting on his own pile of almost a half million.

However, when he was scouting his fourth heist, law enforcement was on to the pattern and was taking the case seriously. He had already decided he would split the northwest after his next score but he wanted one more good hit. The pool of susceptible victims was just too rich and the money was just too good. He surveilled another shop owner, Gary Youngs. He remembered the name of this one. Youngs was the same as the rest of them, keeping his stash under his own roof.

Hopkins watched him for the better part of two weeks. Youngs would leave his head shop at mid-day and at closing with a duffle bag over his shoulder. The bag was full when he left the shop, he would go to his house, and the bag would be drawn and empty when he returned to the shop. On that last day, when Youngs left his residence after the midday drop he let himself into the house from the rear patio. Most of the people he had ripped off had some kind of safe in their home but nothing a crow bar and a hammer couldn't handle. Hopkins had one of each, and a .38 revolver with him as he made his way around the small, one-story ranch home.

It didn't take long to find the stash. A safe sat on the floor next to a chipped and faded desk in the spare bedroom-turned-office. Hopkins paused for a second to listen before going to work on the security container.

Most people do not realize how many different sounds a house makes. They tend to filter out the pipes growling, or the sigh of the fridge when it is their own home. Hopkins realized that when creeping through someone else's place the stillness mixed with the sudden clang, or growl of some aspect of the building added to the excitement He paused for just a moment and when he didn't hear anything, went to his loud work. After jamming the crowbar into the seam between the door and the safe wall, he beat on the crack with the claw end of the hammer, trying to widen the gap, and a dozen or so hits later, mixed with some cranking on the bar, he felt the sturdy lock give way. He dropped the tools with a clang and stepped back to enjoy the view. Then he caught movement out of the corner of his eye.

Youngs was standing in the doorway to the office, mouth agape, eyes wide. Hopkins heard the shot almost before he realized he had taken action. The revolver was in his right hand, the smell of cordite and sulfur burning the air. Youngs took the round in the chest and dropped right where he stood. Hopkins heard a muffled cry as he stuffed the tools and cash into his backpack. Within three seconds he was packed and stepping over Gary Youngs' quivering body. The man wasn't dead. Hopkins looked into his eyes, listening to choked sobs, and a plea to help him. He put a finishing round through Youngs' eye as he walked past him. Couldn't have any loose ends. To this day, and seven additional murders later, Hopkins still remembered that first one.

His take from Youngs was less than a hundred thousand but all in all he was able to net around three hundred K before having to skip town. He bought a used GMC short bed for cash on the way out of Tacoma and headed east. His first stop was Vegas, but after a hooker roofied him and made off with the majority of his stash he had to move on.

He bounced from one town to the next until he ended up in Charleston. He was able to stay out of too much trouble as he drifted east from Washington. When he got to Charleston, South Carolina, he had blown through what remained of his take from the Washington robberies. He had tried his best to settle and have a normal life. He joined the union, took a stevedore job at the port, then the old life came calling.

Most of the guys at the port were good guys, hardworking, just hoping to feed their families. But then there were others, the groups that saw the Port of Charleston for what it truly was: Money. There was no brand of vice that in some form or facet didn't need a smooth transition from international waters to U.S. shores.

Hopkins watched and listened, pushed the right buttons, and eventually ended up at Rutledge Westchase's side. He had to drop Rutledge's former right hand to gain the position, but Rutledge seemed entertained by the incident, and that is after all the rule of the game: Kill or be killed.

In hindsight, while sitting next to the North Carolina mountain man who absolutely terrified him, he might have taken the entertained air he'd perceived from Westchase while they attempted to rob him at the club as a sign he was being played.

They were headed for the old, run-down berth that Hopkins and Westchase used as the offload point for their product. The pier was crumbling and the old tub of an outdated container ship was rusting away in the Cooper River's murky waters. Though it was only a couple of miles from the fourth largest container port in the United States, the approach to their base was secluded and distant from the rest of the peninsula.

Now that he was at his mercy Hopkins was trying to read Hammer. Trying to find an angle, some point through which he could endear himself to these ruthless hillbillies. Hammer was a concrete block in human form; Hopkins got absolutely nothing from him. Hammer simply stared out the windshield like they were travelling to the store for a gallon of milk.

They were only minutes from the dock and Hopkins couldn't help himself. "Westchase is a snake, Mr. Hammer," he said, trying to thicken his own brand of southern drawl. "You think he set those cops on us?" The question made no sense to him after the fact, he was just trying to spark the old man to speak to him.

The sudden impact of a lead filled sap against his sternum doubled Hopkins over and he gasped for breath. His lungs fought for air as he took several more strikes across his ribs, the last of which elicited a crack from somewhere. He felt a massive paw grab a fist full of his hair and yank him backward. He was staring at the cloth-lined roof of the SUV when he felt the cold point of a gun barrel against his neck.

"There is no us, you white trash straphanger,"

Hammer growled, then slammed the side of his head into the frame of the door.

Hopkins fought the fuzziness brought on by the sudden impact. All his instincts screamed to fight but there was a dark place within that told him he was completely at the mercy of this old man. When he looked up, cringing against an anticipated further assault, the vehicle had stopped on the lonely dirt road. He looked at Hammer and started to speak but the man silenced him with an open-handed slap to the face.

"Listen. I agreed to this meeting because I believed you had things in hand. I get here and see that not only have you not taken care of this Westchase, but you also tell me you have a fed tied up in your own distribution point. You're an amateur kid,"

"Bu—" another whack across the face by Hammer's open hand silenced Hopkins yet again.

"One more word and I drop you right here," Hammer growled. Taking the que from the old man Jeh pulled the vehicle over to the side of the road.

Hopkins shifted in his seat, sitting up straight. He was completely at a loss and realized he was at the mercy of this man. The worst part was that he had been the one that brought Hammer and his army of hillbillies into his operation.

Hammer gave a "go" gesture and his man with the ponytail continued toward the berth. "I recognize that working down here would be a much smoother process if we continue to use the resources you say you can provide, so I am going to give you a chance. When we get to that ship, you kill that cop, you find Westchase and kill him and anyone else who knows about me. Once that is done, we have a clean slate and we can start fresh."

"Done," Hopkins snapped.

"Humph. You come out of that ship and if anyone else is left standing, you die right there."

Hopkins didn't reply.

Chapter Thirty-Two

Alex barely missed flying right into a three-foot diameter tree and instead rolled when he hit the grass on the other side of the street until he smacked into a wrought-iron fence. The impact knocked the wind out of him and he felt a crack someplace. It took him a second to regain his senses. When he finally got his feet under him he saw the Porsche across the narrow street. The nose of the once beautiful machine was almost sheared off as the vehicle had spun into a tree, impacting at the front right quarter panel. Coolant and other engine fluids spilled from the under carriage and steam rose in mournful tendrils from the dead car.

Westchase was fumbling with the driver's side door; Alex could see a smear of blood running from his forehead down the crease beside his nose.

Alex started across the street but a howling pain radiated through his entire body, making his pursuit into little more than a hobble. He reached the car just as Westchase got the door open and had one foot on the ground when Alex kicked the door back into the frame. Westchase screamed as the heavy metal slammed his shin. Alex pulled his handcuffs from his back pocket and smashed the shackles across the back of Westchase's head before dragging the man by the hair out of the car.

The pudgy man hit the ground with a *whump*, as though a sack of concrete had been dropped next to a mixer. He was mumbling something unintelligible as Alex put his knee in the back of the man's neck and applied the handcuffs.

"You think things are bad now, asshole, just wait till we get somewhere quiet," Alex said. There was a crowd of onlookers gathering to watch the show. This kind of action was unheard of at this end of the peninsula.

"I want my lawyer." Westchase whined like a

three-year-old wanting his blankey.

"I bet. Get up." He pulled the man up by his hands that were bound behind his back, eliciting a yelp.

Westchase finally got his feet under him and was whimpering as Alex marched him back to the task force SUV.

Farraday came out of the building at a trot as Alex threw Westchase in the back seat of the vehicle. "You got him?"

"Yeah, I got him," Alex said. "How is your guy?"

"In pain but stable. Medics are on their way."

Alex worked his shoulder in a slow circle and winced.

Farraday looked at Westchase sitting in the rear of the car. The man was rocking slowly back and forth like a mental patient. "Let's see what he has to say." He opened the door to the SUV. "You Rutledge Westchase?"

"I want my lawyer," Westchase whimpered.

"I would too, if I were you. Problem is, I have two agents with gunshot wounds today, and two others missing. I think you know about all of that. That means there is an exigent circumstance here that trumps your need for a lawyer. You tell me where my agent is and I'll be more than happy to get your lawyer for you, how's that?"

"No."

"You heard me mention that I have two agents missing and presumed kidnapped by your people, right? I don't get them back and they end up dead too, you face murder and attempted murder of four law enforcement officers. You think any of your friends are going to come to your aid? You think your lawyer can protect you from that kind of legal hell?"

Westchase wasn't rocking anymore but wouldn't look at Farraday.

"Give me what I need and lighten some of the load you're already carrying. It's your only chance."

Stillwater watched Farraday's makeshift interrogation with a growing rage but there was a crowd watching them from the street. There was nothing he could do but back Farraday's play and it was killing him. He wandered over to Westchase's car just to get his mind back under control. The interior of the convertible was a mess but he noticed the satchel Westchase had been carrying and grabbed it.

He started rifling through the bag and whistled at the sheer amount of cash and gold in the bag. Another five minutes and their main subject could have been in the wind. The thought sent a chill down his spine. He left the cash and the gold in the bag but grabbed a cell phone he found in it and turned away from the car. Cell phones had a tendency to be fountains of intel for law enforcement.

He activated the phone and started swiping from one screen to the next. The call history didn't have much for him since he didn't know the case well enough to recognize calls from particular players. He maneuvered to the text messages and saw a stream from Hopkins that had started the previous night. Hopkins had tried to make contact with Westchase multiple times but he never responded. He scrolled down to the last message, it read, "Dangerous package in the hold. You are NEEDED HERE!"

With the phone and the bag, Alex returned to the SUV. Stillwater opened the bag to show the gold and cash to Farraday, then waved the phone in front of him. "Any luck pinging Hopkins' cell?"

"No, these guys are pretty disciplined; they use burners which weren't a big deal since we had Charlie on the inside but they also turn the damn things off and remove the battery whenever they are operational. We tried Hopkins a few times today and got nothing."

"Shit," Stillwater responded. He leaned into the

SUV to Westchase. "Hey, what and where is the hold?" He held the last message from Hopkins up for Farraday to see.

Westchase didn't respond.

Alex was about to speak when Farraday beat him to it. "There are too many witnesses here. We gotta move."

Chapter Thirty-Three

Charlie Bowman hurt. It wasn't the beating, it wasn't the gunshot wound, or the fact he'd been bound to a chair since what felt like grade school at this point, it was all of it. Every fiber of his being rang a dull incessant bell of pain throughout his body. The fact that his restraints had been loosed from his wrists and ankles helped relieve some of the tension from his joints but it didn't do much overall to ease his pain.

He heard Wallace and Higby returning from outside. Every step of their heavy boots served as a countdown.

Mai had given him a chance, this stranger who he guessed at this point had been more tortured since her arrival in this wolf's den than he had ever been, had opened the door for him by cutting him loose and giving him a weapon. The small scalpel was not much but he would take it.

The trust she had shown in giving the implement to him was a giant gamble for a woman who had been treated the way she had been. Maybe it was the fact that he had risked his neck to get that pregnant girl out of this hell that had brought her around. Or maybe she just saw him as a spark of chaos that she could leverage to escape herself. He didn't know.

He did know that he had the skimpiest of a lifeline concealed in his hand, and he was going to make it work. At least that was what he was telling himself.

Bowman's mind was all for the fight, just like always. His body was not so sure, dire warnings trimmed in aches and sharp, shooting pains advised that he was injured and not up to getting out of the damn chair much less taking on two professional bruisers.

The countdown of approaching footsteps ended as he watched the men return from outside. His breath caught in his throat. If he was feeling up to taking on two of Hopkins' badasses, how did he feel about three?

Since Charlie had awakened in that deep, dark, dank shithole, he had accepted the fact that he might be killed. He was damned sure that he would do everything in his power to take some of them with him but the numbers and the fact that he had been shot and bound to a chair were never in his favor. But now here he was with a sharp instrument in his hand and the freedom to use it . . . but against three armed men? For the first time in a long time Charlie felt a trickle of doubt enter his mind.

He remembered the first time he'd heard that little voice in his head whispering, "You're not making it out of this." He was in Ramadi. He and Stills and the others were still trying to settle in, trying to get comfortable in the one hundred and forty degree heat, talcum-powder dust, and broken-down shacks they called home. Within two weeks they started getting shelled. If there was one product Charlie Bowman respected, it was the .107mm rocket produced by Iran and provided to the Iraqi insurgents for the constant antagonism of coalition forces.

The first time Charlie experienced a rocket attack, he and Stills and a couple of other guys in their unit were returning from the dining facility after dinner. Feeling fat on ice cream and the rest of the calorie-heavy food, they strolled toward the "morale and wellness trailers" where base personnel could buy new movies, pirated of course, for a dollar from some local Iraqi capitalists. They were just rounding a bend as the call to prayer played in the distance, when a faint warning claxon sounded. They had been briefed on arrival what the early warning system sounded like, but that was after a three-day ordeal just to get into the damned warzone in which none of them got more than an hour or two of sleep.

Charlie didn't remember a damned thing about that briefing, but he did hear a faint mechanical voice repeating incoming, incoming, incoming. That was all they needed to hear. That first rocket attack was nothing more than a distant rumble coming from the burn pits. The rocket had hit but it had been so distant the Marines started laughing at each other. What had they been running from?

Three days later a Major General showed for an inspection. Every five to ten minutes a rocket landed somewhere on the (FOB) forward operating base. Charlie, Stillwater, and the rest of their unit tried to stay undercover as much as they could but there was always something that needed to be done. They had to change out at the watchtowers spread all along the wire. They had to run errands for command, or respond to calls for help when a particular building got hit. The first time Charlie heard his name called that day was the first time that little voice whispered in his ear: "You're not going to make it. The next one has your name on it."

Bowman tried to look as stoic as possible in front of the lieutenant sending him out into a shit storm. Rockets were falling like rain, some within twenty or thirty feet of the concrete bunker stuffed with Marines.

"The colonel ordered everyone to have response vehicles on standby in case any of the haji's come over the wire," the lieutenant explained to him. "I need you to grab the MRAP and move it over next to here." He gestured to a topographic map of the FOB. The bunkers were marked with a red X. As Charlie followed the officer's finger and the lieutenant talked him through what he wanted him to do, he realized some colonel sitting in a bunker very much like the one he huddled in, was willing to risk Charlie's life to "move the car." He'd never met the man but in that moment Charlie hoped he got the chance to punch him in the face.

Charlie waited for what he hoped was the last round that wet off maybe a hundred yards in the direction opposite of where he was going. He thought it funny that his last thought before charging into a virtual no man's land was of how convenient it would be if the next .107 fired by some Arab asshole hit the MRAP and saved him the trouble.

No such luck. As soon as the crack of the rocket subsided, Charlie dashed from the relative safety of the bunker. The first leg in his run was a good two hundred yards from his position. On his skinny frame he wore his body armor and helmet, which added a good sixty pounds, including his ammunition, med kit, and the three grenades he carried.. It was a dusty, dry one hundred and twenty-five degrees as he ran across the broiling Iraqi dirt. He felt like he was running in quicksand.

He got to the MRAP, gagging and coughing up the fine sand that covered the ground and reaching for the driver side door of the armored vehicle when a steady drone filled his ears. The sound was unmistakable once you heard. Starting as a high-pitched whine, the sound of the rocket motor falls to a low, steady hum as it loses altitude. Charlie caught that falling whine just at the last minute. He dove for the undercarriage of the MRAP as the first rocket hit twenty feet away. The sharp crack and over-pressure felt like it would kick him out the other side of the big vehicle. He cringed, burying his head in his arms as sand, rocks and burning metal pummeled him. Then there was a pause. Charlie, lulled into raising his head and two more landed, followed by another three, all within a hundred yards of him. Hell was erupting all around him.

It was the third impact when that the little voice came in earnest. "Here it comes... You're not going to make it... This is it... Do something!" Whispering, then screaming in his mind.

It was much the same now as, out the corner of his eye, Charlie watched the three men approach him. He wasn't sure he could even stand, much less take out three grown men. The little voice of doubt was there, pleading for him not to move. But there was no other time or chance. It wouldn't take long for them to realize he was loose and once they did, it was over. He had to move on the first one to get close enough to him. Like a gremlin the little voice whispered in his ear that they would cut him down before his ass left the seat.

Then he saw it—in the hands of the thug who'd just joined their little party. It was tough to see at first but it became clear as the man approached. It was a necklace. One he recognized from a few nights ago. The insignificant piece of jewelry hadn't even been an afterthought when he'd seen its glint ever so slightly in the dim light—jade cross trimmed in gold.

Chapter Thirty-Four

Ferris was barely holding it together as he walked up the ramp and into the dark hold of the permanently tethered old cargo ship. He barely noticed the prisoner, really didn't care, and didn't even realize it when he'd walked past Mai. He was out to lunch and silently chastised himself to get his shit together.

The more he thought about what he had done the more he knew he had gone too far. Ferris had done a lot of shit in his life, but hell, that's life. He got his and whoever got in his way lost. That's how life works. He stared at the little crucifix hanging from his fingers. He could see that little round face and those dark eyes as she pleaded to him in a foreign language for the life of her child—as though a monster and a human could speak the same language, foreign or not. That was what he felt like now, a monster. He wanted to run, but how do you run away from your own skin? There was no escaping the fact he had just killed a mother and an unborn baby. Straight up murder of the worst kind.

That was the job, he tried to tell himself. That was the hand he'd been dealt and the hand she'd been dealt. He tried to work himself up, let anger burn away the guilt. Besides, he thought, what had that whore done to end up in the box in the first place? Probably sold by her own old man for coke or some shit. And how many of those bitches, either dead on arrival, or so sick they couldn't make it anyway, had he and his boys taken out? Fuck

***

Charlie caught them all off guard as he sprang from the chair and shot himself like a missile from the rusty old chair, hoping his feet stayed under him until he reached his target. He was within a step of him and the piece of shit was still playing with the fucking necklace. Probably going to keep it as a trophy, Charlie figured, as he plunged the dinky little scalpel as deep as he could into the bastard's eye. It sank in with kind of a splat as the eyeball ruptured. Charlie felt the blade scrape against the back of the socket, trying to punch through to the brain.

Ferris screamed as he reeled back and fell. Charlie fell with him, fumbling for the gun in the man's waistband. He felt like his arms were still tied up. They were slow and heavy from being bound for hours in the damn chair. His fingers didn't want to respond as he commanded them to grip the butt of the 9mm semi auto. The pain in his hip was excruciating and he felt the wound stretching and tearing. He could hear Wallace and Higby behind him, yelling. He steeled himself for the boots to land on his head and pulled on the gun.

BOOM!

His old firearms instructor, Sergeant McAvoy, would have had him doing pushups. His finger had closed on the trigger as he pulled and the gun fired into the bastard's groin. Charlie didn't have time to enjoy the fact he might have just blinded and turned the son of a bitch writhing on the floor into a eunuch at the same time. He had two more thugs to kill. He rolled off Ferris and was crushed by Wallace who crashed down on top of him. Time slowed as a hand wrapped around his and they started fighting over the gun. The big man pinned the gun to Charlie's chest and Charlie thought he might pass out as pain shot from the bullet wound in his hip throughout his body in a tormenting wave.

This time he couldn't argue with the little voice in his head. It wasn't a matter of heart, it was a matter of physics. Wallace hadn't been tortured over the last six hours. He didn't have the energy to hold the big man off. Slowly the barrel of the gun started creeping toward his chin. Charlie felt a panic like none he'd ever known. It came from deep down, from his primitive brain screaming that death was imminent.

He growled and fought, feeling his injured body popping and tearing from the stress. Wallace was staring into his eyes. The man had a snarl on his face and the whites of his eyes glowed in a barbaric pleasure of overpowering the smaller, damaged man.

"This is it, cop," he growled. "Hope it was worth it."

Charlie didn't respond, but he didn't break eye contact, either.

"I'm gonna go to your funeral, the parade, the whole bit, and I'm gonna—"

BOOM!BOOM!BOOM!BOOM!

Wallace's eyes looked like they would bust from his head for a split second and his body jerked and shuddered.

Charlie slipped out an involuntary scream against the report of the gun blast he thought was meant for him. He wheezed under the dead weight of the three-hundred-pound behemoth who up until a second ago had the game well in hand. Charlie withered under the grinding pain in his pelvis. He clenched his teeth as he fought to roll the big man off him.

"I won't be going to yours, asshole," he breathed, inching away from the dead man, using his boot on the man's face for leverage. "Fuck you." Then he saw Mai standing over him, gun drawn.

She was staring through him. Charlie looked into her eyes and for a moment was positive she was about to finish him off. Finally, she dropped the weapon to her side.

"Thanks," Charlie said, voice hoarse as he picked up the gun he'd just been fighting over and checked the battery. One in the chamber.

Mai nodded, then a weak whimper drew both their attention.

Ferris was still alive.

Charlie, either through exhaustion or curiosity,

studied the stricken man for a moment. He lay on his side, shaking. His lips quivered and every couple of seconds the light click of the handle of the scalpel jutting from his eye would tap on the metal floor, each light tap eliciting a new moan or gasp of breath. A pool of blood had spread from his waist and his jeans were saturated. As were the sleeves of his henry shirt as he tried to cover his wounded genitals with his hands. Charlie had barely noticed that Mai had gone to stand over him.

"This man may survive his wounds; the blood loss is not too great. It may have stopped."

Charlie didn't respond.

Mechanically, she reached down with a scalpel of her own and, using her free hand as a guide, sank the blade of the scalpel in between the fourth and the fifth lumbar Charlie watched in shock as the lower half of the man's body shuddered, then went limp. Ferris groaned and cried but didn't lose consciousness as he was paralyzed. Mai rose, wiping off the blood on scalpel's blade on the man's now useless leg.

"I recognized the necklace he carries. He killed a mother and an unborn baby. I have seen him kill others like a child would an ant." She was fighting tears.

Charlie couldn't tell if it was from rage or sadness.

She bent down again and her lips hovered over Ferris' ear, "You may survive this but you will be forever missing your manhood, your legs, and most of your vision. You will be a freak that others will flee the sight of. Death is too good a fate for you."

Without looking at Charlie she rose and headed for the cargo bay door.

Charlie lingered a moment looking at what was left after the woman dispensed her own brand of justice. He would have just killed the man and been done with it. This woman had had a lot of time to plan and plot, and imagine her day of reckoning. He looked over the scene of Mai's wrath and saw Higby lying on his face, a pool of blood circling his head.

***

Mai hadn't thought about what she would do to Ferris in that instant. She had told herself time and time again, from the moment she woke up in that metal coffin that she would not hesitate to kill if it meant freedom for her or the others. But what she had just done was different and went way beyond murder. Simply taking his life would have been quick and sufficient, she didn't know why she'd done what she did, leaving a man to suffer in continuous pain and defilement for years to come.

As she walked toward the light of the outside world with no watchmen or guard for the first time in almost a year, she realized that her actions did not affect her one bit. That scared her. What would Wu think? If somehow she ever made it home would he or her grandfather accept the woman who'd returned? She was in a daze walking toward the outside like a bear coming out of hibernation, only she had a gun in her hand. Still, she didn't see the group of vehicles approaching from the marsh access until it was almost too late.

"MAI!" she heard Charlie scream just as a round pinged off the hull of the ship a foot away from her head. She jumped and saw Billy Hopkins hanging out of the side of an approaching Jeep Cherokee, revolver in hand, trying to steady his aim.

Her first instinct was to attack the man, the target she'd been waiting for since she first hit the shores of the United States. She raised the weapon she'd taken from Higby and pulled the trigger but not before she felt a vice grip take her upper arm and yank her back into the darkness of the ship.

"No!" she screamed.

"Look at the numbers!" Charlie yelled pulling her along. "Run!"

After a moment she stopped fighting him and accepted he was right.

***

Charlie pulled her along as much as his battered body could. As he dragged her away from the fight she wanted, he thought, there men coming to kill them, and they were contained within this crumbling behemoth of a ship. No matter how hard they ran or how they hid it was just a matter of time. They were locked in a box.

Chapter Thirty-Five

Alex rode in the rear seat of the SUV next to Westchase, who stared straight ahead at the rear of the driver's seat where Farraday piloted the heavy vehicle. Alex studied the man who, for all intents and purposes, had hidden away within himself. Westchase's eyes were blank, devoid of thought; he looked into nothingness.

He needed to get to him. Charlie had no time left; Alex knew that as soon as he realized those bastards who'd ambushed them had gotten away. What was it that would hurt Westchase enough to get him to talk? Alex could beat the shit out of him, and probably would have taken great pleasure in doing so, given the day's events and the price of failure. But physical torture was no sure thing.

Alex had only beaten on those two earlier in the day because he could read them, he could see that they only respected fear and strength. Long-time criminals know to keep their mouths shut and that cops can't touch them. Violence was the only tool he had against them. Showing them what he was capable of but more importantly, letting them wonder how far he would go was what worked. It wasn't the abuse he'd handed them, it was the fear of what was to come that got those men to talk.

As he watched Westchase, he wasn't so sure. The man couldn't take a punch that much Alex knew from looking at the soft, doughy bastard. Westchase might give him what he wanted or he might just shrivel up in a ball and cry for his mother. Physical violence against this pussy was too much of a gamble, Alex told himself. So what else was there? Then he saw the man's cufflinks.

"Those are nice," Alex commented on the gold, diamond-encrusted cufflinks.

Westchase did not respond.

"They look old," Alex continued, "and I see the

initials etched into the one there. Family heirloom?"

Westchase flinched just a little and the boyish eyes darted his way.

Game over, Alex thought: "You ever had them appraised? Personally, I can't wait to find out. I bet that's just the tip of the iceberg when it comes to you, big dog."

Westchase was still watching him out of the corner of his eye.

"That's okay if you don't want to talk. I don't blame a guy for knowing his constitutional rights. In fact, it's so rare when they do that I respect them for it."

Westchase turned back to stare at the rear of Farraday's driver's seat.

"But nothing says I can't lay it out for you. I mentioned the cufflinks because they look important to you, and expensive. Rutledge, do you know what asset forfeiture is?"

Another meek sideways glance.

"You do. Good, then I don't have to bore you with the details." Alex turned in his seat and faced his quarry. "Family is important to you, isn't it? Legacy and all that? How many of your ancestors have been taken down for human trafficking, drug dealing, prostitution, et cetera? I bet human trafficking doesn't even count as a crime in your down home ass as long as the humans aren't white." He paused for a moment as his quarry started breathing harder and in short gasps. "Not only are you about to embarrass your lineage in the most public way possible, but you are about to single-handedly send your family to the poor house. You see, I'm taking everything you own: house, boat, real estate, business interests. I can't wait to see how far the Westchase Empire extends."

"You can't," Rutledge whined, turning toward him.

Alex leaned in, they were all but bumping noses. "Count on it."

Westchase suddenly looked out the windshield.

After a second, he said, "Head up East Bay Street toward the Neck."

"Why?" Farraday asked, turning the SUV around in the middle of Broad Street, no regard for the tourists and other travelers he was cutting off.

"They've got Charlie on one of the family's holdings, an old cargo ship. It's been at our pier for decades. It's only used for storage now."

"I would have seen anything like that when I ran your property. I didn't," Farraday grumbled. "Don't fuck around."

"It's not in my name; it's in a cousin's name. A deceased cousin. We've been hiding assets under his name for years."

Farraday punched the accelerator and flipped on his blue lights.

"I'll take you there and you leave my stuff alone?" It was more of a plea than a question.

Alex chuckled. "Depends on whether or not Charlie is still alive. Once we've got him back we'll discuss your future."

"Bu—"

Alex put up a hand. "You aren't getting the position you are in. We don't get Charlie back in one piece, going to jail and losing your family fortune will be the least of your worries. That man saved my life, we've been through the meat grinder together and came out whole on the other end. If he dies, you are one of those people responsible." Alex's voice went gravelly and cold. He was no longer acting. Alex fought the urge to beat the man to a pulp, to punish him for Sammy's death, the wounding of Agent Helmsley, and whatever happened to Charlie and his handler. We aren't there yet, Alex told himself. "If Charlie dies, what do you think I'm going to do to you?"

"Take the dirt road after Magnolia Cemetery."

Farraday nodded as he sped through the streetlight

at East Bay and Calhoun Street.

"You're gonna let me out before you go in there, right?" Westchase asked.

"Sure, stop here."

A minute later, Rutledge Westchase, millionaire shipping magnate was whimpering, handcuffed to a telephone pole on the side of the road.

Stillwater and Farraday were about to turn onto the access road leading to their target when two more SUVs similar to Farraday's fell in behind them.

"Who the hell is that?" Alex barked, reaching for his gun.

"Relax, they're ours, teams three and four. I put out a code on the radio and they vectored in on our GPS."

"We could use the backup," Alex commented.

"It's only four more guys," Farraday told him dryly. "This is gonna be a bitch given what we saw at Westchase's place."

"Yeah, I know," Alex said but there was no one else to call. Alex felt incredibly alone all of a sudden. For the first time in his career as a cop there was no back up coming when he needed it most.

"Better get those ARs out of the back," Farraday told him.

Chapter Thirty-Six

Mai was poking her head out of the ship as they came around the bend and Hopkins saw his chance. He had a mission, to clean out any witnesses, his own people or not, from knowing anything about the connection to Hammer. He fired wildly at her and was amazed when he saw her raise a weapon at him. Then he saw Bowman pull her out of the line of fire. The Jeep skidded to a stop in front of the derelict and he dove out of the rear seat and into the cloud of dust.

The realization that Bowman was loose, and that Mai had a weapon, did not faze him. That if Mai was shooting at him and Charlie had slipped his bonds and that most likely Higby and Wallace were dead. It didn't matter what was waiting for him in there, Billy Hopkins knew what was waiting for him outside. His only chance was through that ship.

Hopkins boarded the cargo ship with all the caution of a man trying to outrun a forest fire. Hammer's four men, including Jeh, filtered out of the Jeeps to take up various positions around the berth. Hopkins charged into the gloom, boots clanking on the rusting deck plates and ducked to the right so as to get out of the light of the large doorway. He found a sliver of cover behind a support beam and waited there a moment for his eyes to adjust. He blinked rapidly and listened for any sound, any indication that Charlie or Mai were on the move. As his eyes adjusted he looked around the cavernous interior of the ship. His eyes scanned the interior as he slipped from his relative position of safety and started making his way deeper into the gloom.

***

It took Mai only a couple of strides before she realized Charlie did not know where he was going. The old derelict was barely more than a hollow hulk and there were very few places to hide. She moved in front of Charlie and took the lead.

Charlie hobbled along behind the woman as fast as his breaking-down body would carry him.

They crossed the wide cargo bay under the dim, orange lights that highlighted the rust and dankness of the relic. There was only one true escape from the cavernous area and it was by the catwalk. Mai was heading in that direction when Charlie stopped her at the base of the decaying metal stairway.

"Not that way," he whispered, trying to catch his breath.

Mai furrowed her eyebrows for a moment then looked at the stairs and understood how open the climb would be. When she looked back at him she hid her dismay at the sight of him. "Your wound has re-opened," she whispered, probing the area near his hip with suddenly delicate fingers.

Charlie spared a moment to look and sighed; his grimy jeans was soaking through with his blood. Now was not the time. "We can deal with that later. Where can we take cover?"

Mai looked around the interior of the hold and after a moment pointed toward the aft of the ship, "The—"

The first bullet pinged off the steel bulkhead between the two of them and she jumped. Charlie's own instinct kicked in and he turned toward the open cargo hold. He saw a form—a silhouette—maybe twenty-five feet away. He didn't have a good sight picture. His front sight seemed to swerve and sway as he tried to track his target. Then, in that split second, opened fire. The figure dove behind a support beam. He felt a tug on his arm and followed as Mai dragged him toward the rear of the ship.

Charlie followed, but didn't take his eyes off the threat.

"Come on," Mai pleaded.

Charlie was moving at barely a shuffle. His legs no longer wanted to respond, the bones in his hip ground together like a grain wheel, and his breathing was labored. He wondered if this was what it was like to be a stricken deer on the run during hunting season. Trying to flee, not giving up the fight while components of its body started shutting down. He realized he was losing it as his mind began to wander.

"Right," he groaned, distracted for just a moment as he fought to keep his legs under him. His left leg was feeling dead, barely responding to him, the muscles swelling and constricting due to the re-opened wound.

***

Hopkins watched the two flee across the decking in a kind of discordant shuffle. Bowman was faltering under his injuries. The assailant grinned as he peered at them from behind the heavy metal support. Bowman was no slouch, he'd seen that first hand last night. Hopkins kept his cover, hoping the precious seconds would not overwhelm Hammer's patience. The last thing he could risk was some redneck taking out these two. Killing the last two people involved in this whole mess was his only chance to save himself from Hammer's wrath. He watched as Mai pulled at Charlie's arm and the two started moving aft. Bowman kept his eyes in his direction until he lost his balance and Hopkins saw the man's head dip away from him. He came out firing.

***

Charlie had screwed up and he knew it as soon as the first bullet blew through his right shoulder. The impact spun him around and in his weakened state he hit the deck plating like a sack of flower. He turned toward the direction of fire and saw Billy Hopkins' dim form creeping toward him, gun trained on him.

Chapter Thirty-Seven

T he approach to the location Westchase had given them sent a collective shiver up both Stillwater and Farraday's spines but neither mentioned it to the other.

Alex sat a little higher in the rear passenger seat, head turning, trying to cover all the angles as they made their approach. There was a berm on either side of the worn, sandy road, with wild marsh grass and other weeds growing five- or six-feet-high to either side. It was a natural shooting gallery fit with blind curves and turns that made Alex hold his breath each time he lost sight of what lay ahead. It reminded him of the way he'd felt every time he'd passed under a bridge or by a piece of garbage on the roads of Iraq. Just waiting for some fool to detonate a bomb or drop a grenade into his vehicle.

They made one last turn and got their first sight of the target location. There was an old container box directly ahead with the doors open. It sat perpendicular to the rusting hulk of an old bulk container ship. A large ramp was open amidships, Alex noted two Jeep Cherokees parked in front of the boat. A man wearing a button-down shirt, suspenders, and trousers was climbing the ramp.

"I'm—" Farraday never finished his sentence.

A barrage of heavy fire suddenly shredded the engine compartment and the front end of their Suburban. Still going at relative fast speed, once the tires shredded under machine gun fire the bare wheel of the vehicle dug into the soft dirt just as Farraday tried to turn away.

Alex braced as the vehicle lurched forward and rolled. The world spun. He had already unhooked his safety belt on the approach to the target and he went rolling with the vehicle as it tumbled.

He concentrated on holding on to his AR-15 and tucked his head as he bounced out of the SUV.

It took a moment for him to regain his senses. The weapons fire seemed to pause for a second as he got on his knees on what had been the roof of the SUV. He looked up to see Farraday cut himself loose of his restraints and drop out of the driver's seat. As the man shuffled toward the passenger side, Alex asked, "You okay?"

Farraday didn't look at him. "Ask me that again when we're the ones holding that fucking SAW," he responded.

The target with the machine gun opened up on them again. The loud pings, and thundering impacts of heavy rounds bouncing off the chassis of their truck spurred both men on. From behind them they heard the chatter of AR-15s belonging to their team answer their attackers.

Alex and Farraday joined the other agents and opened fire on a subject shooting from a prone position atop the container.

"Contact rear!" one of Farraday's agents yelled and Alex dove to the ground as a cloud of bullets smacked into the hood where he'd been standing. He kept moving, falling back on his USMC training and the combat in a foreign land had driven into him years ago. Stillness equals death when there is a guy trying to kill you.

He scanned for a target and found two more subjects behind them. The second SUV had pulled up to the rear and at an angle to their own mangled vehicle. The shooter on the top of the container had him dead bang if he inched his way toward the engine block of the follow car, Alex squirmed across the dirt and sand the other way to the rear of the second SUV and crouched next to one of the agents. He was in a catcher's crouch, trying to clear a jam from his rifle. He saw the name Hayes in a tape strip across the back of the body armor of the agent who crouched next to him.

"Shooter is taking cover behind a truck at our twelve o'clock off the bumper. These guys got us in a pretty solid cross fire."

"Reloading!" the second of Farraday's men, this one bearing the name Rawles, announced.

Alex leaped to his feet and squeezed off a burst of fire meant to suppress further assault as he tried to walk rounds toward his target. He got an eye on a head popping out from behind the engine block of an old Chevy four-by-four fifteen yards away before a stitch of rounds chattered into the vehicle taillights. Alex barked, "Fuck!" as shards of plastic embedded in his face and neck.

He blinked for a moment and realized he could still see. He heard some muffled words between his adversaries and peeked out from cover in time to see one of the men— dressed in jeans and a dirty black t-shirt scrambling to the right trying to get a flanking position. Alex fired on instinct, rounds kicking up dust at the man's feet as he ran. "They're flanking!" he called.

A blast of weapons fire over his shoulder was so close he could feel the over-pressure of the rounds. The overwhelming sound of the explosions deafened him. He watched as the man's shirt seemed to jump just under his shoulder. He stumbled and fell. As the man tried to scramble to cover, Alex put two more rounds into the wounded man and watched as the second threat ducked behind a metal container box.

Alex crouched as Rawles sought another target.

"Good shot," the agent said as Alex looked for Farraday. He found him two feet away, hugging the side of their truck, working an angle millimeters at a time to try to take out the man on the roof of the Conex container box. The position of the ambushers had them pinned down.

"Farraday, we gotta get in that boat!" Alex called.

"Yup," he responded, "working on it!"

"I'm going in!"

"What? No! Shit!" Farraday yelled.

***

Farraday, Rawles, and Hayes heard it but they didn't quite believe it until Stillwater broke from cover. Farraday and Rawles leaped into action and poured .223 rounds at the shooter atop the Conex box and Hayes made a charge of his own toward the second target behind the Jeep. Stillwater's suicide attempt—at least in Farraday's mind, was a successful maneuver. The sudden appearance of the enemy in open ground seemed to surprise the shooter on the container box enough that he poked his head up from the sights of his rifle just in time to have a round empty out his skull.

***

Alex ran. As far as he was concerned every one of the rounds he heard being fired had his name on it. The ramp was a twenty-yard dash but what choice did he have? He'd seen a subject entering the ship with a gun in his hand as they rolled up. Alex believed Charlie was in that ship, and right or wrong, he and Farraday had staked not only their own but Rawles, Hayes, and Bowman's lives on it.

They were at a stalemate sitting in the kill zone between two trucks, someone was going to have to rabbit to give the others something to shoot at. So Alex had dashed into no-man's land. He made it to the ramp and dove through the opening as a round chased him through the wide door and banged off a steel bulkhead. He rolled as he hit the ground and scuttled behind an I-beam for cover.

***

Bowman heard Hopkins chuckling as he walked toward him. He watched through the dim light as the man who'd shot him leisurely re-load his revolver and close the cylinder with a *schnick*.

"I bet about right now you're wonderin' how it was you ever volunteered for this mess," Hopkins said.

Charlie didn't have the energy to argue with the

prick any more. He slumped against the bulkhead, staring at the pistol in his hand. It was a semi-automatic and the slide was locked back. He could see the top of an empty magazine in the chamber. Instinctively, he reached with his left hand toward the spot where his extra magazines would have been on his duty belt. He moved clumsily now and didn't realize that what he was reaching for was not there until he rubbed his hand against his loose-fitting t-shirt.

He figured he must be going into some form of shock as he watched Hopkins approach—a blurry, slow-moving shadow.

Hopkins kicked his foot. "What? No smart-ass bullshit from you?"

Charlie looked into Hopkins eyes and the man looked away ever so slightly. Then he seemed to catch himself his eyes flared. Charlie took pleasure in the fact that Hopkins was still scared of him in some way. He admitted to himself that it was a small victory, but it was still a victory.

"You fuckin' pussy, now that there's no one here to protect you, you don't have shit to say, huh?" Hopkins' voice was rising. Hopkins closed the distance until he was standing right over Charlie. He could smell his breath as Hopkins leaned over and thought the guy might hit him. Then, Hopkins stood straight and still for a moment before looking down at his revolver. "Nah, fuck it." He raised the gun.

Charlie stared down the barrel and thought about Sammy in that moment, and Milligan, and felt ashamed. He thought he'd done all he could for them. He'd tried to fight but came up short. It was his fault they were dead whether he'd gotten this bastard or not. He whispered, "Sorry," softly, but he didn't take his eyes off the gun. There was still that screaming voice in his head to do something but he had nothing left. His body had given out.

Hopkins must have heard him, "You sure are," he

responded adjusting the gun just a bit.

"YOU DIE!"

Hopkins had no time to react before the first round entered his chest. He jumped as he looked up at Mai, eyes wide.

She fired madly, cranking on the trigger of her own confiscated weapon. She fired six rounds, charging out from behind one of the support beams and chasing Hopkins across the ten paces as he tried to flee her assault. He fired one shot in her direction.

Charlie didn't see where the round caught the small woman but it silenced her and she crumpled to the floor. He looked at Hopkins and heard more than saw the man's gun clank on the metal deck. Hopkins stumbled for a moment. He looked confused. He coughed and bright red spittle spilled from his lower jaw. He fell to the ground three feet away from Mai. Charlie watched as he heaved, straining to breathe. She must have hit him in an artery, he thought as Hopkins' heaving turned to a wheeze. Some mumbled whimpers accompanied his last gasps. Charlie closed his eyes for just a second as a wave of relief hit him like a tsunami.

BANG!

Charlie jumped, startled by the sudden sound. When he looked up through bleary eyes he gasped. Even in the gloom of the old dilapidated ship he recognized Hammer's solid form. The old flesh trader stood over the body of Billy Hopkins with a Colt 1911 in his hand; a tendril of smoke wafted from the barrel. Hammer was looking at him with depthless black eyes.

"You're still alive," he commented dryly.

Charlie didn't respond. He watched him like a rat tossed into a terrarium watches a boa constrictor.

Hammer took a step toward him. "You and me woulda been pretty tight in the old green machine, Charlie. You're a fighter, I'll give you that."

Movement at the periphery caught Charlie's attention. He looked at the same time Hammer did to see Mai shift ever so slightly. She coughed weakly and tried to move. Charlie looked at Hammer, who huffed and turned.

"No—" Charlie croaked but his protest was drowned by Hammer's Colt barking in his hand.

Mai's body convulsed as the old man shot her in the back of the head.

He looked at Charlie, then shook his head. "Damned shame," Hammer said. "All this complication. Bad for business." Hammer started toward Charlie once more.

Each rough sound of Hammer's worn work boots stomping on the deck dismembered the fragile resolve Charlie had held on to. Henry Hammer was a terrifying man. His granite, stoic demeanor chilled him.

Charlie fought to keep from shaking as Hammer hovered over him. The Colt started to rise and Charlie knew there would be no hesitation. Charlie was a problem to be dealt with. That voice in Charlie's head screamed at him to do something, anything, to fight. But he couldn't move; he slouched there in a pool of his own blood watching death clad in flannel and Dickie trousers coming for him.

The gun pointed at Charlie's head.

"Nothing personal, Charlie," Hammer said. "I know you were just doing your job."

The shots rang out. Charlie screamed like an enraged bear caught in a trap It was the last fight of a dying man, a refusal to go quietly, no matter what state he was in. But after a moment, he realize he was still breathing. The bite of a heavy bullet tearing through his body never came. When he dared open his eyes he saw yet one more figure shuffling toward him with a slight limp. He blinked away tears and it took him a moment for his blood-starved mind to comprehend that it was Stillwater covering down on the fallen form of Henry Hammer.

"You look like shit," Stillwater said.

"Took you long enough." Charlie coughed and tasted blood. He was done, now he could sleep. As he drifted off, he could hear Alex yelling. He didn't know why.

Epilogue
Two Months Later

Walter Chatsworth hit the button on his remote and heard the confirming chirp as his Aerostar locked behind him. His coffee steamed in his one hand while he swept through the backed-up emails from the night before on his government-issue Blackberry. He wandered through the ground level of the parking garage adjacent to his office building without rush. He was actually early this morning. For whatever reason the kids had been ready with a few minutes to spare. No one forgot their lunch, homework, or book bags, and he had dropped them both off at Wando High School a full twenty minutes ahead of their normally ragged, and tight, weekday schedule.

Walter was relaxed, it was so uncommon for him to not be in a hurry in the morning. It surprised him how good he felt.

Walter continued to scan his phone as he crossed the gap between the garage and his building. Emails about budgets, projected staffing, end-of-year money to spend, statistics, all the regular digital garbage that frequented the inbox of middle management, but no emergencies Chatsworth couldn't handle. He took his eyes off the phone for a moment to open the brass-handled door of the federal building and passed through security with a wave of his identification card.

Back to the Blackberry, he was nose deep in an email chain discussing the latest inspection that would be going on for the next couple of weeks. Inspections were always a bitch, hated by staff and management alike. An inspection meant weeks, if not months, of monotonous, worthless bureaucracy to dot every i and cross every t before the inspection team got their hands on office files. For management, a bad inspection meant losing a bonus,